I TELL OF
GREENLAND

also by
FRANCIS BERRY

Verse

THE GALLOPING CENTAUR
(Methuen)

MORANT BAY AND OTHER POEMS
(Routledge & Kegan Paul)

GHOSTS OF GREENLAND
(Routledge & Kegan Paul)

Prose

POETS' GRAMMAR: PERSON, TIME AND MOOD
IN POETRY
(Routledge & Kegan Paul)

POETRY AND THE PHYSICAL VOICE
(Routledge & Kegan Paul)

THE SHAKESPEARE INSET
(Routledge & Kegan Paul)

I TELL OF
GREENLAND
AN EDITED TRANSLATION
OF THE
SAUÐARKROKUR MANUSCRIPTS

FRANCIS BERRY

ROUTLEDGE & KEGAN PAUL
London, Henley and Boston

First published in 1977
by Routledge & Kegan Paul Ltd
39 Store Street,
London WC1E 7DD,
Broadway House,
Newtown Road,
Henley-on-Thames,
Oxon RG9 1EN and
9 Park Street,
Boston, Mass. 02108, USA
Set in 12 on 13 Bembo by
Kelly and Wright, Bradford-on-Avon, Wiltshire
and printed in Great Britain by
Lowe & Brydone

British Library Cataloguing in Publication Data

Berry, Francis
I tell of Greenland
I. Title
823'.9'1F   PR6003.E7435I/
ISBN 0-7100-8591-5

to
GUDRID

and other of his ladies

CONTENTS

PREFACE

I

In the month of July 1963, I took the bus at Akureyri, ready for the long journey to Reykjavik. Time of departure was 8.10 a.m. and the sun had risen at about two in the morning. It was one of those still hot summer days which are not uncommon on the north Arctic-facing coast of Iceland in July, even when, in the south of the country, it is chilly, grey and raining.

The road is narrow; its colour is black since its surface is crushed volcanic lava. The bus started; there was little traffic; and if one cared one could listen at that hour to the driver's radio; pleasant but undistinguished music from Reykjavik was interspersed at frequent intervals by weather reports for the benefit of the republic's main, if not quite only, primary producers of wealth – its trawlers.

It is that kind of bus which stops to put down mail bags or take up parcels. Or it had that kind of driver-conductor who would pull up when someone at the entrance to a trackway leading to a farm signalled him with a wave of the hand to do so, or even by the simple, stolid stare of a worthy determined to stand no nonsense. At some of these stops, no one alighted, no parcel or chicken coop was handed out, but there would be a ten-minute earnest conversation between countryman and driver, important enough, it seemed, to delay this main artery of national communication. But, at other times, the spoken transaction seemed to be of less weighty significance – the driver would stop to deliver a message to a lady in black, or to a lass, bold enough to show herself in blouse and jeans, waiting at the gate rails of a farmstead in this parish or that. The driver was to enquire the

price of methylated stoves in Reykjavik perhaps? Or the driver was
the lady's nephew and was receiving news of a family illness or a
family engagement? Or the driver was to bear a message to young
Gunnar, who worked in X garage in the capital, that he could look
to take his girl to the American movie showing in Reykjavik – if he
was good? I could not *know*, able to understand little except the
occasional word, but I could guess the significance of tones and
gestures, of a frown, a wink or a smile. A knowledge of Old Norse
is insufficient for following spoken Icelandic today, despite the claims
of the natives that the language has changed so little, that it is still the
language of the Sagas.

The bus was due at its terminus in Reykjavik at 5.15 p.m. but would
more likely, at this rate, end its journey nearer 6.45 or 7 p.m. or still
later. And it was raining in Reykjavik: that much I did grasp, as it
was repeated at intervals over the radio, but here – thanks be – facing
the Arctic Ocean, it was blessedly warm: a long, long day; clear blue
sky; still lovely air. Why do I, cooped up inside this bus, find myself
bound for grey sky, chill air, dull rain at the end of a long day while it
is golden *here*?

When the bus drew up in mid-morning by a narrow side road with
a sign-post pointing to Sauðarkrokur, acting on impulse I asked the
driver to enquire of the farmer, who was putting a massive labelled
parcel on board, whether he had a room to let. He had: the charge
would be twenty krónur for bed and breakfast, sixty for full board.
Thank God, into the sun. Now I'll know what it's like to live in the
country!

I dismounted the bus with a light suitcase in one hand, of which the
farmer took charge and a briefcase in the other containing Halldor
Laxness's *Salka Valka*, Nordal's masterly monograph on the *Hrafnketla
Saga*, paper, pens and pipes. I trusted his black sheep-dog was friendly
to strangers.

On our walk up the lane to his home, I enquired of my sturdy host
the etymology of the place-name Sauðarkrokur. Did it mean '*Saudr*'
'sheep' plus '*Krokur*' crooks? Or did this bend in the lane resemble a
sheep-crook? I added that in English we had Crookdale and Water-
crook, places in Westmorland.

Hr Gunnarsson did not understand. He replied, 'You English not bad
men. I met many in last war when you came here into my Iceland, yes.'

Hr Björn Gunnarsson and his wife, Fru Anna Vigfusdottir, possessed
a scrupulously clean modern house built of boards with a corrugated

iron roof painted green. Their eldest son Björn, to whom they had hoped to leave the farm, had gone to Reykjavik where he was employed in the accounts office of a fish-freezing plant; the second, Einar, was a second-year theological student at the University. If he did well enough at Reykjavik, he aimed at doing post-graduate work in Copenhagen. If he did less well, he might still finish up as one of those admirable Lutheran pastors of a country parish. Meanwhile Einar divided his time in his summer vacation between his theological books and helping his father on the farm: first with the hay-harvest, then at bringing in the rye. Their youngest, Harald, was a weekly boarder at his secondary school in Akureyri, but he was home for the holidays, and accepted as a matter of course that he should rise early during these days of twenty-one hours' sunlight and help his father.

The room I occupied was, to one of my habits, uncomfortably neat. An iron bedstead, reminiscent of my boarding school and barrack-room days; a wooden washstand with a hole in its surface in which rested a washbowl, a jug of cold water standing in this washbowl, a porcelain mug to support a toothbrush; a chamberpot under the bed. Washbowl, jug, mug and chamberpot were all of a set – white with a patterning of pink roses. There was an upright chair beside the bed on which to drape my clothes at night, and a tiny chest of drawers of deal painted in a pretty blue. What more could a man want seeking peace and quiet? Beer, a woman, *The Times* daily? 'Hush you,' I said to myself, 'these must wait till you are back in Reykjavik.' For hot water for shaving it was necessary to go downstairs. Likewise, for other matters.

Except for the clucking of fowls, and the occasional whirr of distant farm machinery, the silence was intense.

The family meals, I remember, consisted mostly of fish – cod variously cooked – or mutton. Kind and considerate as the family was, I thought, as I sat at their table and reflected on that bed in that bedroom allotted me above, three days would be more than enough to satisfy a craving for a quiet holiday.

And so it would have been but for Einar.

Like all Icelanders, Einar Björnsson had a passion for genealogy. How great his devotion to theology was, or how good a Lutheran pastor he would become, I did not know, but I suspected that the real motive for his study was the chance of further training in Copenhagen, and the prospect of stimulating his mind with a variety of experiences far beyond that offered by a small farming community, or even by his country's capital – with its fish-processing factories, two cinemas and a street of banks.

On my telling him at table, and over the baked or boiled cod, that I had been to Greenland in the previous year, and had been present at the excavation of Thjodhild's first church, and at the exhumation of the skeletons from its churchyard, one of which had possibly belonged to none other than Leif Eiriksson, Einar asked me if I had read *Eirikssaga Rauð* and *Groenlendingssaga*. On my assuring him that I had, and many another Old West Norse text beside, we warmed to each other.

The bearded young man, with good English, though he spoke it in a gruff, toneless voice, asked me to visit him in his room. There he asked me which I thought was the more authoritative, *The Saga of Eirik the Red* or the *Saga of the Greenlanders*.

A great scholar, Professor Jóhanesson, has of course decidedly ruled on this question, and I summarized his judgment, but Einar was all for *Eirik* on the ground that it included a longer list of Karlsefni's descendants. I pointed out that both sagas were firm in stating that Karlsefni and Gudrid, with their son Snorri, born in America, had settled, on their return from Greenland, near the very part of north Iceland in which we were now speaking – Reyniness, in the one case, and Glaumby in the other. And were we not at the head of Skagafjord? Was not Sauðarkrokur *near*? 'Were we not', I put it in my possibly exaggerated or romantic way, but which I nevertheless felt, 'on holy ground?'

Einar grew very excited and exclaimed that he was a descendant of Gudrid, and that he could prove it.

I replied that I didn't disbelieve that for a moment but rather thought it inherently probable that he was; that a few families long settled in a small and remote community would have intermarried again and again over many generations.

He was not ruffled by the thought of having to share the glory of his ancestry with others in Sauðarkrokur and Glaumby. Not in the least. He also declared that he was descended from a contemporary of Karlsefni and Gudrid; 'A man not so famous as yet, but who had gone to Greenland as a little child, and who died there, but his son came to Iceland, and he too settled in this part of his country. I am descended', he went on, 'from him, as I am from Gudrid, and if I marry and have a son, I shall name him Ingolf after the one who went to Greenland. And if I have a second son he shall be called Heriolf after that man's son.

'But first I must get my degree, go to Copenhagen, come back here and be a pastor.'

'Very right and proper,' I said.

'It is proper, and what is more, it is right or, as you say, correct.'

He made me sit on the edge of his bed; he opened a small bedside cupboard with a shelf, the sort designed to hold a pair of chamberpots, and drew from thence a collection of documents. These were of an extraordinary character.

II

There were, to start with, eleven stitched leaves of vellum inscribed (recto) by a close and fine writing which I take to be that of Ingolf Mordsson in a typical early fifteenth-century hand, and which I designate as MS.S[auðarkrokur] Ing[olf] M[ordsson]1. My near literal translation of this appears in this volume.

Second, there were three leaves, only two of them consecutive, in an older hand which I provisionally judged to be that of Olav Lawman and to date c. 1300–42. These I styled as MS. S OL2. These I deduce to be a transcript of a small part of the original eleventh-century work of Heriolf Ingolfsson, son of the Greenland teller, on which work all subsequent scribes (except the author of MS.S Ing M1), in some degree, depended. This is the lost *princeps* MS.H[eriolf] Ing[olfsson].

Einar's third exhibit was a very large bundle of MSS. written on paper. This was in a late seventeenth- or early eighteenth-century hand and in the Icelandic of that period. The scribe described himself as 'Ingolf Snorrisson, descendant of Ingolf of Greenland, of Heriolf his son, and of the sons of the said Heriolf Ingolfsson in lawful marriage thereafter to Ingolf Mordsson and thereafter of his son Olav Ingolfsson who was wed to Gudrid Gunnarsdottir, both of them descended of Gudrid Björnsdottir the Good, and thereafter of their issue in generation and in lawful marriage.' This was obviously a transcription, or one in a series of transcriptions, of an earlier document.

I designate this MS. S IS3, and on it my translation is based. The three leaves of MS. S OL2 give support to my rendering of part of what now appears as chapter X, and which is possibly the most critical part of the whole work.

Einar allowed me to take the collection to my own room after I had congratulated him on the fact that his documents had evaded the notice of that inveterate collector of MSS. from Denmark in the late eighteenth century, Thorkelin. But I was not permitted to go till Einar had shown me a genealogical chart, purporting to show his own descent from Olav Ingolfsson, son of Ingolf Mordsson, and of his wife Gudrid Gunnarsdottir.

Next day I cancelled by telephone my reservation of a room in the Hotel Borg, with its Edwardian-style comforts, in Reykjavik and spent three weeks transcribing MS. S Ing M1, MS. S OL2 and MS. S IS3. I went without beer, and even the cricket scores as reported in *The Times*, for that period. This even meant a foregoing of the delicious creatures waiting on the quays of Reykjavik to welcome, intimately welcome, the return of the seafarer. But there is something more important . . . the passion of the dead. I was heroic enough to acknowledge this.

Next year, 1964, I returned to Sauðarkrokur and completed the task of transcription. A full technical description, palaeographical and textual, is being prepared. But this will be a lengthy business.

I am most grateful for the hospitality of Hr Björn Gunnarsson and his wife, Fru Anna Vigfusdottir, on both occasions. Yet I must claim some credit for the task since it was not easy. There was no desk in that little bedroom under which I could thrust my knees. I pulled up that little hard upright chair, on which I hung my clothes at night, and placed it at a corner of the little chest of drawers of deal wood painted a pretty blue. I planted my knees astride a corner of this piece of furniture.

III

What follows this Foreword, then, is the result of many years' study of the transcription of the MSS. and an effort at a translation.

A direct and literal rendering of MS. S [auðarkrokur] Ing M1, though not easy in itself, was child's play compared with the problems confronting the 'Englishing' of the late seventeenth- or early eighteenth-century MS. S IS3. I had my transcription of the three precious leaves MS. S OL2, and Olav Lawman, if he could be trusted, as I believe he could, was himself a reliable transcriber of *princeps* MS. H Ing, though each transcriber had obviously kept pace with the growth and changes in the Icelandic language. The three pages of MS. S OL2, two of which are consecutive, corresponded fairly closely with two passages of MS. S IS3 (both occurring in chapter 10), and that at least gave me confidence that the scribe of MS. S IS3 would be reliable elsewhere, notwithstanding the changes in the Icelandic language and the changes in the notions of what constituted narrative prose between the fourteenth and the late seventeenth or early eighteenth centuries.

On these, and related problems, the learned reader must await the publication of a full analysis of the palaeographical, linguistic and textual problems attending the Sauðarkrokur MSS. In the meantime I take the responsibility *inter alia* as editor as well as translator, for what is to follow: division into chapters (none are marked in the MSS.), the giving of titles to the whole and to chapters, the silent interpolation of connectives between phrase and phrase – where to omit them would lead to desperate obscurity. On several occasions when confronted by a word requiring an periphrasis, for example 'wealth and well-being of the land', I have used, perhaps ruthlessly, a modern term such as 'economics'.

IV

My next remarks are addressed to the general reader rather than to the Old West Norse scholar.

Few who have had experience of both fields would deny that the greatest achievements in narrative prose of the Euro-American world are to be found in two areas widely separated in space and time.* These are the Icelandic Family Sagas and the novels of France, Russia and, to a lesser extent, England of the nineteenth century.

Leaving aside the vexed question of *How far are the Sagas, claiming to be historical, fictional?* and the equally vexed question of *How are the greatest nineteenth-century novels, claiming to be fictional, historical or biographical or autobiographical?* one notices, among many differences, one distinctive contrast between these two fields of achievement.

It is this: Whereas Flaubert, Dostoevsky, George Eliot and Henry James, in their professedly fictional creations, are intent on entering

---

*Notice I say *prose*. By far the greatest achievements of all are, of course, not in prose at all, but in verse, and one need only instance a few names, Homer, Virgil, Dante, Shakespeare – and the list can be greatly extended. Likewise the term 'Euro-American', if not the term 'narrative', rules out the Old, if not the New, Testaments, whether in the original or in translation.

the very hearts, minds and souls of their characters – acts of empathetic analysis or identification – so that we, the readers, do not merely observe but 'feel in with' the purportedly imagined character (the Mme Bovary, Raskolnikov, Dorothea Brooke), the Icelandic saga writer, purportedly dealing with fact, sees his characters from the outside. His prose, historical fiction or fictionalized history or pure history, is nothing if not objective. If the reader does feel 'in' or 'with' or 'in with' the saga person, that is the co-operative contribution of the reader or listener, for it is not supplied, though it is elicited, by the saga writer.

The saga writer of prose is nothing if not objective, leaving the reader, or listener, not to guess but to supply the keenest feelings of the man or woman in the tragic situation. Instead of man or woman, one might have written 'hero' or 'heroine' – for in this vital respect the saga writer is more like an epic poet, Homer. When the dead body of his son, Hector, is allowed back to his father, Priam, by his killer, Achilles, the intensely tragic feelings of Priam (and 'the pity of war,/ the pity war distilled', to quote Owen) are supplied by reader and listener, elicited of him by the poet. In this respect the poet Homer and the prose saga writer are nearer to each other than either is to the nineteenth-century novelist.

Hence, unlike the nineteenth-century novelist, the saga writer does not offer a man's or a woman's soliloquies, thought processes, reflections or streams of consciousness: for how can he presume to know what is going on in a man's head or heart? He may invent – or may not – but he will not follow an artistic convention not yet conceived, and which would evoke at once a listener's protest: but how do you know that Gunnar thought this? that Gudrun felt that?

We are intensely moved when Gudrun in the *Laxdaela* says, 'Of all the men I have loved, I have been least kind to him I have loved most', or when Gunnar in *Brennu Njalssaga* says, '"Fair is the barley ripening in the sun. Now will I not go into exile." And he turned his horse, and rode back to Hlidarend'.

Such utterances are poignant in the extreme in their context: we know that Gudrun knows that she has betrayed Kjartan; we know that Gunnar knows that by not going into exile he will be killed. Yet moving as they are, and whether history or historical fiction, these sayings are being appreciated by the writers from the outside. We, listeners or readers, supply the emotions of Gudrun or Gunnar. The saga writers report their sayings (they cannot *know* their thoughts);

and imply their objective appreciation of words and deeds that we sense as brave, honest, true, and beautiful.

V

In the work to which I have given the title *I tell of Greenland* in my translation, we have something unusual. We have neither saga, nor history, nor novel, but the autobiography of an Icelander who was taken to the then recently established Norse colonies in Greenland in his childhood. There he remained until his death, except for his active participation in two expeditions from Greenland to North America.

An autobiography, though not historical, partakes of history, for the teller is not a student of documents, but is an experiencing centre, recording events in which he engaged. The teller in this case, Ingolf Brandsson, tells of his associations with people of historical importance, with some of whom he took part in actions of historical importance. He tells what he witnessed; he tells what he heard; he reports gossip. To this extent his autobiography, though not history, partakes of history; it becomes in itself an historical document, it becomes material for history. From it, we can learn from someone who was *there*. We learn what it was like to have lived in Greenland in the early days of the European settlement of that country; and to have been a member of the parties that from Greenland struggled to attempt to found colonies in North America. Here, incidentally, Ingolf's account helps to reconcile the divergencies in the two saga accounts of these attempted settlements, though at other times, as a witness in these affairs, he comes down in support of the one account against the other. We learn, too, about other matters. Christianity was introduced into Greenland fifteen years after the founding of the settlements. From Ingolf we discover how especially puzzling many of the Norse Greenlanders found the doctrine of the Trinity. We learn too about the institutions, laws and ordinary habits of the inhabitants – whether Norse or, to a much lesser degree, of the people who, even more sparsely perhaps, occupied the huge country before they themselves came: the Eskimos.

An autobiography is not a saga. We have described some of the major characteristics of the saga. The sagas were objective; they were written down, after oral transmission through some six, seven or eight generations, about two hundred years after the events they relate. But *I tell of Greenland*, though Ingolf corroborates material found in two of the sagas (and material recorded in Vigfusson and York Powell's massive collection, *Origines Islandicâe*), is subjective. Ingolf tells of his thoughts, his hopes and fears and doings, however unrefined and rudimentary these may be, with such immediacy, that we might almost be led into thinking that we are reading some historical novel. But in fact nearly all is authenticated by either such historical documents as the *Annaler* or is confirmed by the archaeological findings of such scholars as Poul Nörlund and Aage Roussell and their successors as published in the successive volumes of *Meddelelser om Grønland*. And for what is not authenticated or confirmed by historian or archaeologist, we ought to trust, I suggest, Ingolf Brandsson since he was there at the time.

We cannot expect, of course, of Ingolf, or of the men and women in his pages, heathen or first generation Christians, that discrimination of feeling we demand of educated twentieth-century men and women, though even in this day there are people who manifest the same kind of hostile prejudice to those of another race or religion than their own, a prejudice born of fear. From a reading of the following pages, as set down by his son Heriolf Ingolfsson, I own that Ingolf and his kind suffered the delusion of not only thinking themselves superior to *skraelings* – the one word was applied to both Eskimos in Greenland and to Red Indians in America – but superior even to the Christian Irish, or to the Celts generally, and to the Semitic peoples of the what to us is the Near, but was to them the remote, East, those of the Biblical lands. Worst of all, it would seem that he even regards the English as not quite equal in strength and vigour. This is deplorable. He thinks moreover that some of the institutions and laws of the English reveal a baseness of mind.

Not that Ingolf is without good qualities, or even a conscience: consider his remorse at siding at a trial against his first benefactor.*

Of the Afterword, a literal translation of Ingolf Mordsson's document, written c. 1412, it only remains to say that it accords with the facts as known, and that the ship referred to was indeed the last known to have visited the shores of Greenland during the life of that remaining European Christian settlement. Hvalsey was in the East Settlement, but the West Settlement, as we deduce from the Afterword, was already extinct.

---

*To go over from one lord or protector to another lord was a wrong and shameful thing to do in the Norse heathen world, even if it seemed prudent to the man who transferred his loyalty. As Christian or former heathen, Ingolf was equally troubled.

Those readers, who are altogether new to the subject, might not find unwelcome a note on the Norse conception of the geography of Greenland and North America.

The West Settlement, we would consider today to lie more to the north than to the west of the East Settlement. We would rather designate them as the North and South Settlements respectively. But the Norse suspected that the axis of Greenland was inclined more on a S.E.-N.W. line than it is. It must also be remembered that their navigators in the year 1000 had no knowledge of the compass. Their probable notions of the alignment of Greenland, which they thought of as a peninsular rather than as an island, and its relation to Baffin Land, Labrador, Newfoundland, Massachussetts and Rhode Island, can best be discerned by consulting the maps of the medieval cartographers, or as late as those of Hondius, which can be found in specialized works on the subject.

Before the translation of *I tell of Greenland* is an illustrated map which I believe suggests well the early eleventh-century Greenlanders' notion of their land in its relation to America. In the preparation of this, I have had regard to Leif Eiriksson's expressive demonstration of two long oars, their hafts planted on the ground, their shafts and blades converging, though not touching.

During the long labour of translation and preparation of this book for the press, I have had help and encouragement from many, and to these I express my thanks. First and foremost I am, of course, grateful to Sera Einar Björnsson. On obtaining his degree *cum maxima laude* in theology and receiving ordination, he proceeded to Copenhagen to specialize in medieval ecclesiastical history. Among other tasks, he is undertaking a scholarly edition of the original manuscripts, with full textual apparatus.

I owe thanks to his parents, Hr Björn Gunnarsson and Fru Anna Vigfusdottir, for going out of their way for making my second visit, for the purpose of transcription, much pleasanter. Not only had they arranged for the bus driver on the Reykjavik run to deliver London's *The Times* daily at their postbox at the foot of the lane, so that the Englishman could keep in touch with the county cricket scores, but, in return for the duty-free bottle of whisky, Hr Gunnarsson had brought into his house a firkin of excellent *vat öl* for my evening refreshment. Moreover, he forebore to complain more than once or twice about the incursion of Hull and Grimsby trawlers within his country's fishing grounds.

For guidance and information in Greenland itself, since, as explained, I had previously visited some of the actual sites familiar to Ingolf Brandsson, I owe thanks to members of the National Museum of Copenhagen who were carrying out excavations at Brattahlid, especially to Fr Karl Wolfe; and to Professor Gwyn Jones; also to Dr C. L. Vebaek who was excavating another site in Eiriksfjord. Neither should I omit mention of a large Eskimo family, and of one member in particular, who admitted me to their shelter at Narssak in the early hours of one July morning when ice had blocked the passage of my launch down the fjord to Julianehaab.

Generations of Danes have devoted their learning and their labour to archaeological fieldwork in Greenland, and the records of these, reaching back for nearly a hundred years, are to be found in the magnificent series *Meddelelser om Grønland*, of which the Sheffield University Library has an almost complete run. To this whole series I owe much, but to two contributors especially: the late Poul Nörlund and the late Aage Roussell.

I owe thanks to my colleagues at Royal Holloway College: to Mr C. A. Ladd who, though he has probably forgotten it, dropped a word of encouragement at an auspicious moment; and to Dr Martyn F. Wakelin, who settled an etymological problem. Mrs Phillis Barry, secretary of the Department of English, despite her multifarious duties, has typed, with good will and accuracy, a manuscript by no means always easy to read.

To Professor Peter Foote of University College, London, and to Mr J. A. B. Townsend, Senior Assistant in charge of the Scandinavian section of the University College Library, I owe thanks for information respecting the *Islandske Annaler*. I thank Miss Kathleen M. Dexter, formerly of Exeter University, my first teacher of Old Norse. Nor do I forget Professor G. Wilson Knight's constant helpfulness.

Two members of my family have assisted me in different ways. My daughter, Melloney, prepared evening meals, thereby enabling me to give the more time to writing. I also benefited from her knowledge of geography. My son, Scyld, discussed *I tell of Greenland* in a companionable way all along. As a student of Arabic, he is alert to the problems confronting anyone struggling to render a text from another language into English; and his sense of, and delight in, what may be termed the droll, has rarely been out of place.

I thank Frau Liesl Railton of Salzburg who lent her professional skill as a painter to the making of the delightful illustrated map to which I have already referred.

I dedicate this book as I believe Ingolf Brandsson would have wished.

F.B.

I TELL OF GREENLAND

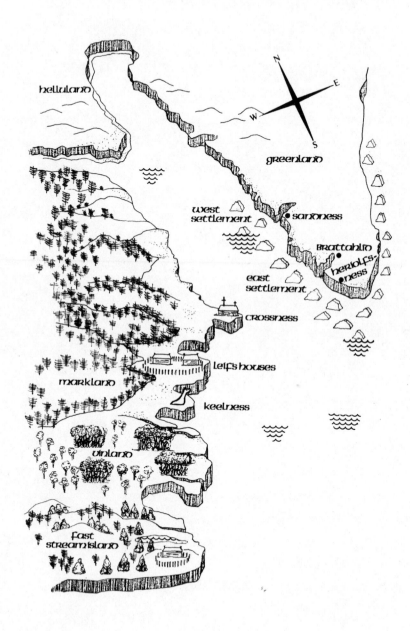

1

MY COMING INTO GREENLAND

I am not important. Nor was my father. But I have seen some big and important things, and these I want to tell before I die. So I must tell them now – for I have lived more than sixty winters, about sixty-four, I believe, and if I leave the telling – go on and on putting the telling off – it will be too late. Whom do I tell it to? And for whom? Well, I tell it to my son. And he writes it down just as I say it because I can't write. He can. So he comes to hear matters – and of matters – for the first time. Each evening by the fire he comes in, and for two or three hours, he says, he will come until he must go away for good. Far away: and I will never see him again – after these three months are gone. It is kind of him – and he's writing that down – to do this, and kind of his wife to allow him to walk over from his own home – each evening, and for two or three hours, and for three full months, he says.

And *for* whom do I tell this? Well, for him, but not only for him. I'd like him of course to know the story of his father – to remember me by, and to pass on to his own children – when he has them. And I hope he does have them and will be very lucky. I think he may be lucky since he has such a good wife. She is good by letting him come here every evening until they leave this land. In their new home – over the seas – I shall think and think of them. He is my only child. So to him I tell this.

But it's not only *for* him, I tell. If it were, there are a lot of things which I would hide, things which a father would not tell his son – things for which he feels shame, bad things and foolish things – and the bad things are often foolish, and the foolish bad – things which a man does not ever even tell his living wife.

Telling through him to others is different. Indeed, one can tell friends – a man can, and a woman, I guess, can too – what one can

3

never tell one's children (for one tells them only those things of which one feels proud) or even one's wife – or a wife a husband. So we need good friends, and my son has to be a friend now as well as being my son. And one can tell strangers, persons one has never seen, nor ever likely to see, things which one would never dare to tell one's friends even. They don't know you, so you've nothing to lose for telling the truth. Interesting things, too. Not all of them sins, I mean. For God – or the gods, which is it? or them? – gives – or give – a person feelings, including the – as they say – naughty ones. Now you put that down, son. And you do understand what I mean by it? So I tell you and your children when they are grown up, and *through* you others we do not know, nor perhaps ever shall.

So, now, dear son and, through you, others, I was not born in this country. My father brought me here. I was very young at the time – scarcely more than an infant – and have few memories of the journey here, but those few are strong, and those few and strong I mix with what others on the journey told me later, when I was eleven or twelve.

I was born in Iceland, as was my father. It seems there was a fairly important man there, called Heriolf, and that this Heriolf had a son called Bjarni. Heriolf farmed, but Bjarni had a ship, and he used to go trading in this ship each summer – Norway, or England, or Denmark or Bremen, somewhere like that. Then he would return home to Iceland just before winter, exchange or sell the goods he brought in his ship, and then he and his father, who had brought in his harvest, would have quite a calm and happy time at home together in the winter. But any routine, however comfortably settled, does not go on for ever. People grow older, unexpected harm strikes or someone dies, children grow older too, and they quarrel, get into trouble, marry, move away. Well, anyone knows this who's had any time in the world.

So this plan of living, of Heriolf farming and his son Bjarni's summer trading with his ship, did not last – or I wouldn't be here, and you, my son, would never have been born.

My father told me that Bjarni came home later than usual one year. He docks his ship, seals his cargo, checks that everything is all right, promises to meet his crew – at the ship – next morning to pay them, and then hurries up to assure Heriolf that he's safe, to explain that he's later than usual – it's October, not September – but that he's had a good voyage, only to find that his father's – gone. Yes, not dead, but gone. Not only that, but he finds a stranger in the house who says, 'Heriolf's sold this farm to me, but you're welcome to put up here

4

tonight, and for a few nights after that, if you so wish. I arranged that
with your father before he went. After all, it was your own home once.
Can't do less than offer a night's rest.'

'But where has he gone?'

'He waited, hoped you'd be back early. You have come back – late.
In the fifth week of summer Heriolf set off with Eirik Thorwaldsson –
the one who was outlawed for three years for killing two of his
neighbour's men. After the three years' sentence was up – and that
was this summer – this summer! but this summer is now passed – Eirik
comes back, to us here, full of the new land he has found out there,
and which he called a green land. A green land! It's more full of ice,
to my mind, than this Iceland, in spite of his boasting. Oh, how he
talked of it as "*my* Greenland". Well, what else could he do, con-
sidering that his own land here was taken over while he was exiled for
those three years? It was a grim killing – by Eirik himself. Two men.
Well, he boasts and boasts of his marvellous Greenland, its pastures, the
plentifulness of land for good, able and strong men. He gulled many.
He gulled twenty-five shiploads – of men, women, children, serfs,
animals – and off they sail. Your father among them. I had never
thought your father – I thought Heriolf a wise, shrewd man – would be
led so. But he was. Of those twenty five ships some turned back, others
were swamped. Some of those who came back saw several ships taking
in huge waters, quicker than they put them out, though twenty or so
people had pails, buckets, basins. They saw ships getting lower and
lower in the huge romping seas, and sink. Lucky those who came back
to Iceland howsoever soaked.'

'And my father's?'

'Your father's ship did not turn back. Couldn't, since he'd sold this
farm and this land to me. With luck he got through. I believe he did.
For your sake I hope he did. Now I was to give you these. Here are the
sailing directions, directing you how to follow after him, and find him.
Exact directions. He expects you in this as in other winters, Bjarni.'

Now my father told me that Bjarni, having thought it over and over
during that night, came over to him (my father) in the morning. My
father had been a tenant of Heriolf, in the dale, and so had been handed
over to the new landlord when Heriolf sold. Sold all his estate. So
when Bjarni, in the morning, came over to my father and said he had
decided to follow Heriolf to this new green land, and 'Would you,
and your son, follow *me*, Bjarni?' my father, not caring for his new
landlord, said, 'Yes, I will.'

5

So it all came about – your fate, and mine, my son. We gave up the tenancy. Rapidly we packed up. Bjarni sold just over half of his cargo he'd brought to Iceland – at a cut price, a loss – and stacked up with a lot of things we had heard, or guessed, we'd need in this new green land. Rapidly, for it was already October, almost horribly late for travelling, with days darkening, nights lengthening, and all that. So I was taken, said goodbye to my home – yes, I am nearly sure now I was nearly seven years old – and we started. Bjarni, my father, a lot of other people in the ship – women too – and of course cargo and some farmstock. And a few animals to kill while sailing. And fresh water.

And, yes, I have flashes of memory of that journey. Frightened, much of the time, I own to it. But I could see that many of the grown-ups were scared too. Their skins drew tight over their faces and the skins grew whiter. That was a sure sign, I learned. Bjarni, who had all the charge of us, and of the ship, was occasionaly scared too, I think. But he was a good man, responsible, a sailor of many years, and tried not to show it.

Now, my son, is that enough for this evening, or shall I go on?

Well, that voyage. Our coming here.

It was dreadfully late in the year to do it for all sorts of reasons. We had been told to steer due west on and on until, after the third, fifth, or sixth day, we saw a black mountain, streaked with snow, or rather ice, to be called Blue Shirt. Why Blue, I don't know. It was merely the biggest of a long, long jag of mountains, all black and streaked with ice. Now, when we spied Blue Shirt, we were to turn south, and follow that line of mountains, but about three miles away from the land because of the drifting sea-ice, until we came to the very southernmost point of the land – which was called Hwarf or Turn – which we were next to round and sail north for a little when we would soon hit upon Heriolf's place, which Bjarni would recognize, for Heriolf had said he would leave a rowing-boat on the ness, with a roll of yellow cloth, wound round a thwart, as a sign, and then we would be safe.

That was the design. But what happened? What happened was that when we were clear of the vik's sheltering headland a strong banging wind came at, and against us, from the north-west, just about as much at as against. The stem of the boat – I watched from under the boards in the stern – with its long blade of a prow-post, went slowly lifting up. I never thought it would stop climbing to the low brownish rainful clouds – that post with the blade. But it did. It seemed to stop and hang, and then it would start to come down, slowly at first, but

6

then more quickly, hitting the water with a thump. That was the work of wind, and so wave, *against*. But the great prow blade was not mounting to the clouds and falling like a long staff held by a walker – straight. The wind and sea – as much *at* as against us – drove at our broadside too. The lifting and sinking blade was at a slant. There was north in the wind as well as west, and as the prow lifted, the ship rolled. The strakes on my left – I, under the boards at the stern, looking towards the way we were striving for – leaned nearer and nearer the water as the wave rolled and romped at starboard, the stem lifting clear out of the water, the blade sloping to the left.

I understand the navigation now, so many years after, but I was scared that the ship would be filled up with water, or that it would dive down into it, or roll over into it. I understand now that the sail was of course furled, that the oars were drawn in, that the ship was simply being driven – backwards and too far south, and that we would never see Blue Shirt. Day and night were terrible, and this continued for many days and nights. It was mid-October and the nights were too long to have ventured on this, with the sky coated under by large hurrying clouds, the stars but barely sighted, between these huge clouds, and then for too short whiles for us to try to steer by.

The wind shifted to blowing from due north, so the prow didn't lift up and up till I thought it would hit a rushing low dark cloud, but instead the rolling was worse, the gunwale running to below the level of the sea, sipping it up. People came to scoop it with large pans to throw it out of the ship, but this was frightening because all these people added their weight to the same side as every huge wave leaned over our ship. I sat at the stern. On the right, and leaned over to the right, as hard as I could, but my small weight could not equal the men and women with their pans. One of the women, amidships, just where the curve of the ship ran lowest, stooped over to empty scooped up water, and she went overboard. The man on her right tried to grab a leg to haul her back, but she had been wearing a long coarse woollen dress, and long soaking from the rain and the salting spray from the sea had stretched the dress so that it reached below her ankles to the floor. If she had been wearing a short skirt the man might have seized a leg before it was too late. Well, that woman paid for her modesty, if modesty it was. We could do nothing for her, but were lucky that the ship didn't heel right over.

The wind backed away to the north-east and so in part it followed the ship, instead of being against our broadside, and the sail was at last hoisted. The wind slackened, so the sea at last grew less rough, but there was still enough wind to sail, and with no need of oars. But no sight of Blue Shirt, so it was clear the storm had driven us much too far south, and it was thought we had already passed the southernmost tip of this Greenland – the Hwarf, or Turn – and would need to bear up, north again, for Bjarni to find the new home of his father, Heriolf. So Bjarni gave the word to steer north, and if he had only a vague notion of where we truly were, small blame to him since none of us had been there before. There was now some mist, still air, and much use of oars. Except for the worry of the men about not having much food and fresh water to last out, I did not mind too much now that it was nearly calm, though cold.

So for some days. Three, four, or, more likely, five or six, then, going north, but too much west as it turned out, we suddenly saw, on our left, a huge block of land, steep-cliffed, so high and yet flat on top. All snowed was that level top. Its cliffs black but striped with ice, and its beach – as far as we could see it, as the breakers broke on it – all loaded with great boulders, broad heavy thick stones. Grey stones.

'No, that's not the place. That's not this green land. That's not where my father is, his new home,' said Bjarni. 'Turn right about, go south, follow this coast at three miles out. I shall call this ugly land Helluland, that is Slab Land or Stone Land, and this is not what we want. Turn right about!'

The men, understanding that there would be no sort of a welcome there – in this Helluland – did turn south and followed the coastline for two or three days. Unwelcoming, I thought, this 'Helluland'.

So we went south, and a bit east, for a few days, sometimes using the sail, and then, after leaving that coastline and crossing some open water, came to something different: a long, long, long sandy beach, white-sanded, a seemingly unending dune. There were trees a league, or less, behind these dunes, and these trees were mostly in dark leaf. They were tall with slender trunks, narrowing to the top, evergreens. We liked the sight of this white-sanded beach, stretching on and on, but Bjarni was certain: 'This is not Greenland.' Instead we were to keep on our course. 'I will call this land Markland, Woodland, because of all the fir trees behind this long coast,' he said. 'But it is not the place. Keep going south. Markland is not the place for which we are bound.'

Then again across an open gulf of sea, and then a great island, with a long ness or point, and we could have gone east or west of this point. But Bjarni was determined we should go east. 'I like the look of this land,' he said, 'and others will come here, because of its trees, with their many coloured leaves – red, black, gold – and its grass, but still it is not where we are to take ourselves. We'll tell others of this land when we get home, settling ourselves, our wives and our children. But this is not our home. Turn east and somewhat north.'

The grown-ups, the men, had little liking for this. 'But there is grass on that island, and there are trees too. It is a green land, greener than we have seen heretofore. It is the best of green lands, greener we think, than your Greenland.'

'Our friends and our families are not on that land,' Bjarni said, 'however green it is. We shall aim for our own new home, and no other land.'

So we turned east and somewhat north, as he said. And with some help of the sail, and with much of the oars, we ferried on under a light high grey cloud cover, rifting here and there for a pale sun, with scurries of slant rain on and off. The sea had a dull heavy heave or swell, thudding our ship's sides, but not frightening.

On the second or third day after turning away from that green land which was not Greenland, and in the first or second hour after noon, the man standing up on the steer-board, at the stern, governing the course of our ship, with his great broad oar, saw something odd, and he called out. Bjarni, from far up near the prow, came quickly down and stood up beside the steersman to look.

Now, son, I was crouching under that board, with my knees drawn up, hands clasped in front of them, feeling rather cold and very hungry, and I heard what was going on between the two men.

The steersman had called out because he saw we were driving towards a reef or rock.

'It's a strange reef, with those spikes on it,' said Bjarni.

'It's a long thin reef, or rock come up from the sea, shaped like a smooth bow, the highest point in the middle. A strange reef!' said the other man.

By now all of us in the ship were looking at this thing towards which we were being carried. A low black bow, like a whale's back, except that it didn't plunge out of sight followed by a great fountain of spray and air because of the whale's breathing.

Our puzzlement was not helped by the weather, though we were now drifting closer all the time. The cloud was now low, and there was a strong very slanting rain which spattered on the sea near the object, lifting a mist. The sun being low, the light was decidedly tricky.

'It's not a whale, for one of those five spines is moving, sitting and waving,' said the steersman.

'And it's no reef or rock,' said Bjarni, 'for it too – the whole long narrow black thing – the bow with five spikes, is moving too.'

'And it's no island then,' said the steersman.

The waving went on, and one of the wavers nearly slid right off.

And so, as we drew close, we saw it was no reef or rock but an upturned ship. Upside-down it was, drifting with five people clinging to the keel. When they were sure we had seen them, the five people sat astride the keel and waited for us to draw up.

So using oars, so that we would not drive hard against them, we came alongside – as near as we could.

Well, we saved five people, four men and one woman, from that upturned ship. It was not easy, for there was a gap of water however close we tried to come to them. Underneath the sea was the ship's widest part and that kept us apart. And the swell sometimes brought us near so that we struck, and sometimes it drove us apart.

Still, we got all five, one after the other, from the keel of their upturned drifting wreck, into our ship.

For the first of the five, one of our crew reached out his oar as far as he could reach, and a man on the keel took a hold of the blade, but it was not a firm grasp, and he was in the water between our two ships before he was pulled in. That was a risk. So then we thought of the long plank we carried, the boarding plank, and it just reached from our gunwale to the keel of the upturned hulk. Two men walked over it, with spread out arms sawing up and down to hold balance. Then the woman. She wouldn't walk, but sat astride the plank, shift pulled up, her hands sliding along the edges of the plank in front of her, jumping herself forward on her bare behind. One of our men cried out, 'Look out for splinters in your you-know-what', and laughed. Another called, 'Is that how you do it in bed?', and there was so much laughter that I joined in, though I didn't know what the jokes meant. But the woman was dank and dirty, and she kept on going in her funny way, but she scowled. Then the last man walked over boldly, not even waving his arms, showing off, and the board was pulled in.

And that was good indeed for Bjarni, his clever seamanship.

The drenched hungry five, one of the men weak and the woman rather complaining (though she was lucky, and owed a lot to Bjarni and to us), were an extra charge on us, on our food and water. But at least they were of some use, for they had come out of the Greenland to which we were going. Weak, weary things, they yet could tell us where to go.

That day, or the day after it, we ran along a coast. Great mountains, but there were gulfs or gaps in between into which the sea softly went or came, and there were fjords and they looked sweet, despite the muffish hang of misty air that hung at the entrance to these fjords.

Bjarni needed no help from the shipwrecked five now. He was looking, like a happy cat watching each food bowl on an eating table in turn, waiting for one to be put down on the floor. He was watching for this or that sign. Then he saw the entrance to the fjord for which he was searching. There! On the tongue of rock was the small rowing-boat, drawn up, for which he was searching. Over the middle thwart a winding of yellow cloth – dulled, because of the wet and rain. 'That's it,' he said, and, with lowered sail, we went up the fjord. This was Heriolf's ness, and Heriolf himself stood on the wharf, waiting for his son. He had stood for several hours on the wharf each day for many days past, waiting. And now Bjarni was here.

2

SHIFTED

I remember, dear son, even after these fifty and more years what hard a winter it was–my first one in Greenland. But so were some later winters.

As to our first one, Heriolf and Bjarni were glad to be together for the season, and Heriolf was glad of the half cargo Bjarni had brought in his ship because all the farmers were in short supply of many goods and these farmers had only been settled in Greenland some four or five months before our own coming.

It did not help that Bjarni showed some disappointment with his father's new homestead, and indeed we were all disappointed, and this marred the good feeling, or happiness, a little. And it soured Bjarni's temper further when it was – though this was later – put about that the five rescued from the drifting keel had been rescued by Lucky Leif, not by Bjarni. And that couldn't have been so since I saw the lifting off (the odd waddling astraddle of a plank in the case of the woman – how she scowled with her dirty face, and dangling hair, when we mocked her) of the five myself. Those five had merely been of a ship's party going up from one fjord to another along the coast, the rest, eleven or twelve, drowning. They had not sighted Helluland, or the other lands, as we had. If I get warm about this, it is not that I do not like Leif – I do – but truth should be told and Bjarni should have the credit when it is his due.

I would not be surprised if it was the straddling woman who first put it about – but I'll let that rest.

Well, Heriolf's fjord was narrow, the sides steep, the soil poor. So –

'But, Father, why did you choose it? You had a good place in Iceland, and you could have chosen better in Greenland. So why this?' asked Bjarni, showing anger for himself, grief for his father.

Heriolf explained that he was not quite the fool his son supposed, that the point of choosing this fjord was that it was *the* point – the point which every ship coming over the water, from whatsoever country, and bound for Greenland, would first sight and make for. They would unload at Heriolfsness, especially when there was floating ice in the upper reaches of the fjords, and he would have charge of the marketing of the ships' goods, and the first pick among them. 'And should all the other farmers in all the other fjords in all Greenland fall short – odd though it seems, and die, as they might – we, at least, shall be able to carry on.' And I dare say he may be proved right in the long run.

In the few months he had been there, Heriolf had made his long house of turf. Meanwhile, a house of thick stone was being prepared for next year.

After a winter in that long house of turf – full of many men, women, children, cooking, eating, sleeping, dying, being born, playing of chess, weaving of cloth, making love, carving of wood for tools or weapons, or dishes, or toys for children, telling of tales or quarrelling, or pissing or shitting on the floor beside the fire instead of doing it outside because it was so cold out there that they pretended they were taken short – some men had grown discontented by the spring, and said they would have no more of it. That was faint-hearted of them; and rude, for Heriolf had given them a roof over their heads at any rate.

My father was one of these grumbling men. He reminded Heriolf that he had been a tenant of his back in Iceland; that he had not liked his last landlord, and so had given up his own holding to follow 'all this way out to Greenland to seek help from my first landlord', and that, 'as far as I can see, all that we have in this cracked-up land is a crowded stinking hall in winter and a dry stony valley in summer'.

'Why, that's odd. I didn't ask you to come here. I didn't, you know,' replied Heriolf after thought, and who was a mild-tempered man unless driven too far, and was wise rather than cunning.

'I've sold up my tenancy holding in Iceland, just to come here.'

'I didn't ask you to. You chose to do it. Odd that. You came here uninvited, and I have put you up all winter – and put up with you, if I may say so.'

'And a fine place you have put me up in!'

'It's all I have, and if you want me to be your landlord here, I could give you –'

'I am not, and shall not take it.'

13

And so, when a trading ship came at last in the spring – and, sure enough, as Heriolf had supposed, it berthed at Heriolfsness – my father arranged his passage and went back east. He told me that he would return some day when he had established himself – either in Iceland again or in some other land. He said this, but never returned. At first I thought he might; and I waited for a long while until hope ended; and then I rather dreaded than wished his return. But, as I say, he did not. Now, I don't mind about this, of course, because I have, thanks to friends, managed without any help from him. You will one day admit, my son, that I have behaved rather more kindly to you.

Now I must pass on. Heriolf, having so many to care for besides my younger self, and thinking the best for me, did, having his son to care for, and minding his own age, begin to plan to see me one day handed over to the charge of some other household. Yes, Heriolf was a good man, careful for others besides himself. After all this time, I can still see him in my mind's eye when he first greeted us. He was not much above middle height, yet seemed taller because he was somewhat narrow between the shoulders. He held himself very upright too. He walked in a strange manner. He lifted his legs, from the thighs to the knees, very high, leaning if anything backwards as he did so. Like a stately horse. He had a narrow face, wore hair on his upper lip, had a rather high forehead. He had some strange tricks of speech. He would seem to listen to lengthy complaints, stories or reports, and whenever the other fell silent would exclaim, 'How odd!' or 'Odd that!' Even if what was being told him was utterly ordinary, this remark would still come.

He was very fond of a special kind of fish cooked slowly over the fire. He liked chess, and was a good player. In the long wait between moves, he would still, when all was quiet, say, 'Very odd.'

Now I found out, in course of time, that the household to which Heriolf had been designing for me to move was none other than the household of Eirik Thorwaldsson himself. Thus I would become a pledge for the keeping of friendship between the two men.

But, before any handing over, I was first to be shown to Eirik that he might agree to having me, when the time came, or otherwise.

On that visit I was in some dread because of Eirik's renown.

During his three years of outlawry, Eirik had closely inspected many fjords up and down this coast, but had early decided on the one which he called Eiriksfjord. So he was at an advantage. For as soon as he came back – leading Heriolf's and thirteen other men's ships, for of the twenty-five that had set out only these had won through – Eirik, using his first house as a temporary dwelling, had started erecting his wonderful and large house of stone. The other leaders had first the job of choosing a fjord each for himself and then cutting turf for a first shelter.

It is famous, but I must tell you how it struck me when I first saw it.

There was the long winding passage up the fjord in our small boat to begin with. Foggy and chill the fjord, at its meeting with the sea. Then the air became clearer, and the sun was shining, but for four or five miles we had to take care because of the ice floes and, worse than the floes, many icebergs. I might even have thought Eirik's choice unwise. But after those four or five miles the water became clear – that is, beyond the point where a great shifting sheet of ice, two hundred feet above the water, pushed itself beyond the edge of its cliff, like dough in a pot brimming over the lip into the fire. But instead of hissing, the huge blocks of ice broke off and flopped into the fjord, rose and rocked with thundering noise and fearful surge and heave of outspreading white curling waves as high as on the open sea. But beyond this glacier's calving the fjord widened, the cliffs, as they leaned back, became less steep, the weather became warm, and soon – there was the Broad Slope. I first caught sight of the turf house, next of the great new dwelling.

I enter Brattahlid, with three others, and am in doubt whether to tell of Eirik first, or of his household, or of his house. But the family and house expressed the man so forcibly, that it must be the man.

Eirik the Red. He was of course striding up and down when I came in, but with a strong limp, mark of a broken ankle badly mended. He glanced abruptly over his left shoulder to look at me, fiercely, I thought, with his strong eyes. Hard reddish-blue eyes. Forehead with deep furrows. Very dark dulled red hair, with grey, and a little black in it, above that wide low forehead. Mighty and heavy shoulders so that he seemed less tall than he truly was. Beard matched his hair, but it had more grey in it.

I said 'of course' he had been striding up and down, stopping to look over his shoulder when I came in. Why, of course?

He undoubtedly sat down sometimes; undoubtedly he slept and, sometimes when drunk, snored; and surely he had lain to beget his children, whether by his wife, or by that other woman to beget that terrible and cruel daughter, Freydis, or had lain with those several other women he went out to in the summer months.

He did sit; he did sleep; he did recline – more and more often as he grew older – but I said 'of course' he was pacing up and down, when I first saw him, and he turned his head over his shoulder to glare at me, because of all the men I have met with in my life, this Eirik – now long dead – and he was over fifty when I saw him – was the one most full of unrestful vigour, life of the body and limbs, life of the brain, and life of the passions – anger, lust, strength of burning hope. How he banged the fist of one hand on the palm of the other, as he would nearly shout, 'Yes, we must', or 'Yes, I must', or 'I shall', or 'I will', or 'We must', or – often to me and others – 'You will.' Such gusts of anger and such energy.

I am right to deal first with the master of Brattahlid. He was the master – truly. And made me feel small, but still proud to be one of his household, rather than the kindly Heriolf's, from now on. If he took to me, and didn't throw me out, that is.

'Who are you?' he said, stopping and swinging round, and, 'Speak up, so that I can hear', he said, when I had scarcely begun to give him my name and remind him that it had been arranged with Heriolf that I should come to be shown that he might settle whether he would later have me.

Here was the greatest man in all Greenland, its founder, and how he had come to be this, I of course knew.

When only fifteen years old he, and his father Thorwald, had killed two men in Norway, the country where they had been born. Neighbours, or a neighbour's men, trespassing over their fence. And if Thorwald had proposed the act, he wouldn't have needed any backing up from young master Eirik, I am sure.

Kicked out of that country, they went to Iceland, late in the day when there was not much good land left unoccupied. They started to farm again and had more trouble of the same sort after some five years. Eirik killed again, and they had to think of something else. But then Thorwald died and Eirik married. As for the match, it was generally thought that Eirik had been lucky, but as to whether he was really so lucky one can hold more than one opinion.

He married Thjodhild, the daughter of a very rich man who had lately died. That's why they said he was lucky. He moved over to his wife's fine big estate, and all went well until he murdered three more men of his neighbour's household, who had strayed beyond their own boundary into his – or Thjodhild's – land. In fairness, it should be said that this neighbour had, over two years, killed two of Eirik's farm workers. When the second was killed, the temper flared and Eirik killed his neighbour's men, two of them, not with a gang but with his own hands.

That had been too much, and Eirik, as you have heard, was out-lawed for those three years during which he had first explored Greenland, later settling there with many followers.

As for Thjodhild. She was a tall and stately and proud lady. Cold, thin-lipped, and bad-tempered. She was scornful. Her temper was not like Eirik's, who would roar out in fierce anger, and then it would all be over – he would be friendly, slapping the man on the back. Thjodhild, a fair woman and pale of skin, was different. Her anger would last longer than her husband's. Indeed, it could be wondered whether her anger would ever die. But it showed itself in clear spiteful remarks. Short remarks, but cruel ones, and they went on all day, and far into the night for all I know. Sometimes she would fix on this serving man or that serving woman as the target for this malice. And the rest of us would hate it – this malice. So was Eirik so lucky, as they said, when he married her? He got her land by the marriage, but then he lost the land by his killings. And there was another grudge between them.

Thjodhild stood up, and walked to within a few paces of Eirik, then stopped to look at me beneath her pale hard eyes half-lidded, for she stood erect. She suddenly drew back the corners of her mouth, and I thought she would smile. It was no such greeting. Instead she slowly walks from one direction to the other, from me to Eirik, from Eirik to me, looking at her husband the while in a wry sour way. She then goes back to her chair.

But what a fine hall it was! Stone walls a yard or more thick, with turf packed against the walls, on the outside, to muffle the cold. A spring of water rose just inside the rear wall of the house and followed a channel in the floor until it reached quite a deep pool sunk in the centre of the floor; the overflow was then led in another channel and conducted out of the building on the south side into the open air. I had never before been in a house with running water laid on. It was a clever idea of which Eirik was rightly proud. No need to venture out of doors in the cold winter to fetch water from a well. Moreover, if enemies should surround the house, there would be no need to send out a man with a pail only for this man to be cut down as soon as he ventured out. Moreover again, if the enemy fired his roof with their flame-tipped arrows, Eirik could hope to douse the blaze from within. Back in Iceland, as I knew, many a family had been either starved to death for lack of water, or burnt by its enemies – and, by burnt, I mean suffocated by the smouldering grass and heather turves which made our roofs.

Down the two long walls were the benches where the men of the household slept at night, or on which they sat in the evenings, warming their hands over the long fire-pit, or playing games of chess, or carving tools from bone or wood, or sharpening weapons.

At one end was the women's place and there the weaving was done. There were as many as three cooking places, and at that time there was still plenty of wood to burn, whether for cooking or warmth.

Eirik, as the greatest of all men in Greenland, and as its founder, was proud of all he had done. Yet he had another reason to be moody apart from his wife Thjodhild's haughty coldness. He liked his drink and there was little enough of beer in Greenland, and sometimes none.

Barley had grown in Iceland and would ripen. It was not for want of trying in Greenland. As soon as settling here, all the chief men had sown the seed. And they had seen it spring from the earth. Even grow tall and rustle in the wind. But the days would shorten, the nights grow colder, and the barley was still not white. Winter would strike and the stalks, still green and sodden, or brown from an illness, not from a late ripeness, would flatten to the ground, and rot. 'Greenland is the place where barley won't ripen and dies green' – was the sung reproach, and it enraged Eirik. But his grief and disappointment were as strong as his rage. 'I'll have the malt brought here in ships, you'll see if I don't,' he cried, when he heard the disgusting song. The jeer was all the more bitter for he felt the loss of beer to his own manly happiness and comfort, the health of his own body and mind so keenly.

I was told that two years after his coming, after the terrible discovery of the failure of the barley to ripen had been made, Eirik was in a great state of gloom as Yule came near, the time when the gods should be thanked with cheer and feasting and merry gamesomeness.

Matters were not improved when a ship entered the fjord and her master and crew came to Brattahlid to request of Eirik their lodging. Eirik was all ashamed to think that his guests might return eastwards after their stay and noise it: 'We were put up at Brattahlid over Yule, and all we had to drink was – water.' The rumour would go all abroad either that Eirik had made a bad choice in his new boasted homestead or that Eirik was mean. The one rumour or the other was hateful, and the likelihood was that Yule, miserable already, would be made the more wretched by the presence of sullen guests and the threat of their reports of 'all that Eirik has in Brattahlid to drink is – water'.

But all came well out of this nasty situation. For his cargo the master of this ship had been carrying a heavy freight of malt, and this was offered to Eirik in exchange for a winter's lodging. Bound for Iceland from Norway this ship had been blown to our Brattahlid. Eirik's change of mood, it is said, was wonderful. He greeted the master warmly, and, 'No, he mustn't try to lodge anywhere else round here – nowhere is so comfortable as my house.' Enormously cheered, Eirik was in great form that Yule. Beer was abundant; all were happy; Eirik laughed, and sometimes nearly cried with laughing. He was friendly to all – even to Thjodhild his haughty wife – whom he thumped once on the bottom in view of all to the hurt of her frowning pride – and there were great games of chess, and telling of stories, and there was a deal of kissing and giggling in corners. And it is believed that Eirik was not slow to partake in that sort of game himself.

'Never have we in Greenland had such a good Yule,' he told the skipper at the end of it, when the ship was about to return east with a cargo of our rolls of cloth and ropes, three white hawks, and one bear. 'And you must come again and again, every Yule, and also in summer, and for your malt we'll undertake to give goods worth more even than your malt.'

That's how it was, my son, but matters are turning out differently. Hopes and promises do not become facts always. Barley not ripening was one blow to Eirik, and though the cheer and larking that Yule were long remembered, still that a ship would always make a timely landfall with a cargo of malt, and that we should always have goods to exchange for it, could not be relied on. And there were years when hopes, eager or pining, failed. At long last a cunning and resourceful man from overseas came amongst us and taught us how to make a strong and fiery drink out of cranberries which are plentiful on the upper slopes of our fjords in the late summer. But this drink, though good in its way, and far better than nothing, was thin and dry, and lacked the fullness and body of real beer. It would make men flushed indeed, and often quarrelsome, and afterwards sad. Besides, because of its tartness it raised thirst rather than quenched it.

We have cause, you may say, to be grateful to the cunning man who taught us to make drink out of cranberries. But this man, despite this boon, was one of the set that occasioned the other great blow to Eirik. He was a priest, Jon Fisherhawk by name. Unlike most priests, he was big and powerful. But all priests had this effect. Thjodhild, not content with being cold and haughty, under teaching – that of the priests – would no longer even share her bed with her husband.

He was surly about this, for the damage to his pride, nothing else. He was furious: 'Those crafty fellows keeping tabs on my wife!' But he put the best face on it that he could: 'Well, it's not that she's all that good now,' he told his cronies, 'there are better wenches elsewhere.' And, however humiliating this was to the great master of Brattahlid, I think he was right, as I discovered myself, as I grew older, looking at the girls, and the older women too, in the neighbouring steads – and in Brattahlid itself.

But the stark fact was that it was Eirik's own favourite son, his second child, who brought this disgrace to his father, and the rejection by Thjodhild of her husband.

Of Eirik and Thjodhild's three sons, Leif, their second, was undoubtedly the most distinguished by his achievements and the most favoured in looks. He was a very tall man, the tallest I have met with in Greenland, but broad-shouldered and narrow-hipped. He had a winning smile. It could be said of him that he was both well liked by men and greatly attractive to all women. That is a rare thing indeed to happen. It happened in the case of Leif because he played fair with men, his word could be trusted, he would not go behind a man's back, and he was upright and just in his dealings. Though he was exceedingly brave and resourceful and strong, he was not a show-off. When he won honour, as so often he did, he tried to reflect praise from himself by praising others who had shared the venture.

So Leif the Lucky was lucky in many a way. Not least in this: that when Bjarni performed that act of rescuing five people – four men and one woman – from a drifting hulk – as he did, for I was in his ship and saw him do it, as I have told you – the credit of the act was taken from him and given to Leif. Poor Bjarni. It was not that Leif claimed the credit. Far from it. It was simply that when a notable deed was done by any man, the honour for it was given to the man already so rich in honour.

Such a man was greatly loved by all the ladies. Of the unmarried women each hoped Leif might notice and then woo her; if already married to another, she might lament her choice and wish herself free or, worse, that Leif might be worked on by a spell or charm. It was therefore widely rumoured that these wives would take counsel of the Little Knowing One, an old hag who dwelt by herself and made dolls, stuffing rags with hair to shape them, muttering – it was said by young boys who had spied on her – to herself the while. I said she lived by herself. In fact she lived with several cats which were striped, ugly and diseased. For payment, she would advise these women on practices or receipts to gain the attention and love of Leif. Yet for all his manliness Leif was still free at this time. He knew enough of the Little Knowing One to be wary when he received a small package containing something eatable. He would suspect that it was concocted by one of these women under direction from this witch. How especially disgustingly one of these sweetmeats was made under prescription, I may have occasion later to mention. However, there were other matters than love that occupied his mind.

Many a person asked, 'How could there be born such a son as Leif with Eirik for a father and Thjodhild for a mother?' For myself, I understand it this way: in Leif were combined the best of his parents, but little or nothing of the worst. Eirik's large build, strength, bravery and enterprise – and energy – were to be found in Leif, but not his mad anger and moodiness. Thjodhild's chastity, sense of what was proper, and caution were to be found in Leif, but not her icy pride and nasty contemptuousness.

It was this man, Leif, however, who further divided his parents, bringing shame and woe to Eirik when Thjodhild resolved never again to sleep with her husband.

It came about in this way. Whilst Eirik had been settling in his Greenland, Leif had been raiding the shores of Caithness, Sutherland, Orkney and Shetland. He had succeeded in loading his ship with a great store of plunder, and then his ship had run for Norway. The King of Norway, Olav, had lately become Christian, forcing those who were unwilling to turn to the new faith either to clear out of his kingdom or die from his sword.

Olav took to Leif when, after docking in Norway with his cargo, he appeared at the court. Leif's fighting ability was admired. The King made much of him all that winter, induced him to accept this new Christianity, and liked him so well that he only permitted him to set sail in the coming summer on the understanding that he would go to the land of his father, Eirik, and convert the people there to Christianity. So when Eirik set out for Greenland in the early summer, he included in his ship three or four Christian priests.

Leif was greeted by his parents fondly. Eirik was ignorant to start with of the trade of the three or four 'sly-looking' – as he later called them – fellows who looked too pale to be farmers and too weakly to be blacksmiths. Still, as they were companions of his son, he was ready to offer them some of his prized beer no less than to the others. They accepted with slight thanks and drank primly. But when it came out that their intention in coming to Greenland was not to do any useful work, either for themselves or for others, but to induce people to change their gods, Eirik was curt with them and next, on knowing more, downright angry. He told them that he 'by virtue of being the owner of Brattahlid, and consequently the chief man in this whole land, was thereby its priest'. He was the godi and 'by Thor, if they had anything in those skulls of theirs, he was not going – if he had anything to do with it – to allow any sneaking fellows from overseas to come into his property and mislead all his people from their loyalty to Thor and their loyalty to Thor's godi'.* By Thor's hammer he wouldn't!' He saw to it that this hammer and the idol of its owner the god – a well-carved idol it was too – were maintained with all its dues in a holy house of good mound turf. He, Eirik, was Eirik Thorwaldsson. His own eldest son was Thorwald Eiriksson, and his third and youngest was Thorstein Eiriksson. Only Leif, his second, was not bound to Thor. If these fellows thought that they could work so as to induce his family and people to betray Thor and Thor's godi and to be paid for it, they were far out. Did they truly think, lousy pale thin-lipped weaklings as they were, that he, Eirik, would stand by and see them do no honest work while they thought to win food, shelter – beer even – by stealing the dues owing to Thor and Thor's godi, through preaching a campaign of treachery?

Did they think that? By his god, Thor, he loved his son, Leif, and had thought hitherto that he was no fool, but he doubted his wisdom for once when he brought such despicable creatures under his roof under the guise of friends.

Nevertheless, despite Eirik's hostility towards them, the Christian priests stayed their ground, and over the months made their gains, baptizing one here, extracting a promise there, among the people roundabout. Their success was not received by Eirik with good grace. And it was all the more cutting since Thjodhild gave the chief example, to the priests' joy. She became a devout Christian. She built a church where she and Leif, and the other converts – these increasing in numbers – worshipped. This little church was built near enough the homestead to be reached easily in winter, and yet carefully sited so as

---

*Godi (Old Icelandic, goði). A chief in Iceland and heathen Greenland who combined the functions of both chief and priest.

not to strike the notice of Eirik if he stood at his doorway, to gaze at his fjord, and so become a daily cause of annoyance. Thjodhild, though not Leif, went to mass daily. The latter would occasionaly remain behind to distract his father's attention, and to soothe him with thoughts of further feats of exploration, and to discuss with him many practical matters.

To add to Eirik's chagrin, it was said that these priests instructed Thjodhild that now she was a Christian it would be sinful to bed with her husband so long as he remained heathen. If this is true, and it may well be, Eirik might have thought that this instruction by the priests was less because of the rules of their faith than their way of getting at him because of his rudeness to them. Perhaps the priests were right about the rule of 'no sleeping together' between Christian and heathen, but perhaps also they took pleasure in getting their own back by stating the rules.

Rightly or wrongly, Thjodhild observed the rule, and withdrew beyond the curtain of the unmarried women's quarters early each evening.

Thus Eirik, thanks to Leif, suffered another great blow, and one that had consequences. Though whether or not it was worse than Greenland being unable to produce its own beer, I cannot say.

I must say something here, though shortly, about Eirik's other two sons before returning to the doings of Leif.

If Leif was well nicknamed The Lucky, the eldest of the brothers might, by contrast, be thought of as unlucky. Thorwald was named by Eirik after his own father. Grandfather and grandson, no less than Eirik himself then, who was the godi, might be expected to be looked after by Thor. Yet it could be said that the god did not look after Thorwald well enough.

The eldest son was neither so tall, nor so comely in any way, as Leif. He was perhaps just above average height, but looked shorter than that by reason that he held himself in a weak and ugly manner – his head thrust forward on his neck, perhaps because of his somewhat poor sight, so that he was hollow-chested and his back was rounded. If he had carried himself upright he would have been a more impressive man.

At a quite early age he became scant of hair. It had never been, they said, thick and rusty red in colour like his father's, nor fair and beautiful like Leif's. Thorwald's hair was fairish but of no special colour, he grew baldish early; and he peered forward.

For all that he was a good and interesting man, and would have been more valued, if he'd not been overshadowed by both his father and his next brother. He was a mild man, a thinking one, and trying to win a reputation on his own account, and thereby he was unlucky.

Thorstein, clearly also vowed to the god, until he turned, like Leif, to the new faith, was the youngest. Like Leif too he was an impressive man, tall and robust, his hair the colour of tow. He was keen-eyed and active. He was much admired, and many a woman felt that if Leif would not have her, then Thorstein Eiriksson would make the very best match in all the land. He had spirit when roused, and was neither so even-tempered as Leif nor such a thinker as Thorwald. I liked him, though I think he was even more unfortunate than Thorwald. Rather than be chosen by a woman, though so many wanted him, he chose for himself. He wedded a fair, a good, a wonderful lady, none other than Gudrid Thorbjörnsdottir, as you should know. Indeed you do know that. But as I was with both husband and wife for a time before you were born, I can tell you – that you do not know enough, or know only imperfectly.

Eirik had more children by other women, both before and after Thjodhild, encouraged by the priests and because of her cold behaviour, refused to sleep with her husband.

Of these natural children I have nothing to say, except the natural daughter, Freydis. Unhappily, her doings must be recounted. There are many bad and wicked people, both Christian and heathen – as well as good, of both faiths – but Greenland never knew a wickeder person than Freydis. It was not that she was wicked because she was weak. Far from it. She had a fierce will, and from the beginning always saw to it that she got what she wanted. Yes, ever since she was a child this was so. Her father fondled the child when he visited its mother, a widow who cherished the help and support that such a wealthy man as Eirik could give. Eirik's headstrong temper could be seen in this child, but such a proneness to outbursts of wrath is more dangerous in a woman than a man.

Freydis took after her mother too, of course. The mother was a big, broad-hipped woman, renowned for angry scolding of both anyone or anything which thwarted her. Renowned for her energy too, and her lust. This widow, if her nature did any thanking at all, was thankful for the attentions of Eirik, though, as you can guess, Eirik allowed no other man near her while he lived. If he had found one, he would have killed him.

If Leif inherited only the best of what each of his parents had to give, it is fair to say that Freydis inherited the worst of what each of her parents had to give.

But Freydis's outbursts did not end like her father's – sulks, laughter, and then good humour. Her rages, started by sheer greed as much as a thwarting of her will, led to an act by her of utter cruelty, such as no man would be capable of, and of which her famous father would have been ashamed, if he had lived to know of it.

It was not that Freydis was not attractive. Despite her bad nature, she aroused the desire of very many men – young and old, heathen or Christian, good and bad – and this she knew. She would trade on it, and play one man off against another, always with an eye to her special advantage. She would be ready to welcome almost any man to her bed, provided he had something more to offer than his love, or desire for her. Thus, if two men were competing for her, she would accept the uglier rather than the better looking, if the uglier seemed likelier to offer in return the bigger reward – a bigger payment of some sort, not necessarily money. She would accept a young fellow of good looks and no prospects only if the visit did not clash with an arrangement with a rich, ugly, much older man – such as the bailiff, or even, as time went on, with the Vicar-General or Archdeacon.

She was, it must be admitted, wonderful in person. Of just over middle height for a woman, her hair somewhat resembled her father's, in his middle years, wherefore he was nicknamed Eirik *the Red*. But Freydis's head was less flaring, they say, than Eirik's had been. It shone deep, coppery red in which, however, there were also some tresses nearly black. Her eyes were widely spaced, staring and of a hard grey. Like her mother she had broad shoulders and broader hips, and she had, as you might expect, very full breasts. She had also, and you might expect this too, large thighs and a positively large and well-curved posterior. Whether for her top, or for her bottom, or for both, Freydis, for all her rages and cruelty of nature, attracted the desire of men, even the supposedly good ones, like the Vicar-General, when she, as well as he, was quite old. If our Bishop had cared to come out to his throne in Greenland he might have found out, and taken to task his Vicar-General and Archdeacon. But not many of our 'Bishops of Greenland' cared to come out to this stern land, though they lived in comfort on our tithes in Norway or other lands. While the doddering Vicar-General, and the Archdeacon – who had received his superior's glowing account – were in the arms of Freydis on their visits, they might have called to mind that these tithes of walrus ivory, falcons and white bears, sold in Norway or Bremen for the costly support of our Bishop, who never came to his see of Greenland, were captured with danger to our lives, and that some of it provided them with their own upkeep, and that the fees they gave Freydis for their fun with her were won at the cost of our fights with the tusked walrus and bloody bear. But we have had some good priests, and one good bishop came among his people too.

Of many women I have known, son, in the way of love – and, you understand, I do not, and would not, speak of your mother except that she was the best of all women, at the same time witty and shrewd, ever my greatest help – two have always stood out in my memory: the dear and lovely Gudrid and the wicked Freydis.

After my visit to Brattahlid, I told Heriolf that I was ready, when he thought it proper, to leave him for Eirik as had been planned. But I added that I dearly hoped I would never have to side with the one against the other.

3

LEIF TO THE NEW LANDS

Very soon after Leif's homecoming he grew restless. Nothing in the way of distinguished deeds could be undertaken before the next summer, or late spring at the earliest, yet still he wanted to be up and doing. In the ordinary way he would have looked forward to equipping his ship, sailing eastwards, and harrying the shores of Caithness, of Sutherland. He would then have sailed, aided with rapid oars, south, either down one side of Scotland or the other. In the one event, he would have raided the coasts of Northumberland, and perhaps – depending on the weather, the pluck of his crew, and the space left in his ship for plunder – would then even have penetrated the broad river as far as York, ransacking that very rich city. Or, in the other event, sailing down the west side, it would have been the fate of Chester, or parts of Ireland, to suffer from the skill and strength of Leif. Then, with autumn near, he would turn north, make final attacks on Orkney or Shetland – or on the Western Isles, again depending on his sea-path – before running homeward with a full ship.

This was his routine when his family lived in Iceland. But now it was different, not only because his family had migrated to Greenland.

The trouble was that he was now a Christian. You will remember how Olav, King of Norway, had persuaded him to be baptized the previous summer and how he had given passage to those three or four priests to Greenland, where they had done their work to the annoyance of Eirik.

Now those priests, or their like, possibly even Olav himself, had put it to Leif that it was no longer seemly to break into monasteries in England, kill the monks and steal their treasures, or to rape the women and girls in Scotland – however long he and his crew had been at sea –

for these were all Christian people, had long been so, and he now shared their faith. No, he must think of something else. But honest trading was dull. Moreover, it would mean a big cut in his income – to pay for the goods. There was this decisive disadvantage to himself in becoming Christian. And he was an eager man.

So very soon after his welcome at Brattahlid, and loosing his priests about their work, and dutifully admiring his father's new homestead, Leif chafed. It was then that, as we say, he heard what was in the wind. I was told that he seized hold of a middle-sized, middle-aged owner of a middle-sized farm in Eiriksfjord, spun him round and said: 'What is this talk of new lands? Out there – yes, further to the west? And of this Bjarni Heriolfsson having found them? Or, they say, having just seen them? Seen them merely?' So Thorir Glupsson, this farmer, repeated simply what he had 'heard' – about Bjarni Heriolfsson, about the journey from Iceland to Heriolfsness in that very ship in which I had been a passenger.

Well, there could be other countries in which people who were not Christian lived with their wealth.

Leif, in this winter, despite the mass of hard sea ice, somehow got through in a small boat to Heriolfsness. There he confronted Bjarni.

I was still at Heriolf's when Leif turned up unexpectedly, and was now of an age to note how one man could overbear another. The good old Heriolf, my fosterfather on my father's so early forsaking of Greenland, rose and told his son to stand up and greet the visitor likewise. Bjarni did so, and though brawny and well-seasoned in experience, and older than Leif, he was rather at a disadvantage in this meeting with the magnificent second son of the great Eirik. Besides he was caught unprepared, whereas Leif had it burning in his mind – what he was going to say – on his journey from Brattahlid.

He told Bjarni that he had heard that he had spied the outline of the new lands on his voyage from Iceland to Greenland when blown off his course – spied the outlines, but had lacked daring to set foot on them. Very well, he (Leif) had enough interest, and to spare, in these lands, and would Bjarni be so kind as to give an exact, a minute, account of what he had seen – and when, and call on his memory for the precise details of distances and wind directions, and so on. Then he might make a proposition, 'strike a bargain'.

At this point, Heriolf, wanting to come to the aid of Bjarni to give him time for thought, so that he might be less liable to commit himself rashly, put in with, 'Now it so happens, Leif Eiriksson, that this young fellow made the voyage with my son in the very same ship. Odd that! Come here, Ingolf, and say what you remember.' Heriolf grasped me by the shoulder and led me up to join the important men. I was proud but shy, muttering my childhood memories about Helluland first, Markland second, and Vinland third, but then chattered about a floating rock with people on it; and of how this floating rock turned out to be an upturned ship with people standing or sitting astride the keel; and of how a woman among them straddled the plank between the two vessels, and came jumping towards us on her bottom in a funny way so that we all laughed at it.

I hope I did help father and son a little. Leif had a witness in me of three lands at least, whatever he thought of the joke. Leif said he would offer so much for Bjarni's ship for a voyage next summer, providing that he was given all the particulars that either of us – Bjarni and myself – noted about those three lands westward. He understood that Bjarni had no taste for further adventures now that he had settled down with his father in this somewhat stony fjord ('such a narrow one compared with my father's') but that if I, though so young, should care to come with him, Leif Eiriksson, in this voyage to the three new lands in the summer, he would take me. It might be that I could be useful if – child as I then was – I remembered certain landmarks.

But I did not go. As I look back, I think this was partly because I was too much in awe of Leif but more that I did not much like his making out Bjarni to be poor-spirited in front of his father. I was fond of the old man.

So I pleaded that I might then miss my own father's return to Greenland, though I had in fact long ceased to believe, or even to wish, that.

Heriolf understood, and spoke for me, saying that 'the lad was too young'. Nevertheless this meeting led to my going straightway from Heriolfsness to Eirik's household at Brattahlid.

And, anyway, I was to go to these lands later. If not among the first to set foot on them, I had been among the first to sight them (with Bjarni, in his ship), and I was to set foot on them too within a few years.

Bjarni and Leif struck a deal. Leif would take Bjarni's ship, and would straightway make payment by means of such and such goods forthwith. Furthermore, though the ship would henceforth be his to keep, Leif undertook to make over to Bjarni a fair share of all or any commodities he brought back in the ship from the new lands in the west. To that he gave an oath. Bjarni knew this was a good deal on two accounts.

First, Leif was a man of his word; and second, Leif was born lucky.

It was arranged that Leif would return to collect the ship not later than the first week of summer, that it would then be taken to Eiriksfjord where it would be speedily manned and provisioned. It was also fixed that I would accompany Leif back to Brattahlid there and then, that though I would not go with the expedition next year, I could be of some use to Leif when he tried to woo his father over to leading a great undertaking himself. 'This young man can at least swear to my father that he *saw* these new lands from Bjarni's ship – which is to be mine – with his own eyes, even though Bjarni had not the heart to set foot on the new lands.'

Heriolf felt the sting of the hurt against his pride in his son and suffered for Bjarni's pride in himself, but said nothing. I knew this by looking in Heriolf's face, and was sorry. Nor did I like saying farewell to Heriolf, and I liked Bjarni well enough too. However, I thanked him for his goodness, and set off with Leif from Heriolf's door.

I have told of my first entry into Brattahlid, and of my first impressions of Eirik and his household.

Leif had done damage to his father by bringing in those priests, but in spite of that Eirik and Leif were good friends and talked much together. I would watch them.

As I understood it, Leif said nothing to disturb his father's sense of achievement in exploring, and then settling, Greenland, and becoming the chief man here. Certainly, he had done magnificently, but –

'But! What are you trying to say? But what . . .?'

Well, Brattahlid had wonderful and large grasslands for cattle – the byres for forty head of cattle in the winter were enough to show this. He agreed too that the upper slopes made good feeding for many sheep . . .

'And the fjord for fish, salmon even, many fish?'

Yes, Leif agreed, there were fish to catch, and seals too – as was proved by the excellent meal they had just had – and Father would ever be praised and envied for what he had done, and what he had made . . . but was there not something missing?

'What do I miss? What do you, or what does any man miss that I haven't got?'

'Well, there's beer. The barley won't – '

'What does it matter, if the ships bring it in? I can let them have wool, walrus hides, tusks, falcons – white bears, if it comes to that, every time the ships bring in the stuff for ale or beer.'

Father was not to get angry, but he must face the fact that the ships –
ice, storms, silliness of merchants, their stupid undervaluing of our
goods – may not always – or often – come in. That last cargo of grain
was a boon, but would it last? And it was not only a matter of beer – it
was a matter of bread. Bread was made out of this same stuff too, and,
speaking for himself, he did not think this loaf made of fish-meal,
with a lot of grit in it to grate the teeth, was quite as good as fresh good
bread made of barley. What did Father think?

Then there were other shortages. What about timber? The tallest
tree here was only as high as a man, with perhaps a child sitting on his
shoulders, and hardly thicker than a man's forearm, where it met the
ground. They had indeed been comfortable and warm that evening,
and a good seal supper had been cooked, but how long would these
small trees last, since we cut them down day after day?

'When they are all cut, we can burn the dung of the cattle from the byres.'

'Still not enough! And when that dung burns slowly, to give us a
luke-warm supper and a chilly talk afterwards, the cows will not grow
so fat because their dung should be put on their grazing grounds to
fatten the grass. Now, what Bjarni saw, not far away in the west
there – three or four days' sail with lucky weather – and I, like you, am
lucky – was a land covered with trees, tall trees, which he called
Markland. And these trees we could axe down and bring here – home –
for nothing. We wouldn't then have to trade our Greenland goods –
costly furs, ivory, I don't know what – for timber (for rafters, for the
making of boats, for weapons, for farm tools, for burning to keep
warm, for cooking) when we can get as much wood as we want for the
axing. Free too, for if any people live in that Markland, which was
seen by the boy sitting there as well as by Bjarni, and try to stop us
felling the trees, we can kill them. We can kill them, for they will be
but heathens – like these skraelings you know about.

'We need timber, Father, for these trees here are few and small. Cut
them, and burn them as we are doing, we'll shiver in a few years'
time – the dried cowpats will scarcely warm up thin gruel. If the ships
don't bring the wood, we'll die; if they do bring it we'll have to pay
for it at their price.

'Let's fetch it freely from this Markland.

'And iron! For axe and blade, for nail and sword, we need that. We
smelt inferior bog-ore here, burning up charcoal to do it.'

Eirik was given to understand that though he had done well in life
he was not yet too old to do better. The secret of his son's deal for

Bjarni's ship came out, and Eirik was asked to lead the expedition in the new year: 'Would you, sir, lead? With you we'll be sure of luck.'

Leif had put his case well. Eirik was touched by the kind things Leif had said of him. He grumbled, said he'd think about it. And he did think about it – throughout the winter, taking his son, Leif, into his confidence, and growing more and more keen. He'd show them – those who jeered that Greenland brought forth only green barley. Why, just beyond a strip of water, he would hold a backyard, stocked with timber, iron, and corn for beer and for bread, too, come to that – and wine even. And he'd get away from those priests for a while! And from Thjodhild! He'd have to leave his friend, the mother of Freydis, for a while, and he'd have to forego seeing the girl herself. Never mind, let them wait.

Spring came. Leif set off with a small party in a boat to Heriolfsness, and returned in Bjarni's ship, towing the boat. The crew was mustered, thirty-five men in all, among them Tyskir – a short shifty-eyed black-browed German who was always grinning – with Eirik as the leader and Leif his right-hand man. But not before Eirik filled a casket with gold and silver which he buried, with no man watching, in a part of his land.

It was but a short distance from Brattahlid down the slope to the ship. But Eirik would ride ahead, and I was to be bridle boy, and lead the horse back, when the brave party had embarked.

Eirik was in high spirits, but half-way between house and ship, the horse put its forefoot in a fox-hole and Eirik was flung off. He injured that same ankle-joint that was hurt before so that he cried out he could not put foot to ground. And in the fall he had broken a rib also, and damaged the arm where it met the shoulder, as he tried to guard his fall.

He said: 'I am not meant to discover any more countries than the one I am in now. And I am now old. Here we must part, my son. May the luck be with you, so we shall meet in life again, and you shall tell of your findings.'

The ship, under Leif's command, set sail. Eirik, with my and another's help, returned home. When his injuries were healed he went to the secret place and recovered his casket of gold and silver. He hid the casket at a place outside the house. Thjodhild was told nothing of this affair.

4

SUMMER HUNT IN THE NORTH PLACES

The arm bone was thrust back into the socket of Eirik's shoulder, the loose bit of his rib knitted; the wrenched ankle, though his limp was hereafter more marked, healed. For two or three weeks he had had to lie down, or to sit, a great deal more than he liked. He would shout at the cowherds and shepherds as they came for orders, and at the tenants when they came to render their dues. Occasionally, he would strike at the behinds of the maids as they'd pass by the bench where he sat. Not altogether good-humouredly either since, far from sounding out these new lands – which he had at last been roused to eagerness to see – he was housebound, fretting at his helplessness, and worried about the safety of that casket which he had buried outside. Would any man accidentally hit upon it?

Recovered to the extent that he could once more limp up and down the long hall – thumping once the bum of an aging serving-woman as she was stooping to clear the fire of ashes, so that she fell over the fire and was nearly burnt – Eirik resolved that he would at least, in that very same high summer, go to the northern hunting grounds.

These journeys are still followed, son, but more rarely now, because of the danger from the skraelings. They yearly grow more spiteful.

This summer I was to go too, for the first time, and in Eirik's boat. In readiness, Eirik sent up his youngest son, Thorstein, straightway to his place in the West Settlement. This place in the West Settlement was called Sandness, and it was on the Lysafjord.

It took then, as it does now, six men rowing for six days to get from Brattahlid on Eiriksfjord of the East Settlement to Sandness on the Lysafjord of the West Settlement. So Thorstein, twenty-seven years old and strong, set off with six men for the small property which Eirik owned at Sandness. That property was looked after, during the absence of members of Eirik's family, by a namesake of Eirik's son. This man was Thorstein the Black and he made a striking contrast to Thorstein Eiriksson. Whereas our Thorstein was handsome and well-bred, scarcely less favoured than his brother, Leif, the one nicknamed The Black was a rough and rude fellow, as one might expect from a man who looked after someone's lesser house in return for the right to till a smallholding. As a sideline, Thorstein the Black did the work of a smith at which he had some skill. He had a forge in which he beat iron to shape from ore obtained by smelting the reddish stone dug at the edges of a bog. Because of this work, he had heavy shoulders and very thick forearms. These forearms were covered by long black hairs, as also was his chest which he bared when he struck the glowing metal with his hammer. The hair of his head was likewise black, thick, and grew so low down on his brow that it almost reached the eyes. He had gaps where teeth should have been in both the upper and lower jaws. When nothing annoyed him, he could be easy enough, but was very surly, forthrightly gruff, when it suited him. He had a wife, now dead – but I shall tell you about that – whose name, for some odd reason, I have difficulty in remembering. But I am certain of this: her name was either Sigrid or Grimhilda. Sigrid or Grimhilda? She was a gaunt woman, tall though she bent at the shoulders, as though inspecting the ground two yards in front of her. She had a long nose, thin lips, and wore a sort of scarf over her head which didn't fully conceal the faded yellowish straggle of locks on her forehead. More of this hair could be seen from a rear view of this Grimhilda – or Sigrid – and from that view it but looked grey.

Her husband, beside tilling the smallholding and working with hammer and anvil, did a little fishing within the fjord – Lysafjord.

Our Thorstein, as I can't make too clear, was noble in his build. He was fair, or rather his hair was the colour of pale new rope – tow-coloured – but it was noble and fine.

A week after Thorstein's going, Eirik himself, and six others including me, followed. We were accompanied by two other boats with the same complement of men. One was led by Thorkel, after Eirik the next biggest farmer in Eiriksfjord, and the other from nearby Einarsfjord. Thorkel was a big broad-faced man, somewhat bald. He was good-natured, was said to be hospitable. He had a wide mouth and liked to smile.

Our three boats made for Lysafjord. It was a long journey, and I must say that Eirik did more than his full share in pulling at the oar. At night we moored in the creeks along the coast. Eirik, from his three former visits to the grounds, knew exactly where the best stages were to be found. We chewed salted fish, and managed as best we could. We had sweated in the sun, now low at midday, but shivered as the dew fell. Eirik was bold and kept us in good heart.

We reached the Lysafjord after the regular six days, and in its calm water gained Sandness. Thorstein had done his job well. Thorstein the Black, under his orders, had re-ground and sharpened all the spears and given a freshened edge to the knives and other tools. He had de-rusted the chains and shackles. His wife – this Sigrid or Grimhilda – prepared a meal and gave us the provisions for the hunt, provisions which would need to last until we could relish the new meat.

In high mood, Thorstein Eiriksson's boat now joining ours to make a fourth – making a party of some twenty-eight men – we moved early next morning, northwards to the hunting grounds. Days passed and each one grew colder. There were more and more ice-floes, between which we steered bravely and with skill; the sheer face of the mountain on our starboard became barer and blacker, set off by the streaks of ice. Gulls were many, and gannets sprang from their cliff-nests high up, and I saw an eagle.

Eirik, and the other experienced men, knew exactly the signs and omens. And they knew the creeks, and the landmarks. Eirik handed over his oar to another, standing up in the stern of the boat, the sooner to catch sight of a particular creek and a particular spur of rock projecting from the northern shore of that creek where it met the sea. Then he spied the creek and the tongue of rock. We were above half a mile from the cliffs, and he told us to lift our oars. For a while our boat rode up and lowered on the heave of the swell, moving, it seemed, neither forward nor backward, and with the oar blades drifting. Eirik, and the leaders in the other boats, were all standing, and the one next to us was actually standing on the thwart. This man nodded to Eirik and made a sign. Elbow touching his side, he lifted and dropped his right hand to the level of his shoulder some four or five times, fingers divided.

The sign gave Eirik satisfaction. He seated himself on the stern-sheets and, with the ball of the palm on his right knee, dropped and raised his fingers, loosely divided, some four or five times.

35

At the signal from Eirik, Thorstein Eiriksson's boat rowed further out to sea, passing beyond the spur of rock. The three other boats, at the same time, turned in close to the shore and, as we rounded the southern point of the entrance to the creek, we could hear great bellowings and barkings, though I could see nothing, which came from the direction beyond the spur which ran out from the northern point. In file we proceeded about half a mile, or more, up the creek. We drew to the shore, moored, and then Eirik explained. Just beyond the spur of rock behind us was a great flat table or shelf of land, just above the level of the sea. But it would be swept by high waves and, he warned us, slippery. It would, when we came to it, be pitted with small pools. The roars and barkings that we heard gave him delight. We could take it, as he knew from three earlier journeys, that there were between some thirty and thirty-five walruses – or whale-horses, you surely know what the word means, son? – on that shelf, and that the roarings and screams that we heard were the result of savage males in dispute with each other for one of two rights: either for land – a fight as to which of the two should own a part of the flat table of rock or, more likely, at this time of the year, as to which of the two, by bloody battle, should have the right to become the husband of between eleven and twenty-one shes. He guessed, if the sighting of the steersman who had stood on the thwart was correct, that we might find between twenty and thirty full-grown beasts and an uncountable number of mothers suckling their young. 'These few males are still fighting each other as to which will have the right to mate with the females and become the father of the next brood of the year, even though the wives are still giving milk to their first lot of children.'

We, at first light in the morning, were to scramble over the lowest part of that spur of rock, with a spear in one hand and an axe in the other. You must imagine a woman lying naked, but prone not supine, on a bed. She supports her upper body weight on her two elbow joints. The highest points are her shoulder blades, the next highest are the top points of the curve of her buttocks. But what is the lowest point – from the thigh downwards not reckoned?

'I'll tell you,' Eirik said, 'it is her waist, the small of her back – unless she's beastly fat – and such is not this rock. You are, the whole lot of you, except one in each boat, to scramble over the low waist of this rock – beware of the slipperiness – with spear in right hand and axe in the left – change over afterwards as it may come about. Attack, first, the males – or they will kill you – next the plumpest females.

Their children are not worth much, but take some. My son, Thorstein, is standing off shore, in this dark – but, there, he's just burned off a pitch flare for us to see he's there – for two reasons: first, as he rows to shore, to frighten the whale-horses from escaping by plunging into the sea, and second, to frighten off the skraelings if they show up, and try to interfere.'

I am very excited, and can hardly sleep. It is cold; the stars shine; and the roarings of the animals fighting or mating is heard. And heavy splashes and thumps as when one or another plunges into the sea.

Very early, our boats are prepared, weapons ready – spears and axes, the poles and chains stretched along the keelboard – and we move quietly down the creek. One man is to stay in each boat since the Lying-on-her-Belly-Elbow-Supported-Legless-Woman Rock would not take mooring-stakes. Coming alongside the waist, the rest, one after the other, step over the gunwale. Now I see the flat shelf smothered by the tusked beasts. I have been told where to thrust with the spear. I forget to be wary of the slime on the rock, but lift myself at once after pitching foremost, not noticing the hurt to knuckles clench-ing spear and axe.

Rending are the roars of the beasts. Men shout. Violent the strength behind the spear as its point is thrust behind the bone of the fore-member of the beast where it joins the body. Gnashings and screams as, point withdrawn, blood floods out of the hole to mingle with the slime of sea and beast on the shelf. More slippery then. Don't fall, or the tusks will come down from above into belly, or throat, or through back.

Some of the beasts plunge off the shelf into the sea. Spray drenches. Thorstein, out at sea all night, is closing in. After the males, go for the suckling shes. A man, not able to dodge to the side of the beast as she lunges at him, thrusts his spear down her gullet, as she lifts up her head high with her horrid tusks. The point of the spear comes out at the back of her head, and the shaft of the spear snaps as the head is lowered in the grab of pain. Farmer Thorkel, broad-faced and of late middle years, I see – and he's smiling – does his job skilfully, deftly skipping left to right, like a dancer, in his special rock-gripping thin-soled shoes. He notices that I see him. I go on with my work. Wounded and groaning, blood-pouring bodies are many. And dead ones. The young ones squeal. Go for them last. Easy to take.

All through it, Eirik was as strong or stronger than men much younger. And lame a bit, as he was, more crafty in the work than all the rest, more skilful even than Thorkel with his clever side-stepping ways.

But even Eirik had had enough. A few of those which escaped, by plunging into the sea, came rolling in with the waves, watching the killing of their tribe, but unwilling to clamber on the shelf to meet us. Of the sucklings, Eirik told us to slay the youngest, but to push or kick those nearly weaned into the water. 'Come back next year and we'll take you for meat and ivory,' he jeered.

Barely half of an hour since we began our attack. But now there was much work to do. The poles were dragged out of the boats, set up and lashed together, and the chains slung from them.

With wedge and axe handle the tusks were wrenched from their sockets. As the beasts were slung head down from the frames, the hides were cut from them, and sliced into strips. Beheaded, the animals were split open, and their entrails – hearts, lungs, livers, kidneys, guts, all their entrails – drawn. The gulls, gannets, and other birds of prey, flocked screaming from the black cliff and mobbed us in their hundreds, even wheeling between our axe blades and the flesh the blades struck at. There was a gathering of particular bones of the beasts: of the two-foot-long begetting bone of the male, later to be driven into the walls of the stables of horses for the hanging-up of halters; of the broad thigh bones for use as shovels; of rib bones to act as handles of the pots fashioned by our womenfolk. Six of the skulls, their tusks drawn, were scraped for burial in the dwelling of the idol Thor. 'Or I'll plant them in my wife's churchyard. She may then believe that her worshipped one, no less than my Thor, brings in the herds for our summer hunting', said Eirik.

The thick blubber was being heaped into one mound by the waist of the Lying-on-her-Belly-Elbow-Supported-Legless-Woman Rock, ready for carrying in buckets over the waist to a spot where we might set it into flame for the cooking of young walrus steaks – a meal for which we were in need, though only now were we beginning to feel hunger. Then Thorstein Eiriksson, still riding in his boat seventy or eighty strides from the coast, makes a sudden sign to his father, holding an oar blade aloft, waving it from side to side three times and then pointing it towards three or four small black quickly moving things. Soon there were many more than three or four, and we could see that they were many very small boats with one sort of man in each, or so it seemed. Some were already darting around Thorstein's boat, and he was shouting at them, threatening. The strange men in the little boats would lay down their paddles, and take up a sort of bolt and shoot. A man standing up in Thorstein's craft, cursing and shaking his fist, appeared to be hit, falling overboard. I saw Thorstein grasp his comrade's hair, as he surfaced, and, almost at the same time, with but five rowing men, ram one of the nimble little boats so hard that his boat's prow, and then the keel, rode over it. Then others of the swarm came nearer to the shelf of rock, where we had been toiling and stooping over the bodies of the slain beasts, and started shooting their bolts at us. I say bolts. They were strips of fine bone, or splinters of bone, and they were tipped with something hard and sharpened that was not iron. One of the wretches had come in so close to the ledge that he landed, though at the furthest point, and came towards us. He was making faces, speaking a strange speech, nodding or shaking his head, showing his teeth and his tongue. Waving his hands too; but in one of these hands was a weapon. Eirik walked straight towards him, though limping, but when he was near, brought round the axe, which he held behind his back, showed it, and then flung it with all his force at the wretch. It hit into the neck, and the man fell. Eirik followed up, recovered his axe, and killed the thing.

Meanwhile Thorstein, ever active and resourceful, had rapidly rowed close in to shore, and now moved, slowly but carefully, in a line between the shelf on which we were gathered and the remaining crowd of small boats. His man who had been shot overboard, I noticed, if alive, would not drown. His head must have been in the bottom of the boat; his arse drooped over the gunwale; his feet must have trailed in the water. With but two of his men pulling at the oars, Thorstein himself and the three remaining men were drawing their bows, and shooting arrow after well-aimed arrow at the men in the little nimble boats. And they killed several of these men, as it was easy to see, some of their boats turning right over – an arrow sticking in the breast of the man – and floating upside-down.

To our yells and tauntings, the wretched attackers withdrew, those who survived coming together and paddling out of sight.

Nearly all the others had met skraelings in earlier huntings far away up in the north. But they were something new to me, and I was curious.

The one Eirik had killed with his axe, in such a bold fashion, I examined with my eyes. 'Like one, like all,' said Eirik. 'Apart from the difference between a man skraeling and a woman skraeling, they're all alike.' And the others agreed.

This one was of good moderate breadth between the shoulders, had a full chest and strong shoulders, but his legs, stout enough, were very short indeed. If he had had legs to match the length of his body, he might have been more like one of us in stature – or not very much less – but this was not so. This one standing would scarce reach to the height of our bosoms, if that. His arms however were more decently in proportion, perhaps because of all the paddling the skraelings did from their boats.

The man had tough black hair on his head, a low brow, and eyes which were almost black and which slanted towards the corners, shaped like the shells of shut mussels. The face was so boned as to be ugly, and of a dark dirty colour, like the sides of some wooden jars. The bones of his cheeks stood out and the top of his head, despite the broad face, was narrow, and in its centre was a curious ridge which I felt. There was no beard or hair on the upper lip, yet they did not shave.

Eirik pointed this out, and he then stripped the man. There was no hair on his chest either, and scarcely any under his arms. The body was all this strange wooden colour. The nose was a curious shape, nearly level with the face where it met the brows.

'A woman would look like this, except for her womanness, and her wider hips and narrower shoulders, and her smaller stature, and yet wider head,' Eirik said. 'But there might be another difference.' He turned the body over so that it lay face down. 'See where I put my foot,' placing it at the lowest point of the back. 'In the women skraelings, and in the young children whether boy or female, you may see just here a blue patch. It fades with the men children as they grow up.'

I looked at the garb of the creature. Hood and tunic, trousers, footwear – they were all made of one animal skin: sealskin. What held up the man's breeches was a sinew of the seal, and garments were sewn by other sinews.

His little boat, from which he had landed on the shelf, was made of sealskin stretched over a frame of seal bones, bound tightly together by seal sinew. Except for a hole in which the skraeling sat, the boat was covered by the stomach wall and other membranes of this animal, so that, when the boat turned over and over, the water would not enter. The bow or bolt from which the arrow sped was a bone of the seal, treated to make it vibrant and bendable. The string was made of a long muscle string of the seal, folded for strength. In this wretched craft, which yet rode the waves lightly instead of cleaving them, I saw a blown-up bladder. It was a seal's bladder and with this thing, when it floated, they lured seal or fish, or rorqual or the narhwal.

He was an ugly little man, and our people said they did not much care for their women when the chance came, for their breath stank of fish or seal or whale-horse oil, and that they were too small to be much good, and that their legs were clammy since they ordinarily never took off their clothes. They had sorcerers among them who sometimes made them mad, when they would scream, roll their eyes, writhe their bodies.

What did they eat?

Well, they ate, I was told, seal mainly. But they went also for walrus. That explained our fight with them. They sought to take away what we had earned for ourselves by our killing. They liked the flesh and made ornaments of the bones. When one of these people died, his fellows, far from putting him in the earth in a cleanly fashion, reared a low little hut over him made with stones. And they left an eating bowl, made of soft stone, beside him, and a charm carved out of one of the chain of small bones, joined up by the main thread, forming the back of a seal or whale-horse. The trouble was foxes would muzzle between these stones and, dislodging them, would devour the flesh, dragging the man's leg or an arm out of the hole they made. Therefore these little low stone abodes of the dead were smelly places. And Eirik said he had seen some of these places, and bits of their boats, and other nasty scraps, near Brattahlid when he first settled his homestead. So he knew the skraelings had once passed near there. He was 'ready for them', but he rather believed they had slunk away far to the north, and hence we only encountered them when we, as we were doing now, went far up the coast to undertake our summer hunting of the sea-beasts.

At times the skraelings hunted and killed the white bear – for its meat. But, he believed, they died from it, because they did not know that the liver of the white bear was poison.

There was talk as to what to do with the man's body. Thorkel was for letting it lie where it fell on the ground since it would draw the attentions of the gulls and gannets, while we rested in our boats laden with tusks and whale-horse meat. Eirik was against this, since there was a chance that the skraelings might return to fetch off the body. So the body was pushed off the ledge into the sea, and we could hope, if only for a while, that the gulls would follow the corpse rather than the meat we had claimed.

Much hurried work then. Our three boats, each with its single oarsman, and Thorstein's boat with its six living, and one dead, man – he had by now altogether been withdrawn into the boat, and we were later to see a stone arrow head lodged deep into the side of his head – drew alongside the edge of the shelf.

We piled into the boats the block, poles and heavy chains, then the tusks, the hides, the stripped bodies of the beasts, and all the things of the killing worthy of saving. We embarked and, rowing round the hanging head of the Lying-on-her-Belly-Elbow-Supported-Legless-Woman Rock, we proceeded up the creek to rest for the night.

But first, before it was dark, we found a soft and level piece of grassed and damp earth. It was not long before we struck stone. But it was deep enough. Over the grave of Thorstein's man we then heaped a small cairn, and on the largest stone one of his friends then cut a single rune.

There was much blubber. Over the several fires we cooked the stripped bodies of many of the infant walruses. There was nothing to drink except water. A spring gushed from a rock and we were thirsty. I felt as though I had never been so thirsty before.

And we feasted. We drove our stakes the length of the suckling walruses for roasting, enjoying the first fresh meat we had had for several days. We were happy. Untroubled too, before darkness, by the gulls, which had enough to gorge upon from the offal and the bloodied insides of the beasts we had left behind us on the ledge or shelf.

I had to stand watch first since I was the youngest but, when I was relieved, I slept well despite the coldness of the night.

But we were forced to wake early. In good cheer, in our four, now heavily laden, boats, we passed the famous rock. Eirik raised a merry greeting to her, the Rock – 'Still be kneeling like that, lass, when we come back, and I'll see what I can do for you' – and made for the south and home as fast as we could, however deep in the water our boats were, taking care of the floating ice, threading our way.

Eirik, in our boat, was in good spirits, pleading his years as a reason for doing the steering, instead of sitting on the thwarts as he did coming up, taking his full share. 'This is my fourth trip, and it is likely to be my last; let me steer and think a bit,' he said. We agreed, but he took his place on a thwart later, while another steered. For all his reputation as an ungovernable man, he was companionable as well as mighty.

We made first for Sandness on the Lysafjord in the West Settlement, for there Eirik had that house looked after by that overseer, a namesake of his son's.

Thorstein Eiriksson, our Thorstein, standing on the steering bench, kept abreast with us for a while – the water just there being clear enough of ice – each boat struggling for a lead. But Eirik took his place on the thwart, telling another to steer, for he was not going easily to be outdone, even in a game, and our boat gained nearly half its length over the other. There was about the space of a nine-year-old boy's stone throw between the two boats. Eirik shouts:

'You didn't do too badly, Thorstein, at the shelf, did you, my son?' Then after five or six great tugs at the oar: 'And though little enough – of this meat we're taking home – is owing to your efforts, yet –' straining hard, our boat even increased its lead by a little – 'yet you did succeed in killing a few of those skraelings.'

Thorstein smiled. He knew at heart that his father was pleased with him.

'Which is why', Eirik larked, 'you think you can take things easy now, standing up there, pretending to steer, letting your men do all the work – '

'Well, that's right, for of all the skraelings killed, I killed the most,' Thorstein protested.

'And lost one of your own men in that deal,' roared Eirik. 'And that is why, perhaps, your being one man short, we're beating you in this race.'

On that hint, we gave six yet mightier tugs on our oars, and drew yet further ahead, Eirik laughing in proud happy joyous fun. Thorstein, taking it all in good part, waved and made a mocking bow. Father and son were good friends, even though Thorstein, like his mother and elder brother, Leif, and even the eldest, Thorwald, had become Christian by now.

But Eirik couldn't keep this up. Complaining about his years, and muttering about a pain where his arm had become unlocked from the shoulder when he took the fall from his horse at the start of the summer, he gave up his oar to another, and sat for a while on the steer-board.

So it was that Thorstein overpassed us, without too much difficulty, a little later. Thorstein, still standing, called:

'And you haven't done badly yourself, Father.' And then kindly: 'But take care, sir, you're getting on in years.'

Eirik lifted his hand as a token he had heard, and thought well of the speech, and then we rowed on in silence, Eirik even becoming gloomy, content to be second. Indeed, it was agreed that Thorstein should speed forward to give notice of our coming.

43

When we at last staged at Sandness in Lysafjord of the West Settlement, we were more than half-way to Brattahlid. Sandness looked a meaner place than Eirik remembered. As its owner, he called the overseer, Thorstein the Black, to task. The surly fellow had little to say except to grumble about the poor summer weather. The green hay harvest had been scant, and it was this, not his neglect, that accounted for the sickly condition of the cattle. If 'Eirik Thorwaldsson wanted a better milk yield, he – the landlord – might be so kind as to grant a few of his superior livestock from his own fine farm to graze at Sandness'.

Eirik replied that poor weather might account for sickly cattle, but it did not excuse ill-kept outbuildings. The man had better look out. Nevertheless Eirik was less than harsh, because the man – ill-favoured, but strong of frame, as befitted one who also did the job of a smith in the forge – looked hardly fitter than the animals he was to maintain.

Sandness was small compared with Brattahlid. Because of the harsher winters here, the house was divided into rooms opening on to a central passage. Thorstein the Black and his wife gave up the best room, as was fitting, to their chief guests. Eirik, Thorstein his son, Thorkel, two others and myself were quartered in this room during our stay. On each of the four boats slept some, the rest being sent to farms round about. The overseer's wife served supper. She was not comely enough to merit Eirik's friendly advances – far from it, and indeed it would have needed an attractive and lively woman to have roused Eirik from his low spirits on discovering the poor plight of his Sandness. And the supper Grimhilda served was as poor, thin and ugly as herself – a warmed up gruel followed by dried and tough sea fish. Hungry and weary men, who had fought the seas, monsters of the seas, and skraelings, were not in the mood to take kindly to fare of this sort. Eirik ordered joints of the meat stored in his boat to be fetched up and cooked, whatever the hour. Grimhilda 'could eat the gruel herself, give the fish to her husband to stodge himself with, and for a special favour he would let the couple have a slice of the meat'. The bent thing said nothing but did as she was told.

Late that night, father and son sat talking over the embers of the fire.

Eirik, wanting assurance, began by asking his son what he thought of Greenland: 'Was it not a fine country, with an abundance of wealth to offer the settler?' And 'What about Brattahlid?' He did not think that Thorstein would have found an equal to *that* if he had stayed on in Iceland.

'You have done remarkable things in life, Father, that I will say.'

'And all the kings and earls in quite distant lands have heard of Eirik of Brattahlid?'

'They have; and they have heard of the rich grass for your cattle, and the great number of cattle you have; and the hugeness of your byres necessary for the stalling of so many in the winter. But – '

'But – ?'

'For all the riches of Greenland, it is a pity that the barley won't ripen; and that there would be no bread for us if the ships didn't come in.'

'And no beer.'

'I was thinking of that too, Father, but wished to turn your mind from that shortage.'

'Well, what is to be done about it? I can't go back to Iceland to be scorned. They would kill me as soon as see me. Or they would laugh at me as a failed man ("Is Greenland not so green, then, Eirik?"), which would be far worse. I cannot go back to the land of my birth, Norway, either. The life-ban against me holds there too. And, in any case, I am too old to begin all over again.'

'But we have riches that Iceland has not got, nor other lands.'

'Handsome women, you mean? There are not so many of those.'

'You know, Father, what I mean. I mean not ladies, but what we've been doing all these last days and nights. Food from the sea. And not only the fish, and the sea salmon, and the lake salmon. Iceland has those and we have them too. I mean the meat – and we've just had some – of the whale-horse. Not only that beast. We catch and eat seal too. And narwhal. Sometimes the whale. And it's good strong meat. There we're lucky.'

'Yes, my Thorstein, but think. Think of the toil and heart it has cost us to catch this meat. Not much sleep. Cold. Hard rowing many days. This was my fourth trip, and I feel fagged by it. And you lost a man. You were lucky. Earlier times, we lost more men than one: one man gored in the belly by the tusks of a whale-horse – slipping in the blood and slime down onto his back, and the beast down on him; another man slipping in the slime, falling into the sea, being carried away; three men – no five, last time – killed by those unutterable wretches – skraelings; another man having an eye knocked out by a stone; another with an arrow in his groin and unmanned. Yes, we do have this meat, which other lands haven't, but it is paid for – and the weather grows harsher and the skraelings greater in number, and more vicious, each year we hunt.'

'Yes, Father, but it is not only the meat we shall enjoy for ourselves. There are the hides of the whale-horse in our boats, and from these hides we'll make ships' ropes which we'll sell for grain. And of their bones we have use for many things in stable, byre, field, cooking place.'

'And then there are the tusks – ivory, Thorstein?'

'Besides the whale-horse, whale, seal, and the wealth of the sea, we take in Greenland the white bear's young, and it sells for a whole load of timber to kings or earls in the east over the sea. Or we kill the grown bear, and its skin sells for scarcely less. Or we trap our white Greenland falcon, and that is worth a load of the iron we need from the Swede.'

'You have done well indeed, sir, and are famous.'

'I mentioned, Thorstein, the tusks of the whale-horse – ivory. And you turned to white bears. Why? I know, as it happens, why the easterlings will pay heavily for those tusks we have brought back in our boats, and which are now in Lysafjord!'

'Sir, be not too bitter. You are going on to say that the Christians in Denmark, Norway, Bremen, Iceland itself, make little boxes out of this ivory, with a little window made of pig's bladder put in the front of these little boxes. And that Christians peep through the windows to worship bits of bone, or other relics of saints – '

'Bits of an old woman's knickers, or an old man's sneeze rag – '

'And these boxes, made of Greenland ivory, Father, are called reliquaries – '

'And other trinkets they make – the Christians – out of our ivory: crosses, and other such things – gewgaws.'

Thorstein, who knew only too well, that Thjodhild's acceptance of the Christian faith had led to division between his parents, tried to steer the matter into talk of economics.

'But you will agree, sir, that this ivory is one of our Greenland's greatest riches. In exchange for it we gain, besides what we need, things which delight – best quality malt for the making of the strongest ale . . .'

Yet Eirik, for a while, was too set on muttering about what he called the Creepie-Crawlies – men who did no work, but hung round his wife; men who instead of being proud of honest names, called themselves Sera Peder, or Sera Pál, or Sera Mattias: names, he understood, of dark little people with hooked noses who lived far, far away in hot lands. And even his children! Leif first, then 'you too' Thorstein, and – who knows? – his eldest Thorwald last – all doing the dirty on Thor, whose godi he was, and betraying the other gods. Not that his sons held off from him as their mother did, but it was bad enough.

Happily Thorstein, knowing his father well, and liking him much, did manage to get Eirik into good humour again. This he did by cunning and sound economics. So that, in due course, Eirik was roaring with laughter as he exclaimed:

'Well, that's all right, Thorstein, don't mind me. If your Christians overseas want to pay me high prices for my ivory so that they can make little boxes with pig's bladder windows for the faithful to peep in at a patch from an old lady's knickers or an old fellow's sneeze rag, that suits me – even if it also costs us a man or two, thanks to the skraelings, in the getting of the stuff.' And then:

'Thorstein, as you like my land, you ought to find a woman, settle down, and have sons to follow on. I'd like that before I die.'

Thorstein replied that he understood as much, and it suited his own plans:

'But, since you are in laughing mood now, Father dear, I must tell you that the woman I seek as a bride must not only be handsome, and, as you said, there are not so many of those in Greenland – '

'Stuff!' said Eirik, thinking of the mother of Freydis, and forgetting what he had said.

' – but must also be Christian.'

'Well, have it – or her – as you like,' said Eirik, willing now – for he was tired too – to be easy. 'But have a her – and it – you should soon. I'm getting on, and you are the youngest of my three sons.'

They then talked of the other two, Leif and Thorwald, but more of the former.

'If Bjarni Heriolfsson, and some of those with him, spoke truth of the lands sighted out there – on their coming to Greenland – there may be wealth for us to fetch from them – to bring back home here, Thorstein.'

'You say, they all say, Bjarni was too faint-hearted to set foot on those shores. So much in a hurry he was to greet his father, Heriolf, that he played the part of a weak man.'

'So much the better. It's left to my Leif – and if it hadn't been for that unlucky fall from my horse, it would have gone to my fame to claim those riches for ourselves.'

'They say he saw trees growing. Many, many trees along the shoreline, for miles behind white sand, and waves breaking on that sand. They say it. And he says it. So he actually called the place, Markland. Now if that's true, Father, why did he sell his ship, for not such a big price, to our Leif?'

'Perhaps there were no trees at all.'

'But, then, further south, he says – and they say – those that were with him – they saw another land very well grassed indeed.'

'We'll know about the truth when Leif returns. He may be already at Brattahlid. He may be home before we get home, Thorstein.'

'But if he's not?'

'Then he's lost – I hate and dread that thought – lost, and all those with him – or the new country is good, and his coming home with the news will not be before next early summer.'

'Well, we'll be knowing soon enough.'

'Now that lad over there. He came over with Bjarni.'

'All that he remembers is an upturned ship, four men walking the plank to safety, and one slut female astraddle the plank, jerking along as though leap-frogging. It struck his fancy.'

'That's all he says he remembers, I dare say. He's a friend still of Bjarni's.'

'I'm going to wake him up, and find out what he did see.' And Thorstein came over, grasped my shoulders and pulled me roughly.

Now, as a matter of fact, I had not been asleep. I had heard them talking; but, so tired, I had just begun to drowse off to their voices. And in that short drowse, I had had a dream – of what it was I had once seen – of a long line of trees. I dreamed that I had seen the trees go on for mile after mile, and day after day. But they were misty, and going up and down. Or perhaps it was that I had seen them from a ship, and it was the ship that was going up and down. Whichever it was, when Thorstein pulled me upright so that I sat on the bed, and said to me, 'Did you, or did you not, see trees on your way to Greenland? And land covered with grass? Trees! Did you see trees?', I said, 'Yes, I saw many trees – miles of trees, shimmering between a long white sand on which waves broke, which is why Bjarni called it Markland.'

'Well, why have you only said that now, instead of babbling about a plank and a silly woman?'

'I don't know. Because it was funny. But it has all come back. There were trees.'

Thorstein pushed me back on the bed, and he and Eirik talked again.

Eirik was now eager. If Leif found this Markland, then we could fell the trees and bring the timber back to Greenland. Then we needn't buy the wood from Norway, depending on the ship from that country reaching us. Moreover, if there was land with plenty of grass, it might grow corn, or take our barley that would ripen. We'd cut it and bring it back. It would be ours to cut. No bargaining with foreign merchants! Bread for the making!

'And beer,' said Thorstein.

'And beer,' roared Eirik with a great jovial laugh. 'And beer. Lots of it. And there may be other things.'

'Such as?'

'Good things! Wine even!'

And then he said that if we would sell these hardly won goods, such as our whale-horse ivory, falcons, white bears, not for necessary things – malt, timber, iron – but for costly, dainty goods, then we could live out here in Greenland more handsomely than kings and earls in Norway, Denmark, England, anywhere.

'That is, if there are no skraelings in Markland, or those other lands, to try to stop us getting and fetching the goods home,' said Thorstein.

'If they're no fiercer there, we'll kill them, if they try to stop us, as we kill them here,' said Eirik.

'But suppose there are more of them there than there are here?' said Thorstein.

'Then we'll kill them all the same,' replied Eirik.

The talk turned again to marryings.

'I'd like to see you wedded, Thorstein, providing that the woman is both comely and brings a dowry that a son of Eirik can rightfully expect. You say she must be Christian too. I'll give way so far as to say, whatever my feelings, that I would allow that – for I see that in this country our own gods are doomed to their death – but she must be handsome and she must be rich. You ought to be married; and I ought to see you settled and with sons before I die.'

'That meets my wishes too.'

'As you know, all the girls are running after your brother, Leif. And married women, I hear, are even paying that old hag they call the Little Knowing One for wicked love charms. I know the secret of one of those charms – and how it's made. You're too young, my dear Thorstein, to know about such things, but one day I'll tell you about it, if you're good. The charm is called. . . .' He stopped. 'And it is made in this manner. . . . One day, I'll tell you.'

'But the wenches can't catch Leif!'

'Now these girls are nearly as mad about you as they are about Leif. You are the next best catch, for Thorwald, older than either of you and still unmarried . . . well, I have scant hope of his getting married and getting children, while I am still alive. He is too short of sight to see pretty faces. And he thinks about other things than pretty faces. He looks towards the ground. He may, I fear, be unlucky.

49

'So it's up to you, Thorstein – to up a wench, I mean.'

'And I share the thought.'

'I want to see this Sandness, where we are now, better looked after. Take a wife, and I'll make it over to you. It shall be yours. You'll be the owners when you are married.

'And the sooner the better. This swarthy fellow, this sour namesake of yours, is doing less than he might to build the place up. Namesake of yours "Thorstein". In my thoughts I call him "Grim-looks" and his wife – let's see – "Old Pole-axe". With you as master here, they'd work harder.

'I'd like you at Sandness since the West Settlement altogether is likely to grow bigger and richer. And I'll tell you why.

'By my reckoning this Helluland – Slab Land – which Bjarni Heriolfsson first saw when he wandered astray at sea in his search for his father's home, is due west of where we now are, and a short distance away at that.

'If Leif hits on those riches in the new lands, many ships will be plying between Greenland and Helluland, Markland, Vinland. And all those ships will take farewell of Greenland *here* and, returning from these new lands, will first pass great Greenland *here*.

'Here the ships from the East Settlement will take on food and water. They will ask for a re-grinding of tools and weapons *here*. Thorstein the Black must do that grinding, and to that extent I'll humour the fellow.

'Ships laden with the timber and other goods from the new lands will call here, and, if you look after Sandness well enough, you, son, will have first choice in the deals. Through you, Thorstein, I will be as strong up here at Sandness in the West Settlement as I am at Brattahlid in the East Settlement.

'That lad, over there, may be sleeping, and if he isn't, I don't care.

'The fact is that old Heriolf thought to do me out of the best site in all Greenland. He chose a narrow, stony fjord. He was a fox. He wagered that all ships from Norway, Iceland, and everywhere else would either home to his place first, or – if bound for me but finding Eiriksfjord full of ice – they'd fall back on him, unloading at Heriolfs-ness.

'Cunning old fox. But if we do not have to buy, but can freely take our greatest needs from the new lands, those ships will load and unload at my place in the West Settlement – Sandness.

'So I want you to look after the profit and riches of our family here.

'And if that boy is asleep so much the better. He was fond of old Heriolf and of his son, Bjarni, who did not dare to set foot on new lands he was the first to see.'

I fell asleep.

In the early morning, Thorstein the Black and his wife were summoned. They were warned to manage the household and outhouses better and to render the smallholding as ably as they worked the forge; that before a year had passed it was likely that Thorstein Eiriksson, with the authority of his father, would become master of Sandness.

The surly man's wife put much of the blame on the meanness of the place, and the blame of the plight of all the dwellings in the Lysafjord as a whole, onto the bailiff, Gurdar.

Gurdar was called. While he was being fetched, the wife of Thorstein the Black, 'Old Pole-axe', declared that Gurdar had the power of casting the evil eye, and that 'he has cast it on me'.

'And why would he want to do that?' asked Eirik.

'Because he wants my body – to use it,' said Grimhilda.

Eirik supposed she was mad. That any man's lust should rise for her was improbable. But he gravely asked:

'And does your husband know of this?'

'He knows of it. But he does nothing about it. Thorstein behaves as though he was not unwilling that Gurdar should use me.'

Gurdar entered. He was a tall man with strange eyes. One of the eyes was fixed, unmoving as though dead, and of a whitish colour. The other, dark, roved about the room. He had a thin large bony nose. He held a whip in his hand. He wore trousers and his long thighs were as thick as bolsters. He had wide hips but narrow shoulders. A flat chest. He had a high, very sloping forehead and the back of his head sloped likewise. The top of his head was flat. He had a skin blotched as if by scorching. Grimhilda watched him as though she couldn't do other than watch him. The eye of Gurdar that was not fixed fastened on her first, then flickered over all of us in the room, and afterwards sent its beam at her again. At the second time, she dropped her mouth agape and, with a strange sound, spread her legs wide and made water on the floor. Gurdar lifted his upper lip at this, showing his teeth, and made a sound too – a kind of hiss.

Gurdar and Grimhilda were the only ones standing. I looked at the husband. That Thorstein, for all his hairy swarthiness, was pale-skinned, and the skin of his forehead glistened.

The mighty Eirik and Thorstein Eiriksson had said nothing. I had never known Eirik short of words. His son looked tired, sick, much older.

Then this Gurdar, a bailiff merely, lower even than Thorstein the Black, turned about and left the house as a rain-cloud might shift from its blotting of the sun.

Eirik roused himself. He was kindly: 'Cheer up, man, this fellow can't be much fun for the ladies, not even for your good wife who's done what she shouldn't on the floor.'

'He does it to all of us,' cried out Grimhilda. 'Gurdar with the whip. Every house in the Lysafjord knows of his coming. And neither my husband there, nor any of their husbands, does anything about it.'

'Wipe up the mess you've made on the floor, woman, first, and we'll talk of it.' Eirik had taken charge.

I had been sorrowful over what had been said about Heriolf and Bjarni last night; and now I felt fear. I think the others felt fear too, especially Thorstein the Black and his wife who had to live in dread of visits from Gurdar their neighbour. All of us, whether Christian – both the Thorsteins were Christian, and the Black one wore a little wooden cross on an iron chain which he had forged and which hung about his neck – or followers of Thor and all the gods – Eirik or Thorkel (who was quiet throughout but whose broad fair face glistened with sweat) or myself, at this time – felt that there was in Gurdar a strong rod of wickedness. I wondered if this rod of wickedness in him ran down his arm into the whip that he carried. Or had he been in touch with the skraelings – one of their sorcerers – and learnt their arts?

Eirik ordered us all to gather belongings and repair to our boats. I felt some pity for Thorstein the Black and Grimhilda when we left, and even more for Thorstein Eiriksson now that his father was bent on his taking over Sandness within a year, or as soon as he got married.

With all speed we made for the East Settlement and Eiriksfjord; then Brattahlid and home.

5

GUDRID COMES TO GREENLAND

The boat from Einarsfjord turned off; of the rest, Thorkell's moored at a lower point in Eiriksfjord; those led by Eirik and his youngest son threaded the floating ice, thick below the glacier, and with strong hearty strokes had almost reached home.

Approaching Brattahlid, Eirik had longed to see Leif's ship safely moored from its voyage to the new lands, that had been spoken of, in the west. But it was not there, and it was now late – very late – in the summer. The sun was setting earlier and the cold, soon after its setting, was now bitter.

'He is lost, and all with him, or he is spending the winter in the new lands. I shall tell the god that it has to be the second of these two, or I shall take the hammer which he grips and do his idol damage,' said Eirik.

The two boats had moored – Thorkel's had made for home earlier in the fjord – with their fine cargo from the northern hunting grounds – just below Brattahlid, and Eirik looked for news and welcome from his family.

Thorstein Eiriksson stepped on shore and advanced towards Brattahlid, his father awhile staying on board, giving directions to the crew, but glancing now and then towards his home. From its doorway appeared the mistress of the household, accompanied by the eldest son, Thorwald. They greeted Thorstein half-way on his upward path. After talk among the three of them, Thjodhild waved to her husband, turned and returned to the house with Thorstein. Thorwald continued his journey down the slope to join his father at the waterside. Without changing his name to a Peder or a Pál, Thorwald had become a Christian too: this Eirik knew. Nevertheless the hope was expressed that good terms would remain between them, no less so than there existed – so far as he knew – between his father and the brothers, Leif and Thorstein. Eirik, who had wished that at least one of his sons had remained a sturdy friend to his own god, took this well and said he 'mightily wishes this to be the case – that they would stay in kindness with each other'.

Father and son then hurried on the task of seeing to the unloading and safe stowage of the cargoes and the rewarding of the crews. They told each other the news, the father about the results of the voyage to the northern hunting grounds – the plunder was there to admire – the son about the goings on meanwhile at Brattahlid. It was a blow to Eirik to learn that the hay harvest had been bad, and that consequently the health of the cattle during the coming winter months was menaced. There had been some sickness amongst them already, four or five had died, and the milk yield of the herd had been low. There was no name for the disease, but the beasts were thinning, and foam was dripping from the mouth. Perhaps an ill-wisher had put a curse on the grass so that it had become poisoned. All the more therefore was Thorwald pleased to see the large supply of walrus meat – the harvest of the sea – which his father and brother had brought back from the north. And the ivory, too, for it could be exchanged for a noble supply of barley grain if a ship should call from the east. Yet it was now late to expect a ship this side of the winter. And even if a ship did reach Greenland so late in the year, Eirik feared it would berth at Heriolfsness 'where that old fellow would buy up the entire freight, and re-sell what was beyond his own need to us perhaps, but at a profit to himself'. Thorwald had waited eagerly for news of Leif, but there had been none. There was great hope of commodities from those much talked of lands in the west, but no sight of them, nor of Leif himself yet. It was no less late in the year for him than it was for a trading ship from the east.

It was not long after his homecoming that Eirik paid frequent visits to the woman who was the mother of his daughter, Freydis. Her dwelling was small indeed, but, besides Eirik being very happy with the woman, and fond of her daughter, the woman had a store of ale, it was said, and that gave him comfort too. How she came by it no one was certain, since beer and ale were alike scarce. But it was rumoured that she had always put by a proportion of what Eirik had given her all along and in addition she went short in other things – and she only drank sparingly herself to keep him company. She made sure of the ale as a means of holding Eirik. Moreover, it truly pleased her to please him. The hours of silence while they were together could be understood. But how else explain the roars of happy laughter that followed the periods of silence?

Eirik, as the god's godi, planted four of that season's walrus skulls in Thor's sacred enclosure. This was an offering in the trust that the god would make abundant the animals of the sea for future slaughterings. On the next night, partly as a lark and partly to spite Thjodhild, though it may be doubted whether she would ever have discovered the doer of the fierce prank, he dug a pit inside the earthen wall that ringed Thjodhild's church, and in which already lay several Christian dead, and into this pit he sunk the last two walrus skulls – touching cheek by jowl, but one facing east, the other west. He patted them and covered them up. Prank, or to spite his wife? There was maybe a bit of dare-devilry or devil-may-care in his mood too. 'Now we'll see if my wife's three-fold Christian gods are as effective as my Thor', was the run of that mood. 'Now Thjodhild's threedom, show your stuff! If Thor and you bring a very big harvest of animals from the sea next year, I have a mind to believe in the lot – the three of you. But I have at least two others besides Thor, mark you that!'

The days began to shorten rapidly, the frost in the nights growing keener, and we all had less and less hope of Leif's ship – of seeing him perhaps ever again. The sickness of the cattle, now stalled in their byres, grew worse. There was stronger competition among the farm-steads in the business of cutting and gathering fuel; and there were few trees taller than a man left uncut. There was much ill-health among men, women and children in the East Settlement. How they were faring in the West Settlement we did not know, as the sea along the coast froze.

But just when matters were very gloomy, and we were preparing for much misery in the coming months, Eirik caught sight of a sizeable ship coming up the fjord. Surely it was bound for Brattahlid and nowhere lesser? There was a lifting up of all our moods into gladness, even after it was ruled that the shape of the ship meant that it could not be Leif's. The mast was shorter and the sail the wrong cut. Still, it was sizeable and it was low enough in the water to show it carried a handsome cargo.

The ship had come from Iceland. It was a trading ship with a welcome load of barley meal which the skipper was willing to exchange for the ivory wrested from the walrus that summer. The skipper took also some of the woollen yarn woven by our women, and seventeen bushels of the walrus hides, material for the making of ropes and of rigging, and in return we had an assortment of iron weapons and farm tools, and also two large casks and one small cask of wine. These Thjodhild wanted to be given to the priests for their use in her church. Eirik allowed the small cask for this purpose when Thjodhild pleaded for the wine in a dutiful and wifely manner, lowering her eyes and letting some tears escape and be seen. He was in high spirits because of the ship, laughing at Thjodhild for her earnestness about the wine, pretending that he thought she wanted it all for herself 'to keep yourself warm in your husbandless bed', and when she said, 'No, not for that', Eirik rejoined. 'It is a good faith where the chief act of its worshippers was to bib wine and to eat bread, scarce things both in Greenland. Why didn't they try beer and walrus meat?' Not that the former was all that common, but at least 'it would give those Creepie-Crawlies [for so he termed her priests] some muscle'. Eirik was in the main in that mood when we all liked him most. But at this time the mood lasted but a short while.

It happened that while the dealing of ivory for corn, hides for iron, wool for wine was going on briskly, a man, whom Eirik had known long ago, rose up from the middle of the ship, a young girl behind him, and, crossing the plank from ship to shore, where the dealing was going on, claimed acquaintance.

Approaching Eirik, he said:

"If ever I can help you as you have helped me, then ask and you shall have" Do you call that to mind after so many years, Eirik Thorwaldsson?' And he thrust his hand forward in greeting.

Eirik was taken aback. Then said that he was glad to see an old friend – 'Isn't your name Thorbjörn Vifilsson?' – and asked what he was supposed to do.

The man, who had smiled, explained that he and his daughter – the girl who now stood beside him – had come out to Greenland as settlers; and would not Eirik, in his renowned Brattahlid, please to give them house-room till they had found a piece of land, and reared a simple dwelling, and so established themselves?

Eirik was gruff. He said, 'Sorry, I've no room to spare just now. Full up. Never mind, Thorkel, my neighbour, will manage. He'll do it. He'll do what I tell him. Come with me, and I'll introduce you.'

I saw that the man was astonished. He looked stern, but he could do nothing other than take what Eirik said in silence. Hand in hand with his daughter he went to meet Thorkel.

I thought that Eirik Thorwaldsson had been rude, had damaged his name for great-heartedness. But when I learned more of the facts, I was sure that he had been wrong and ungrateful.

There was, of course, one excuse one could put forward on behalf of Eirik Thorwaldsson. If this ship had come through to Eiriksfjord, why, may not his son Leif's vessel yet come through before the winter had utterly sealed the fjord with ice? And if Thorbjörn and his child were inside Brattahlid, how would there be room for Leif after his great journey?

Still, it was no good excuse, and to understand this, we must go back in time.

Long ago when Eirik had been adjudged guilty at the Thing of the slaying of three men, he had been outlawed for three years. Between that sentence and his setting out to find what is now Greenland his life was under threat.

For the sentence meant that he was cast outside all protection of the law; it meant that anyone – man or woman – could kill him without fear of penalty of any kind. If Eirik were to be killed, no fine, no atonement whatsoever, would be imposed by the Thing on the killers.

Now many men, and not least the kinsfolk of the three men whose lives had been taken by Eirik the Red, were more than willing; urged on by their women, they were eager to exact their revenge on the killer. It was not safe for him, after the verdict, to return home. It was not easy for him to go into hiding for he was notorious; and the colour of his hair and beard rendered a disguise a hard task. And he was a proud man.

He would almost certainly have been quickly slain, and perhaps our Greenland would then have remained undiscovered to this day, but for the help of two men, Thorgeils Uppsson and Thorbjörn Vifilsson. The latter had a farm in Drangaland, in the bleak north-west of Iceland, but he had also, unknown to most, grazing rights on a small island, two leagues from the coast. This was Ellida.

To this island Thorbjörn ferried his sheep in the early summer, and from it he fetched them back to the mainland at the end of the grazing season. Also, at intervals during the season, he visited his flocks for shearing, carrying the fleeces to his homestead in a boat.

It was Thorbjörn who gave Eirik shelter after the verdict, thereby endangering his own life: first, at his house until nightfall, and then, during the three hours of near darkness, on Ellida. He ferried the outlaw over himself, since even Thorbjörn's servants could not be trusted not to betray such a secret. The servants, in fact, could have sold the knowledge of Eirik's whereabouts, if they had it, for gain to his pursuers -- so much was Eirik hated. But Thorbjörn cunningly kept the knowledge from them. His farmstead was searched, and thoroughly, but the searchers did not find the man they wanted.

Throughout three anxious weeks, Eirik lay concealed on Ellida, in a shepherd's hut, or a roofed pen for the dry storage of freshly shorn wool, his bare needs being supplied by Thorbjörn, travelling from the mainland after dusk had fallen.

At the start of this period of hiding, Eirik made his plans. This was where Thorgeils came in. Thorgeils was a close friend of Thorbjörn and was willing, for that friendship's sake, to assist Eirik. He was no friend of Eirik himself, was known indeed to dislike him, and that was an advantage both to Eirik and Thorbjörn as it happened. Thorgeils was under no suspicion of trying to aid the outlaw.

Thorgeils had a property in the Laxdaela, not far from Eirik's home, where Thjodhild and the three sons, all of them children at this time, remained. So Thjodhild received news of her husband, at careful intervals, from Thorgeils as it was passed to him by Thorbjörn, after his visits to Ellida. To mislead those who had remarked on Thorgeils's ridings to Eirik's home, it was given out that Thorgeils rejoiced at the verdict of outlawry on the manslayer, and that he rode to Thjodhild as to a woman soon to be a widow, a woman who would soon need to sell some or all of her late husband's assets for the support of herself and three fatherless children. 'So', it was said, 'Thorgeils rides over to make offers for the buying up of much of the manslayer's land to add to his own.'

Thorgeils did much more yet to serve the wishes of Thorbjörn, though the source of the instructions was of course Eirik. The orders were to prepare and amply victual a fair-sized ship as for a long voyage. The ship lay at the mouth of the Lax river. The job was to be done as unflauntingly as possible, but since a thing on this scale was bound to attract some notice, he was to say that the ship was being prepared since he – Thorgeils, that is – had a mind to travel later that summer to visit the kinsmen he still had in Norway. Because Thorgeils had often boasted of these kinsmen, and since he was renowned as being no friend of Eirik, whose wife or widow he was pestering for the sale of her land, this would excite no suspicion. All this Thorgeils undertook to do, receiving some payment from Thorbjörn, but largely on the ground of a simple promise of eventual reward, which was accepted, for Thorbjörn was indeed a man of his oath.

Mustering a crew was a tricky matter. Under pretence that Thorgeils would be in command, and that the ship would be bound for Norway, some men were engaged for the voyage. Thorgeils was helped in this because the time had come when all the best farming land in Iceland had been settled, and there were two classes of men ready for the chances of a sea-faring. There were the younger sons who saw little ahead to their profit when their fathers died; and there were the late-comers to Iceland, disappointed enough with the state of affairs they saw on landing to risk an even chance on doing better by going back from whence they came which, for the most part, was Norway.

Following the linking of counsel – Eirik to Thorbjörn, Thorbjörn to Thorgeils – the ship, crewed and provisioned, set out from the entrance to the Lax river to Flat Island with Thorgeils on the steer-board. Off Flatey they cast anchor on some pretext thought up by Thorgeils. While they thus waited, Thorbjörn rowed Eirik from Ellida to Flatey at the dead of night. Landing on Flatey, Eirik bade his friend to get the news through to Thjodhild and his family that he was safely leaving Iceland to serve his three years' sentence of exile, by exploring for a new land; that with luck he would find it, and, when the time came, they, and many others, would wish to settle there.

Then he shook Thorbjörn Vifilsson by the hand, and swore:

'If ever I can help you as you have helped me, then ask and you shall have.'

With that, he boarded the ship that Thorgeils had now left, and by a great exertion of humour, frankness and daring, seconded by ringingly confident assurances of reward in the form of first claims on rich grasslands waiting to be staked out in a country he knew to lie in the west, his will prevailed.

After his three years' brave and resourceful exploration of his 'Greenland', the time-expired Eirik, a free man now, one who could walk and talk in all safety, returned to Iceland, and canvassed far and wide the merits of the new country with the results that we know – and but for which neither you, my son, nor I would be here.

During that tour of Iceland of Eirik's, proclaiming the excellence and richness of his Greenland, there were of course meetings with both Thorbjörn and Thorgeils.

Thorgeils was cold: he 'had done what he had done for the sake of Thorbjörn', for it was he who had asked it of him. He was glad that Eirik was satisfied, but, 'No, he did not yearn to leave Iceland.' He was 'doing well enough, content to live and die where he was'.

With Thorbjörn it was different. He minded the oath sworn by
Eirik on Flatey in the dusk three years before. Nevertheless he declined
the venture to Greenland despite his friend's glowing account of that
country. He had reasons for this: he was prospering well enough, but
more particularly he had a wife, whom he dearly loved, who was soon
to give birth. He could not risk the health of his wife and the unborn
child by undertaking a long sea-journey and the hardship of settling
into a new country, however rich, just now, which was the very time
Eirik had planned for his large emigration of twenty-five shiploads.
'But if ever, later, it should happen that my circumstances should
change, and my needs should alter, I shall come to Greenland, and
remind you of the kind words you said to me when we parted from
Flatey some three years ago.' 'That holds,' said Eirik, and they had
shaken hands on it again.

But later the circumstances of Thorbjörn *had* changed, and his
needs sadly altered.

The young girl, of some fifteen or sixteen years of age, who followed
him as he stepped ashore at Brattahlid, was his daughter. Her name was
Gudrid. Thorbjörn's wife had indeed given birth to a child within a
week of the great sailing to Greenland. But then Thorbjörn's wife,
after giving birth, had died, and Thorbjörn was hard pushed to manage.
After a while, he was obliged to find a foster-mother for the child.
He found a suitable woman, not many miles away, one who was a
heathen, as nearly all were in Iceland in those days. But as soon as the
Christian faith came to the country, the young Gudrid was baptized;
and she tried to persuade both her foster-mother, to whom she was
attached, and her father, whom she saw at his household as often as she
could, also to adopt the new faith. They did so, yet Gudrid retained in
her mind – as was natural – many of the heathen sayings that her
foster-mother had taught her while they were still heathen. Both before
her baptism and after, men remarked on the child's beauty. They also
remarked however on her powers: she was said to have the gift of
the second sight.

Losing his wife, and parting with his only child for fostering, led to
further misfortunes for Thorbjörn. Unaided by a wife, and having to
give much time to that side of the running of a household which falls
more naturally – and so more easily and pleasantly – within the
management of a woman, his farming and business affairs went to the
bad; and from bad to worse. It was then he remembered what he had
done for Eirik the Red, and he pondered on the words of Eirik's

oath, both when he was an outlaw and when he was a free man. Then he claimed Gudrid from her foster-mother, sold his entire property, and took passage for both in a ship going to Greenland. He did not go quite empty-handed. He took with them the implements, the seed, and some livestock necessary for starting afresh. And he took a deal of corn, as an offering to Eirik, for he had heard that 'Greenland was a land where the barley stayed green'; that it would not ripen there to a fair waving whiteness such as he had known it to do over so many years, both good and bad, in Iceland.

Not only Eirik was taken aback; Thorbjörn was too, as he received Eirik's cold form of greeting and, holding Gudrid by the hand, he went to meet Thorkel, a stranger, under whose roof they were to bide for a time.

6

GUDRID AND
THE LITTLE KNOWING ONE

Thorbjörn was a mild-mannered man for otherwise he could have been expected to have shown more annoyance than he did. Here was the owner of Brattahlid, the largest house in the whole of Greenland, refusing to take in as his guest a man who had claimed old friendship. Yet Thorbjörn had seemed more hurt than angered, and more hurt on behalf of his young daughter – whom he had at once tried to comfort – than on his own account, though they had both endured a long hard voyage – had suffered cold, poor food, rough seas, scant sleep, damp clothing from rain and spray.

And Eirik had shifted a burden onto Thorkel that he should have borne himself.

Despite the rebuff, Thorbjörn did not charge Eirik with being an ingrate, or an oath-breaker. Striving to hide the hurt feelings which showed on his countenance, he shook Thorkel by the hand, thanked him for the room-space, and introduced his daughter. How much Eirik had gone back on his word was never mentioned by Thorbjörn, nor would it have been wise of him to have brought it up then and there, but it came out later.

Fortunately, the two men, Thorkel and Thorbjörn, took to each other, which was just as well, minding the cramped quarters of Thorkel's house compared with those of Brattahlid. Yet Thorkel was a considerable man, second only to his mighty neighbour throughout Eiriksfjord. Thorkel was a bland sort of man – broad-faced and cheerful as I noticed when, burly as he was, he had side-stepped and skipped like a dancer when fighting the walruses. Thorbjörn Vifilsson, for his part, had not quite the same easy-going humour of Thorkel; besides he was worried, as any man might be who in late middle years was having to start all over again. He was conscious of the extra load placed upon his host, and did all he could to help. The measures of barley grain he had intended for Eirik, he made over to Thorkel. And Thorkel was delighted with this, since he enjoyed drinking beer in good company.

Gudrid Thorbjörnsdottir helped her father by helping in the household as much as she could.

Her father clearly cherished her of course, but everyone else realized she was a rarely beautiful and strange, and though strange yet good, young girl. Thorstein Eiriksson, ashamed by his father's behaviour, was one of those who had instantly admired Gudrid as she stepped on to the wharf. It may be thought that he deplored his father's conduct less for his disloyalty to an old friend than because of his unkindness to someone as fair as Gudrid was. But in truth Eirik's attention was on the father, not on the daughter.

Thorstein paid a visit to the house of Thorkel, offering as an excuse that he had come to avow his own sorrow for his father's unkindness to Thorbjörn in one respect and to Thorkel in another respect, but his chief motive was to have a reason for seeing Gudrid Thorbjörnsdottir again.

Now I, who was to see Gudrid so often and know her so well, must try to describe this remarkable and famous and lovely lady – though but a mere girl as she then was when she came into Greenland. But I fear I cannot speak of her as she deserves.

In person, when I first saw her, she was a long-legged girl, reaching just above the level of her father's shoulder. She was slender of build. Her hair, which was bound in plaits, was so fair that it more nearly resembled the colour of silver than of gold. Her breasts had but lately begun to form and scarcely showed under her dress. A great change was to take place in her within the next few months of her coming to Greenland, but of that there can be no wonder. Her skin was so pale that there seemed to be no red in her face, yet when the sun was low, near to its setting, and shone on her, her skin appeared to reflect its warm burnish. Her voice was the most charmingly tuned of any woman's voice that I had heard. That is to say normally. But Gudrid's voice was able to do strange and frightening things, as I was soon to learn.

As for her eyes. Those can never be forgotten, since they revealed all that was going on in her mind and in her soul. From their altering expression one could read the feelings in her heart, the moods of her soul, the thoughts in her mind. From hour to hour they told the life of Gudrid.

In colour, when heart and soul were at rest, they were neither blue nor green nor black, though they seemed all of these at other times, but grey. Set wide apart, they were very long and somewhat narrow. They appeared to be slightly upslanting towards their outcorners. It was early said of Gudrid that she had 'the second sight'.

She was devoted to her father.

Thorkel, like his guest, was a widower; and they were much of the same age. He had a fair-sized household, consisting of men who worked on his farm. Some of the men's wives worked within the house. Gudrid took her place among the women, and did all she could to earn her and her father's keep.

All the men at Thorkel's, and in the neighbouring farms likewise, young and not so young, early admired Gudrid. Those who were single would have liked her in marriage, yet there was that about her which told them she was not yet ready to be approached in that way, that there was a very particular fate reserved for her. This restrained the men despite of her comeliness. Men from quite far around, hearing of her fairness, came to call on Thorkel on some pretext or other in the hope of seeing Gudrid.

As I have said, among the first comers was Thorstein Eiriksson. He judged his father's behaviour to the new settlers to be more like that of a churl than that of the most mighty of the freeborn, and he feared that his reputation abroad would suffer for it. So he put it to his father, that he would allow him to go to Thorkel's to smooth matters. Thorbjörn had done so much for the good of his father in the past, that amends should be made. Eirik was not unwilling that this should be done.

Thorbjörn was a good-hearted man and, though he could not forget what Eirik had done, he was willing to forgive it. Thorstein carried this news back and Eirik then undertook to make over a sizeable piece of land to the new arrivals after the end of winter.

There was still no news of Leif.

Now started in earnest the worst winter in the memory of everyone in Greenland since their coming into that country. The fjord became fast frozen and no fish could be caught unless a man smote a patch of ice with a pole-axe for the length of an hour, so thick was the ice to break. Those who had stored too little fuel, whether for cooking or for warmth, were punished for their heedlessness of the signs; and many of the old men and women, whose children had left them on marrying, died early during that terrible winter. Now it was believed that

Gudrid, knowing little about Greenland since she was a new arrival had foreseen all this, as we later thought by the look in her eyes. It was as though she saw both the near and the far together.

There was not all that amount of snow, after the first thick grey skies and heavy falls of it. Later, the skies were bare of cloud and that was worse, for it became much colder and the snow on the ground froze into the hardest ice immediately, and neither mattock nor spade could open the ground for the burying of the dead. Instead stones were heaped over the corpses on bleak land, as far removed from dwellings as possible – much like the vile skraelings do for their dead. There they were to lie until the earth in the churchyard should soften in the spring. Yet even so, it was thought that the corpses spread, through the fissures between the stones, their diseases among living men. There seemed to be no hope for most of us, but those who had hunted the sea-animals up in the far north during the previous summer were now thankful for the meat they had salted and stored, but we ate but sparely of it so that it would last the longer. The whole settlement must have been thinking of Eirik with reproach, since he had lured us all there with the promises of a wonderful land.

'Have we exchanged Iceland for this?' they seemed to say. 'Greenland and Iceland should fairly swap their names.' Whether they did or not, Eirik could counter with, 'Who knows if Iceland in this winter is not as badly off, or worse, than we are here in Greenland?' 'Maybe, but at least they have their ale to cheer them there,' would be the answer. In truth there was no one who knew what the conditions were in Iceland now that sailings between countries were over for the next five or, if lucky, four months. The days became very short, and the Christians went to mass and prayed, huddling in the church. Eirik had not that comfort, and he felt the unspoken reproaches against him of the people very deeply. He longed so keenly for the return of Leif, with a report of wealth in the new lands to offset the blame of having persuaded so many to follow him into Greenland. He was low and gloomy; and the weather was so bitter that he even visited his friend, the mother of Freydis, less often. It was rumoured that he was sickening.

More serious for the community as a whole than the deaths of the old and feeble was the murrain among the cattle. For, with the shortage of fish and fresh meat, we depended much on the cattle for milk, butter and cheese. But the animals had been so famished by the poor crop of grass in the summer that they yielded little or no milk and so they more readily caught the diseases in the stalls. The disease spread from cow to cow, and from byre to byre. Nor was it safe to eat the flesh of the carcases of the animals that had had this murrain. Some people, who had so far been healthy, dared to cook and eat this flesh and had then died.

Eirik, renowned for his strength and vigour for so many years, took to his bed.

Christian priests or no Christian priests, the neighbourhood now agreed in thinking it best to obtain some advice from the Little Knowing One, the old witch woman who lived alone, and of whom it had been said that she prepared love potions for the girls or women who had desired Leif to make love to them. To her also went women who were still barren after marriage. She sold charms, told fortunes, and gave instructions to those who sought her help for the recipe for the making of a food which unfailingly aroused lust in man and which was called Sweet Lovebread.

Only the Little Knowing One's reading of the future, it was decided, could enable men to know whether their wives, their children and themselves had a fate that would lie beyond the bounds of this direst of winters.

The vote carried, it was next discussed as to when and where and how the Little Knowing One's foretelling could be drawn from her; for she was a proud old lady, could raise fears in many a strong heart - even those who made to laugh at her in her absence adopted a respectful air in her presence – and she would demand a handsome reward.

'When?' It must be as soon as could be arranged, 'for men, cattle, women and children were dying every day'.

'And night', a man said, 'and I fear my old woman will die under me if I should have the strength to get on top of her.' There was a laugh from the rest at this. But it was a hard and dreary sort of laugh. And another shout came of, 'Sooner the better!'

'Where?' That raised grave problems. By rights, it should be at Brattahlid, but the master of Brattahlid was sick, and Thjodhild was widely known as a cold and lofty person, a serious and fanatical Christian, and no friend at all to what she would call 'wicked and backward heathen superstition'.

It could not be held at Brattahlid, but where else?

A man at the meeting mentioned Thorkel's. He was 'the next greatest farmer in these parts after Eirik Thorwaldsson; so Eirik needn't mind too much if we met the Little Knowing One at Thorkel's. We could tell, or not tell, Eirik the result of the meeting after it was over – depending on his health.'

This suggestion was carried, especially after a farmer had pointed out that at Thorkel's was staying a lass who seemed herself, by all that was said of her, to be gifted with the second sight.

It was agreed that Thorkel should be approached and asked to hold the meeting at his house as soon as possible. It was also agreed that all attending should contribute towards the reward to be paid to the Little Knowing One, except Thorkel who should be answerable only for her entertainment.

The question was brought up again as to whether Eirik be, or be not, informed of the projected encounter with the Little Knowing One at Thorkel's. It was carried that as a sick man, Eirik Thorwaldsson may, or may not, hear of the meeting, but that no special ruling as to that should be voted on.

A carrier to Thorkel of these findings of the meeting was then named, and it was agreed, as wise, that three men should there and then be chosen to assist Thorkel in approaching the Little Knowing One at her dwelling and seeing to all the arrangements that she would insist on. Three were named: one was as stupid as a stone; the second one thought he knew about everything and knew scarcely anything, but talked a good deal; the third was an elderly farmer of sound mind but who had a hare-lip and cleft palate.

Thorkel, sensible man, took the matter into his own hands. He went to her dwelling. The dreadful old thing had a cat's carcase, stripped of its skin, hanging from a hook. Of a joint from this carcase she intended making a meal. Three live striped cats were to share this meal, and one of them stood perched on her shoulder, snarling, when Thorkel knocked. The old woman was also the midwife to the wives of the settlement, and had some gruesome objects on a crude table.

Nevertheless, as she was widely known and feared and respected, Thorkel entreated her with great honour and she consented to appear and to read the omens, providing she were as well paid as she should be.

The next evening the neighbouring farmers were seated on their benches along two sides of the hall – or so we heard since no one from Brattahlid attended. Thorstein sat by the bed of his sick father, and Thorwald held it as a slight that the affair was going on at Thorkel's. At one end a special stool was set up on a low platform. On the stool was a cushion stuffed with hen feathers. In front of the stool was placed a small table. The long narrow fire-pit was freshly heaped with twigs and branches and these flamed up in the hall. Outside it was all dark.

Thorkel met her at the entrance, bowing slightly, and rubbing his hands together. He brought her into the hall, and showed her the special stool on the low platform. She was wearing catskin: catskin fur her hood, and of catskin fur was a kind of shawl or scarf. She had glass beads about her neck, and these glittered in the light of the flames. So did her eyes. She looked very old and was wizened.

Thorkel louted low, and said: 'Please, Wise Woman, please to cast your eyes over the hall, and all your friends here seated, and tell us the omens.'

The flames flickered; our shadows moved on the walls as we leant forward or sideways on the benches; but she said nothing.

Then Thorkel: 'But first, meat! Meat you shall have!' and he clapped his hands. The door opened and a meat dish was put before her on the low table. Thorkel explained to her that the dish was made up of bits of the hearts of all the animals that were to be found on the farm: calf, sheep, goat, horse, fowl.

She nodded, and ate. To do this she took out of a small bag, hidden among her garments, a spoon made of brass and a knife. The knife had a handle made of walrus bone, and it had two bands of copper about it. The point of the blade was broken – the handle had two rings of copper bound about it – the blade was short and jagged at the end. We all leaned forward as she ate, watching her. Thorkel most attentive, nervous.

When she had finished, he neared her as if to ask if she would read the spells. Before he had spoken, though, the Little Knowing One knew what was in his mind, and explained, before he put his question: 'No, she could not do the spells before she had spent one night in the house.'

The men on their benches sighed and leaned back and Thorkel was downcast, for he would have to provide good quarters for this guest overnight.

All this was reported next day at Brattahlid; and it was decided that Thorstein should go over to Thorkel's for the next evening, and that I was to accompany him. Thorwald would stay by his father the while.

Thorkel received us well notwithstanding that he had given house-room in this hard winter to the Icelanders, Thorbjörn and Thorbjörn's daughter – people to whom Eirik owed so much. But Thorkel was an easy man and took Thorstein by the hand and led him in. When Thorstein's eyes fell on Gudrid he looked at her long but did not speak. I believe this was because he could not, because he was wondering how his father, who had made love – so it was said – to many women in his time, could not but beg Gudrid, so fair she was, to enter under his roof. Yet even if Eirik had noticed her, he might have feared the jealous wrath of the mother of Freydis if he had taken Gudrid to Brattahlid; or maybe it was because he was even then sickening although he was yet to take to his bed.

Thorbjörn still felt enough slighted by the man, whom he had helped, to do no more than nod in a cool manner towards that man's son, and he then seated himself at the opposite side of the hall to where we had placed ourselves.

As it had been told to us last night so it happened now. All the leading men, and others too, were ranged on benches set against the two long walls. The fire-pit, now newly heaped with fresh twigs – for logs as thick as a man's ankle-joint were scarce – had been dug down the middle of the floor, dividing the two ranks of benches. The smoke rose and the twigs leaked their hissing sap into the bed of the fire.

At one narrow end of the hall stood the women, Gudrid among them. At the other end, on a platform raised slightly above the level of the floor, was a small table and, behind it, the special stool that I had been told about. On it was the famous cushion stuffed with hen feathers. Darkness had fallen, but, when Thorkel brought in the Little Knowing One, the fire burst into flame at the moment it seemed that he brought her in, holding her right forearm just above the wrist. Sparks floated upwards into the smoke, the flames leaped up from the surly fire, and we could see the faces of the men sitting opposite us. Thorstein – I sat on his left – threw a glance towards the end of the room where the women stood. It was only a glance since what the Little Knowing One was going to say would mean so much to all of us. The witch was wearing the catskin hood. And now she wore catskin gloves, and the glass beads she wore glittered in the firelight. She was a little woman, and was very old, it was said, though no one knew her age.

Thorkel conducted her to her stool, then went down from the platform, bowed to her, and said:

'You have had one night in my house, and so honoured it, O Wise One, and have again been fed from a dish made up of all the hearts of all animals that are bred on this farm, so now I ask for the sake of all those who are gathered here, that you will tell us what you foresee of our fate – what with the sickness of men, starving of our cattle, no wood for our fires, death of our grass. No fish caught. Ground hard frozen. Miscarriages of our women. What can you foresee? Whether what you foresee be good or bad, I vow to pay you your due reward.'

There was a silence. And then the Little Knowing One replied:

'You ask me your fate, yours and that of all of you here. I cannot tell you your fate unless you have one among you who knows – or will utter – the Charm-Spells, the Spirit-Songs, the Ward-Locks. Is there no one with the cunning of that mystery here?'

Thorkel replied:

'Sorry, but no one in this room has that cunning. Very sorry. None of my household knows the secret of those spells, nor any of my friends who have come into this room.' Moreover, since she had mentioned this earlier, he had made it his business that day to go over all his outhouses and to enquire of all his servants, free or bound, men or women, asking them one and all whether they could do these spells. None of them could. Nevertheless, he hoped that because of the Little Knowing One's skill, and because her reputation was so wide, that she could yet manage to foresee – as far forward at least as the end of this terrible winter and the coming of the sun after that end – without the aid of one who knew these spells – for such a one he had failed to find though he had tried hard.

'O yes, there is such a one here in this room who knows the Charm-Spells, the Spirit-Songs, the Ward-Locks and can do them,' she answered. 'And if you shift yourself – for you are blocking my sight – I will look at her,' she said.

Thorkel had no choice but to shrug his shoulders slightly and sit on the benches opposite Thorstein and myself, but at the end of the bench nearest the Little Knowing One. He bowed his head, leaning forward.

There was again a silence.

'O yes, there is, there is such a one amongst us who knows.' She was staring straight down the length of the room to where the women stood.

'Let that one own to it.'

We all turned our heads to follow the Little Knowing One's gaze. And there was no doubt but it fell on Gudrid.

No one spoke and there was no sound but for the murmur of the fire, which sank low but glowed red, and there was a kind of short sigh from among the mountain fells outside.

And then Gudrid took two steps forward, and cried out:

'O, I can do them – the Ward-Locks, the Spirit-Songs. My foster-mother back in Iceland taught me them while she was heathen. But forget them I should now, because we are Christian.'

And Thorbjörn, her father, suddenly stood up at the other end of the room, where he had sat near the Little Knowing One. He was in much distress and waved his right hand, palm open, from above his shoulder in a sweep downwards and, quickly, to his thigh, and looking at Gudrid the while, as if to say no.

'Forget them, I should,' shrilled Gudrid, and then she sobbed.

'Poof! Poof! What nonsense,' replied the Little Knowing One. 'It seems to me that you and your father are owing a lot to our fine Farmer Thorkel here who provides you both with bed and board all this winter until you get started. What say you, Master Thorkel, have you not invited all these people here to know what is in store for us in Greenland?'

It was a shrewd blow. For Thorbjörn had been feeling awkward and uneasy, feeling himself and his girl burdens on their host for a long stay in such a grim winter, as a result of the breaking by Eirik of his oath, in spite of the bland friendliness of his host.

Gudrid knew the feelings of her father, of the need to pay back something of value to Thorkel, I suppose, and that was why she walked quickly from her place at the end of the room among the women and stopped, just before she trod into the fire, on the lip of its trench.

Then the Little Knowing One rose from her special stool. She lifted her upper arms to the level of her shoulders, forearms bent forward from the elbow-joint. Her hands hang downwards, fingers spread. Then she suddenly lifts her right hand, fingers upward-pointing. She says a word to Gudrid, a word I had never heard before, and no one knew its meaning, and then Gudrid sings.

How she sang I shall never forget. What she sang is a different matter, and it seemed not so much that Gudrid herself was singing, but that someone or something else was singing through her. And there was a kind of wild music while she sang. At other times a kind of deep rough growling so that the floor shook. And there were other voices besides, both inside the building, and also outside – it seemed from the fells whence there had been that kind of sigh earlier, and also from the fjords – a sort of grinding noise. Some of her words we knew, and the song was skaldic* – a strong beat, so that some of us stamped our feet to the rhyme or answer words, or clapped, or swayed to it. There was a 'something, something, something HORSE'; and then 'and

---

*Like that of the *skalds*, Icelandic poets.

something, something WALRUS', with a thump on that '-RUS'. There was 'GLASS' – at which the fire blazed up, showing her face, and then – to match it – 'GRASS'. And we couldn't help it but join in, stamping and thudding. And the fire blazed up or sank with the answer words. And all the time there were in the hall other men or things besides ourselves, and these others were whispering, or they were laughing, or they said unclean things to each other, chuckling.

Then Gudrid began shouting rude and wild things, which she could never have heard or uttered before and whose meaning she could never have known. And then it all became dark and only her face was seen. But the face changed, and with that change her voice changed. A deep cruel man's voice roared out of her mouth, and it said grave and terrible things that no good woman, or even good man, could say or know – but still in skaldic verse.

And then it all ended suddenly. I believe Gudrid fell to the floor, but then stood up. Her face then looked quite white in the firelight which then resumed its even glow.

And then the Little Knowing One spoke. She said: 'Well done, my fair Gudrid. You did the Ward-Locks, and now I can say that many many spirits have been here, and so I can tell all of their fate out here in Greenland. And then I will tell you yours, Gudrid. For Gudrid, so I was told by those spirits who were lately here – while you sang – is your name.

'Well now, Farmer Thorkel, and all you good men gathered here, I can tell you, thanks to the Ward-Locks, that things are going to look up, out here in Greenland. Better luck, less lack. This cattle-thinning, or weakness, whatever it is, is going to slacken off. Better grazing. Bulls will mount, cows calve. More fish to be caught. More seal. More walrus to kill. So much for the next spring, the next summer. I give cheer to your hearts that have housed gloom. Frown not, but remember the one who now foretells of better days to come. Come to my dwelling, and give me the right thanks.'

The men did not quite know how to take the news, but shuffled their feet and nodded to her and muttered their 'thank-yous'.

'But as for you, Gudrid,' the Little Knowing One cried out to the girl, who was still standing before her on the other side of the fire – and Gudrid lifted a bowed head and the men's shuffling stopped – 'as for you, I will tell you what the fates hold in store for you, my child.

'First, you will cease to be a child within this hour, and become a woman.'

72

Glowing with beauty, Gudrid half-turned at that moment to look –
not at me – but at Thorstein. And her eyes spoke to Thorstein, and
Thorstein answered hers.

'And you will soon become a bride. You will make the next but
best match that you could make in Greenland. Think of that! With
all but the very best of all. But that match won't last long' – and here
Thorstein bit his lip, paled – 'because I see illnesses and ghosts – and
so you'll wed another, and with him you'll journey. You won't love
your second man as you loved your first, but you'll be happy enough,
and will have a child. And your child will be the father of a great one.
And your second husband will die, but you, Gudrid, will live to be old.
And you will not die in Greenland – for back in Iceland your later
lines lie. You'll die where you were born. I can no more, but I see a
big light shine for you. A white light shines.'

That's all she would say. She made a sign that she wished to go.
Thorkel went up to her, and took her hand and led her out.

Thorstein and I, late though it was, hastened to Brattahlid. In the
morning Thorstein sat by the bed of his sick father. The eldest,
Thorwald, was also there. Eirik asked for an account of the goings on
at Thorkel's. When he had heard all about the evening, he brightened
up a bit and told the brothers scandalous stories about the Little
Knowing One whom he referred to as 'Old Hag'.

'And those wenches – married baggages too – who were after my
Leif (I hope to live to see him again), do you know what they did,
Thorwald? You don't? But Thorstein at any rate should know about
these things.

'Well, they went to Old Hag and asked how to make – so I've heard –
how to make that sort of cake to rouse a man's lust. Now what did
Old Hag call it? Ah yes, . . . not cake, but Sweet Lovebread, Hag
called it.

'And they say, she showed them how – for a fee, of course. First, she
kneads a great slab of dough, made of fish-meal, and then she plumps it
up until it is a sort of pudding right in the middle of her little table. And
she bids the silly girls and fat women watch. Up then – would you
believe it? – she hops on the table, plants a foot on each side of the lump
of dough, pulls up her skirts, squats down, and kneads the dough to and
fro, back and forth, with her buttocks. "And then you bake it," she
said, "and send it to the young man you want to fancy you. If he eats
of it, you can be sure of his lust for you. It always works. And for that
secret you must give me – oh, so much, of this and that." So the wives

would steal the this and that from their husbands, or the girls from their fathers, to give Old Hag her fee to know how to make Sweet Lovebread.

'O, so she held forth last night at Thorkel's, did she? And what was she paid for it? Still, that young woman you tell me of – Thorstein, you like her, don't you? – seems to have stood up to her well enough.'

Thjodhild these days was not so cold but that she visited her husband more than once while the sons were there, laid her hand on his forehead, but at last angered him when she asked him whether he would not see a priest.

Weak as he was, some of the old strong temper awoke in Eirik at this, and he told his wife that she could keep her priests to herself and 'use them as you like, go to bed with them if you wish'. And: 'I guess you do bed with them. Since who else do you do it with. These years, these years of nights, you have shut me out.' And then, fiercely too, about these Christian priests being 'outlanders, who don't even speak our language, and idlers, wanting pennies for doing no work'. And, 'By Thor, if one of those fellows comes near, I'll rise from my bed and kill him, weak as I am.' So Thjodhild left, but wept outside his door.

But then, I learned, Eirik called to mind his talk last summer with Thorstein about their trip to the northern hunting places. He said he held to what he swore then, that he would not quarrel should Thorstein wish to marry a Christian: 'And I don't mind if it is with this Gudrid. From what you've told me about her singing deeds last night, she's a girl of some spirit.' And:

'Come to that, bring her here soon to see your father. Better sooner than late, I warn you.' And:

'There are two reasons for that warning, Thorstein, my son. One reason is that if you bring her here later rather than sooner, I'll be dead.

'Or there's another reason. If you bring her here later, I'll not be dead; but I'll be strong again, and in that case, I'll be the one who'll take the girl and not you. So be quick!' And he laughed. And then:

'And what about you, Thorwald? Are you not going to marry, like Thorstein? Or are you not going to discover new lands, like Leif? You stoop, and are a sad man. Are you only a scholar who will write books?'

Now I think, my own son, to whom I'm telling this, that this was wrong of the dying man to say, for Thorwald, who was short of sight and who did stoop, was yet to prove himself a brave man, but what his father said hastened the eldest son's death too.

Eirik, it was thought, was friendly to Thorstein's marrying with Gudrid because this would in some measure atone for his rude rebuff to her father, the friend and helper of his youth, to whom he owed his own life, and bring them together again before he died. And this is why he urged speed of Thorstein. He reminded Thorstein that he had sworn to bestow on him Sandness, his property in the West Settlement, as soon as he had a bride to take there. 'And you, Thorwald, my eldest, must have my Brattahlid, my great house, the greatest in all this Greenland of mine.'

It was also clear to his sons at this time, that their father yearned to see his daughter Freydis again before he died. As for his mistress, the mother of Freydis, it was a difficult matter. He seemed to mention what we believed was her name several times, smiling as he did so, but tenderly. The difficulty was whether Thjodhild would admit either of them, but especially the mother, into Brattahlid. Nevertheless, it was agreed between the two brothers that they should try to persuade their mother at least to allow Freydis into the house to see her father.

But most of all, Eirik seemed concerned about Leif, yearning to welcome him home from his voyage, and to hear his report on his winter in any new lands that he had found. And once: 'If he returns to Brattahlid whole of life and limb, while I still draw breath, I might almost believe in my wife's three gods and, like her and you, become a Christian.'

But this was not to be. Eirik Thorwaldsson died before the spring and the warmer weather came.

Yet, true to his word, Thorstein did bring Gudrid Thorbjörnsdottir to Brattahlid, rather sooner than later.

Eirik lifted his hand from under the bedclothes, and the girl took it and clasped it. And indeed she stooped and kissed him, and spoke to him in beautiful and kind tones, saying what honour he gave her to receive her so.

Eirik was much moved, but to hide it he said as boldly as he could that he swore Thorstein was the luckiest of men to be so betrothed, and he only wished he 'were strong and young enough to cut him out'. Gudrid took this in the right spirit, and it was clear that Eirik was glad of the promised match between Thorstein and Gudrid.

And before Gudrid left to return to Thorkel's, he bade her give his kindliest greeting 'to your father, my old and good friend Thorbjörn Vifilsson'.

If Eirik was disappointed at not lasting to see Leif, he was also disappointed at not seeing Freydis, or the mother of Freydis, before he died. The brothers did what they could, and Freydis actually came to the door of Brattahlid. But Thjodhild would not admit her, calling her 'the wicked offspring of a sinful union'.

Freydis had to accept that she would not be admitted, but she would not accept the hard words. She had inherited her father's fiery temper, and before the door was closed against her, and after too – so that she was heard by all of us within – we heard her curses.

She shouted at Thjodhild, declaring that it was no wonder that her father had preferred another woman, who made him cheer, and took him for what he was worth, before Thjodhild, who was 'a wife who is not a wife . . . an icicle . . . worse than an icicle . . . a broken spiked pitchfork . . . a sow's intestine stood on end with a face like a bladder . . . a grating clogged up pipe . . . a pallid streak of frozen piss . . . a so-called woman without enough warm blood in her to lift any man's cock one little bit in greeting . . .'. The sick man heard, and was somewhat proud of Freydis's spirit, and amused by her curses, but he could do nothing, for he could no longer see to it that the orders he gave would be carried out. The stern Thjodhild had taken over the rule of the house in her husband's weakness.

I have sometimes wondered whether Freydis's later devilish cruelty might not in part be put down to Thjodhild's spiteful treatment of her when she came to try to see her dying father.

7

GUDRID MARRIES; LEIF'S ACCOUNT; FREYDIS

Eirik Thorwaldsson, 'The Red', died before the fjord became un-frozen, before Leif's ship was seen coming home in the spring to Brattahlid after his great voyage. And between the death of Eirik and the homecoming of Leif, Thorstein Eiriksson and Gudrid Thor-björnsdottir were married in the church of Thjodhild.

Great the happiness of all the inhabitants in Eiriksfjord – for so it will always be called despite the death of its namer – as their guess that the vessel seen stemming proudly up the mid-stream should be none other than Bjarni Heriolfsson's, with Leif Eiriksson in command, turned out to be the truth.

The ship neared her berth at Brattahlid. The crew lowered the sail, threw out ropes, shipped their oars, the vessel was moored, the boarding plank thrust between gunwale and bank, and Leif the Lucky – or Happy – stood midways on that board, and looked at his home, his family, his friends. He looked at once for Eirik and saw that his father was not among the many grouped there to welcome him. Still, it was not possible for us not to show our joy, and our relief and pride too, when we saw that the ship seemed laden with a great cargo, that she was low in the water from the weight of goods that she carried.

Leif, after greeting us all from the landing-board, moved on to shore. Thorstein made known Leif to his sister-in-law. Gudrid saw that Leif stood even a full hand's breadth higher than her tall Thorstein, and that Leif's hair shone like gold. Nevertheless, all her life she was to love Thorstein above all men, even after his death, except perhaps one other. Leif's face was weathered from strong suns and keen winds and his eyes were the colour of an unclouded sky or of the deepest sea when the sky is clear.

Thorwald told him of his father's death. Leif recalled how Eirik's horse had put a foreleg into a fox-hole when they were riding to ship last summer, and had declared, 'I am not meant to discover any more countries than the one I am now in.' Thorstein then informed his brother that at least Eirik had made a great hunt in the north, after his leg was mended, and that they all owed much to him this last winter that had now been overpassed, because of the supplies brought back from that hunt of the sea-animals.

All of us, including Thjodhild who loved Leif most of her sons, and all the crew of the ship, then climbed the slope to Brattahlid. The ship would be unloaded next morning of its full cargo – we had all peered at the timber in the hold. The timber could be left but Leif carried with him a branch, on which was fruit withered on the stalk, up into the house. A sailor followed, carrying two great oars.

Everyone gathered together in the great hall that spring evening and Thorwald Eiriksson allowed in several of the neighbourhood to hear Leif's story of his voyage. One of those that came was Gudrid's father; another was his host, Thorkel.

Leif told us that, in Bjarni Heriolfsson's ship, he had followed the path of Bjarni when that man had at first missed our country while trying to reach his father's dwelling from Iceland, and had hit on other new lands. He turned about and found the Greenland he was seeking but had not dared to set foot on the other lands he had had sight of on the way.

What Bjarni had seen, but not risked the testing, was true. There was a Helluland, or Flat Slab Land, far to the north-west beyond the sea; and there was a Markland, to the south of Slab Land, on which there were trees that were always green, growing on low cliffs behind beaches of white sand – stretching for many miles. Now those trees would be good for building in Greenland when felled and fetched home to Greenland. Their sap could be drained for the making of pitch for the sealing of ship's sides. The trees there were so many that they could be burned freely as common fuel.

But he had gone beyond Markland, to the south and west of that land, and he had hit on land of huge wealth. He had borne home to Brattahlid samples of that wealth to show: to show and to prove. He had named that land Vinland. He and his men had made houses there. They had wintered there. They had lost a man in the winter, but they had killed three skraelings there. He allowed that there were skraelings in this rich land, but of a different kind from the kind that we meet with, in our summer hunts up north in Greenland. He thought the skraelings were weaker, and might be fewer in number, in Vinland.

'Nevertheless, though I went to Helluland, to Markland, and to Vinland, the way of Bjarni, I have not come back the way of Bjarni.

'Bjarni no doubt will be here tomorrow, or on the day after the morrow, to claim his dues, a share of the cargo in his ship which I have brought back, according to our deal. And he shall have his dues. On that I shall not go back, for no oath should ever be broken.

'But I shall tell him this: that his father's choosing of Heriolfsness to settle was not so wise.

'For when it came to homing with a laden ship I risked another route. And that route I found to be both safer and quicker.

'You must know that Greenland and Helluland, as both countries run the northwards, lean together so that, if one sails far enough north, there's but a narrowing strip of open water between them. Go from Greenland to Helluland that way, or come from Helluland to Greenland that same way, and a seafarer, if wind and wave be friendly, should not be out of sight of land more than two days. Like this – '

And here Leif seized two mighty oars, one in each hand. The butt ends he grounded on the floor, a yard away from the side of each foot, but he let the blades of the oars nearly kiss each other above his head.

'As the blades above my head come near to touching', he said, 'so do Greenland and Helluland in the far north come near to touching; and as the butt ends on the floor are far apart from each other, so are Greenland and the new lands far apart in the south.

'Our father, Eirik Thorwaldsson, had a place, Sandness, in the West Settlement. Henceforth any wise and cunning voyager to the new lands will fare from here northwards along the coast to Sandness. At Sandness he will take on water and fresh food. From Sandness he will sail due west – the sun hard above his port beam at noon – until he draws near to Helluland. He will then veer south, and with land nearly always in sight – after Helluland and Markland – will come my Vinland of much wealth.'

So it seemed to us that we in Brattahlid could fetch timber and wild corn from Vinland. And also grapes, for the branch Leif showed was the branch of a wild vine, and therefore he had named the country as he had. We could also bring back wine from the new land, he thought, and at no cost but for the fetching.

And how would old Heriolf and Bjarni, in their narrow stony fjord, fare then? The goods that ships from the east unloaded on his headland for a high price, and which he then sold to us at a yet higher price, we would no longer need. He would need to make a living from the farming of his flinty fells, or die.

'And, who knows, but some of us in Eiriksfjord might shift over the narrow water with our wives and children, settle homes in Vinland, and live and die in a country where there were wine and corn, grassland for cattle, iron for weapons, trees in vast plenty ready for the felling?'

Leif displayed to us the branch which he said had borne grapes at the end of his summer in this Vinland. And he showed seeds which he said were the seeds of wild corn.

So the Little Knowing One was right, we thought then, when she foretold that 'things are going to look up, out here in Greenland'.

And before Bjarni arrived to reckon, and take away, what he declared to be his share of the profits of the voyage, we had what was called a 'Te Deum' in Thjodhild's church. Not everyone could crowd into the church and it was resolved to build a bigger church of stone for, since the death of Eirik, whose scoffing had held back many, nearly all the families in the fjord had become Christian; and Leif's lucky voyage was seen by the rest as a token that Leif's faith was the right faith. Thjodhild too had given every encouragement to the priests. These priests performed a few of their ceremonies in our own tongue, though many of the outlander priests could not speak our tongue properly by the end of their days, but other ceremonies they performed in another tongue. This 'Te Deum' was in the foreign tongue, and was a 'thank you' to the new Christian god, or rather the new gods, all three of them.

After the mass, as it was called, and the 'Te Deum' – which words mean something dirty in our own language, as you know – we all went down to the ship. We wondered at the richness of the cargo as we unloaded it. There was no doubt that Vinland was exceedingly rich in trees and in a kind of wild corn, from the evidence of the seeds, and that it would be good for the making of bread and of ale – in Vinland, if not in our Greenland – was our hope.

There were also branches of the vine and the dried grapes which had grown on the branches. While we were looking at these, Leif called for Tyskir to explain to us how he had found them.

Tyskir was an ugly little black-haired man with a low forehead, but good-humoured. He was always grimacing or winking. He was a merry man. He was not born in the north, but his first home was in the far south, by a great stream called Rhine, in a country called by us

Tyskland, a place which grows very many vines. Leif had met and taken on Tyskir on one of his journeys in the past, and made of him a comrade as much as a servant.

Leif told us that in Vinland he had parted his crew into two: one half, day and day about, was set to build the houses; the other half was to roam the land to find out its resources, but the foraging gang was to keep all together.

But there was no holding of Tyskir. The foraging half came back one evening and Tyskir was missing. A search party was sent out for him. The little black-haired fellow was soon found, but was rolling his eyes and staggering. He professed himself to be drunk, having found the fruit from which, in the part of the world where he was born, wine was made. It was because of this finding that Leif called the country Vinland – a Land of Wine.

There was much teasing of ugly little Tyskir by all of us that morning as the tale was told. We laughed at him and pushed him around from man to man in a circle, thumping him on the back, or pummelling him on the upper arms, as if we ourselves were already drunk, at that early hour, at the mere thought of a country from which wine could be made and fetched without cost.

Bjarni arrived while we were playing in this way. He stood by the ship, eyeing his share of the riches of the voyage.

I watched how Leif and Bjarni would greet each other. They shook hands but Leif was lofty in his bearing and Bjarni felt he was being looked down on by the folk of Brattahlid. Bjarni was my old master, and I hoped he would call me to him. I wished to know about the health of his father, Heriolf, and to find out whether those at Heriolfs-ness had withstood the hard winter. Bjarni did not call to me. He saw me from a distance of seventeen or eighteen paces. He nodded, but not in the way of old friends who like to see each other. I made as if to move towards him, to speak to him. He noticed this but he turned away at once to someone else. The new faith, as I learned later, says how hard it is to serve two masters. But I found the truth of that then, for I owed my coming to Greenland to Bjarni, and his father had been good to me in my earlier years in the land. Yet now I was with the people of Eiriksfjord who would gladden when the people of Heriolfsness had no stroke of luck. 'Old Heriolf', they said, 'with all of Greenland to choose from except Eiriksfjord, chose badly.' And yet, my son, as things grow harsher in this country, I still think that the sons of the sons of Heroilf may outlast us all.

And once more, I will say that I think the credit for rescuing four men and a woman from the keel of an upturned drifting boat should have gone to Bjarni and not to Leif. Leif has justly earned the praise for deeds he has done, and done so well, and unjustly earned it for deeds done by some others too.

But when I think of Gudrid, whom I love, and love dearly, I cannot for long repine at the exchange of my friendship with the family at Heriolfsness for my dealings with the family at Brattahlid.

Leif liked his sister-in-law, Gudrid, as did all men, and treated her with kindness and good-heartedness. Even Thjodhild began to admire her, and say, 'I wish my other two sons would find themselves brides as comely and good as Gudrid.' But there seemed little hope of that. Thorwald was deep in thought as to how he could win his father's approval. Even though that father was dead, the taunt of being called bookish, because he was short-sighted, irked him; while Leif, the greatest catch for any girl in Greenland, seemed set rather on more deeds of fame, however much the girls paid fees to the Little Knowing One to be shown how to make the 'cake' or 'Sweet Lovebread'.

Leif was a good man and, despite the objections of his mother, Thjodhild, he did feel that his father's bastard daughter, his half-sister by blood, should be provided for by some means. So, soon after the disposal of his share of the voyage to Bjarni Heriolfsson, and the stowing of the remainder of the lading at Brattahlid, he called at the dwelling where Freydis and her mother lived. He did not tell his brothers of the visit: and he had overruled Thjodhild on the matter, who wished to have nothing to do with her husband's bye-blow child, still less her mother.

His visit was unexpected. The half-brother and -sister made a strange contrast. As against Leif's great height and manly strength of build, Freydis was only a little above the usual stature of a woman. She was wide-hipped and, for a woman, wide-shouldered. She had very full breasts. Leif was tall above all other men. The difference so far was but the difference between the comely man and the attractive woman. The real difference lay between their colouring, their manners and tempers, and their souls.

In colouring Leif's hair was as fair and bright as gold and the blueness of his eyes showed up against the sun-beaten ruddy brown of his naturally white skin, whereas the colour of Freydis's hair reminded men of her natural father's in his young and middle years, except that it was less of a flaring red than a dark but glowing copper which, amidst however were some tresses or locks nearly black, showing up against the copper. Her eyes were long and were of a hard rock or winter-sea grey, but they became black with flecks of red when she was enraged. And that was often. And that mad anger – a hot, not cold, anger – she owed, it was supposed, to her father who was so hardy, self-willed and hot in his youth. When angered, she feared no one, nor cared what she said nor did. Indeed, angry or not angry, she had a high mood, got what she wanted as a rule, and was both braver and crueller than any man. Her half-brother, Leif, on the other hand, had full control over his wrath, never yielded to it however provoked. Neither did he need to yield, for everything fell in his way. Like his mother, he was a true and faithful Christian but, unlike his mother, he never made a point of that being everywhere known.

On entering the house, Leif observed its slatternly upkeep. The mother of Freydis cried:

'He was such a great man, your father, and such a true kind friend to me. He gave me money, much and often, and I gave him happiness here – in this room, in my arms, and now he's gone. I don't know what to do, or how to support myself or his daughter. You see your father in her, do you not? I have refused many an offer of marriage over the years for your father's sake, you know.'

Leif bowed, and spoke to her kindly, but he was too shrewd not to grasp that the house would be dirty and untidy, whether or not his father were alive.

'And you, Leif Eiriksson, have come back to your home, full of fame and wealth, so full of riches – all the neighbourhood says so – and that reminds me of your father in his great and proud years.' And she seemed to weep. And then:

'He was the greatest love in my life, and this is our daughter. Is she not like her father?'

Freydis stamped her foot at this, and told her mother not to be a weak fool. She told her brother:

'What a man can do in this Vinland, a woman can do. Give me a ship and I will do as well as you, my half-brother, and bring home as much.' And her eyes turned black and the red flecks in them showed. Leif guessed that Freydis would spurn a gift of a sack or two of kindling wood, or even a half carcase of a sheep, or a whole carcase come to that. Her pride was like her father's, and her temper too.

He had been resolving that any gift of foodstuff or fuel should go to the mother rather than the daughter, whom nothing less than the rule of a ship and a new country would please, when a stranger came to the door. The mother looked much worried at the sound of the knuckles on the door, but the interruption took not Freydis this way at all. She laughed, showing her teeth, and the more startled her mother looked, the more she laughed in a kind of cruel triumph, staring straight into Leif's eyes.

Leif judged he should leave the dwelling. After a few words to the mother, to whom he pledged he would send some goods in kind on the morrow, which she acknowledged hurriedly, and a farewell to his laughing sister, he left the house. Outside the door he met the Archdeacon.

At this time our Greenland had no bishop of its own. The Bishop lived far away in Bremen and never set foot in Greenland, but he appointed one of his priests from Bremen, a German, to be his Archdeacon in Greenland. He was short, a fair but scant-haired, stocky man who spoke our language, but badly.

This Archdeacon seemed taken aback by Leif, who was famous everywhere, who was leaving the dwelling as he himself was about to enter. Leif greeted him shortly, but with the due respect that he owed as a Christian to a priest, though he had quickly guessed the purpose of that priest's mission. The Archdeacon, in his faulty language, tried to explain that he was about to call on the women in the house to teach them more about the new Christian faith.

Leif had replied:

'It is my hope and prayer, Sera Archdeacon, that you will teach them only our Christian faith, and that both of them will take baptism.' In the pride with which he uttered this there was something of the cold pride of his mother, Thjodhild.

From within the house, he heard Freydis laughing still more loudly about 'the fool that is my brother', and the Archdeacon, who had a nearly bald head and a round face, was blushing.

Leif had noticed, among the sluttish disorder of the house where his father had enjoyed happiness and comfort, the laundered under – garment of an ill-shaped man. He saw that it would fit the girth of the Archdeacon very nicely. He understood now his half-sister's laughing about the discomfiture of her mother. A mighty and straightforward man was Leif Eiriksson. He let the tubby priest, waiting outside the door to the house, know by his looks that he – Leif – understood his aim in calling on the mistress of the dead Eirik.

Nevertheless, he decided he would still send the gifts to the house, but by another hand than his own – mine.

Next morning the gifts of foodstuffs and firewood were loaded on a packhorse which I was to lead to the dwelling of the woman who had been no less than Eirik the Red's mistress but now had sunk into becoming nothing more than the lover of a Christian priest from Bremen. I wondered what Eirik would have thought of her now, but then I remembered that she had at least given the founder of Greenland happiness in his later years, though she had now taken into her bed one of the class for whom Eirik had hatred and contempt. Yet Eirik had loved his daughter, Freydis, and perhaps the laughing of Freydis, which Leif had heard, was the laughter of one who now scorned her mother.

When I reached the door, I was welcomed not by the mother but by Freydis. She had been watching from the window – I believe they both had – but she declared that her mother was out and would be gone for one hour or more. She paid little heed to, and no thanks for, the gifts Leif had sent, but helped unload the bales, which she did not so much as untie to see what they held. She tethered the animal and, taking me by the hand, drew me in and shut the door.

Now I am not boasting, my son! for indeed I made a sorry lover, having then but slight knowledge of the way such a woman as Freydis could behave or, come to that, such as I myself could behave. But what happened should be told less as a warning than to cast light on the nature of a woman, who did such things later in Vinland as can never be overlooked.

As soon as the door was shut she clasped me around, fumbling at my clothes, and kissed me in a way I had never known. And that was not difficult since, at that time, I had never been embraced before by anyone, neither by man nor woman – no, not by a mother.

But a young man, as I then was, cannot, however raw he may be in these matters, stay unmoved for long by such kisses and fumblings with his clothes, though not dreaming of it in his thoughts before, but taken by surprise.

When I left the house, after one hour – or two – I wondered why I had received this treatment from Freydis. She had hardly seen me before I had been sent on this errand, and I knew Leif would not have sent me had he thought this would have followed. I did not think Freydis, despite her being born out of wedlock, could have been starved of suitors. I still believe, to this day, that she did not wish to be tied to one man in marriage. Rather, I believe she was eager, like her father had been, for riches, or renown, or for both, and that she thought by making me the slave of her body, she had made a friend of someone at Brattahlid, someone who would tell her of all the plans about Vinland that were afoot there. I think it was for this that she told me to come to her again, and that, when I did, she hoped that her mother would be out of the house again. She told me, as I left the house, not to tell anything about what had happened between us – neither to Leif, nor to Thorstein or his wife, nor to Thorwald, and: 'most of all, say nothing to Thjodhild – that cold rake-bones of an old woman would upbraid Leif surely if she heard that goods were coming from her house to mine'. And:

'Never tell Thjodhild anything. Even the priest who comes to my mother – friendly meetings only, to say prayers together – has said he would never trust Thjodhild. He says she is a gossiper rather than a good true Christian, and he should know. For, as he told my mother, "Thou shalt not bear false witness" is a great commandment, and of that sin, Widow Thjodhild, in the manner of all widows, is likely not to be guiltless.'

Of course, I felt sick and disgusted about what Freydis had said – she but a natural child of Eirik – about the lady of Brattahlid. I felt I was being used; that I should go no more to Freydis.

Yet the feelings I had had in her arms and, later, with her on the bed, were such that I knew it would be hard not to go to her house again – with or without a packhorse laden with gifts. And I must admit that she taught me much that has stood me in good stead with other ladies in later life. But, I must also add, that no other has come near to the mad heat of Freydis in the making of love. She was as violent in lust as in fighting. Her hunger was outrageous and would outwear my strength now, though not then. She was greedy, and savage, and bit and clawed and yelled in anger for more – and more.

I cannot believe that I was the only man then. Who the others were I do not know. She would assuredly have despised her mother's old Archdeacon as a weak and flabby half-man.

After these years, I see her still, baring her teeth, her face white beside the dark red of her hair, with its black tresses, and still hear the sounds which came from her throat – curses more often than endearments, or foul words and curses – as she leaned her head backwards and jerked.

Seeing that I was rather white and drawn when I returned to Brattahlid, and knowing from where I had come, there were those of the household who teased me. Leif did not. He looked at me keenly, without smiling, but then – I think – put down my paleness to other causes: the day's journey to and fro, and the lifting of heavy bales from the horse.

And, of course, after the success of the voyage of Leif, there was very much talk of Vinland, and many the plans and schemes discussed. Many were urged forward because the lovely late spring and early summer weather lifted up men's hearts. Yet many of the cattle in the byres had died during the winter. Those that had lived through it were so thin and weak they had to be lifted out to grass. So, at the same time that we were happy, we could not forget the appalling winter. 'Another will come like the last', men said, and they thought of the west, of a still stronger sun than was now warming us, of corn and of wine, of timber plentiful for the mere axing of it – and of iron too. Iron is for killing or for cutting crops that ripen or for gelding cattle. And the thought of the killing brought them often round in their talk to skraelings. There were skraelings in Greenland. Whether households would shift from Greenland over to Vinland, or whether Vinland would merely yield in summer sailings those goods of which Greenland was so scant, would rest, it was thought, on whether there were any skraelings in Vinland and, if so, how great their number, the state of their weapons, their skill in fighting, and their disposition – whether they were quarrelsome, or so frightened that they would suffer what was done to them and their land, without any answer except to run away. Yes, Leif had said there were skraelings in the new lands.

'When we go up north in the summer to kill whale, walrus, narwhal and seal, we meet skraelings, and clash with them, because they want what we want – to slay sea-animals for meat. But, if there are skraelings in Vinland, is it known that they will want what we will take from them? They might just watch and laugh while we fell trees and gather corn, tear up vines, and smelt iron.'

That is what one said, and another:

'And if they steal, annoy, interfere in any way, kill them. It will be no sin since they are but heathen, bound for hell.'

Leif showed himself much wiser than the others. Despite all his strength, he could be more kindly than others with less than a half of his own knowledge of other lands and men. As a heathen, he had ravaged and slaughtered in Scotland, England and Friesland as few others had. He was still free to kill heathens but now, as a baptized person, he was no longer free to raid and plunder those Christian lands.

Nevertheless, he was milder in mood than others who had seen less of the world than he had. He had Greenland's best interests at heart.

He thought indeed that it was both right and needful to take full and quick advantage of his own findings in Vinland – yes, soon, this very summer. But he warned about easy killings of the skraelings there – no doubt but they were many there – for the sake of all Greenlanders, either those who go now or of those who might settle in Vinland in future. His counsel was to avoid fighting at all costs, rather to nod and grin at any skraelings that might show themselves, and to trade them beads of glass or other trifles, worthless things for things of worth.

In those lovely months of spring – the Little Knowing One had not been far out when she said 'things are going to look up, out here in Greenland' – the masses of ice and snow on the fells by the fjord loosened in the warmth of the sun and ran and thumped into the waters of the fjord with a sound like thunder, and the sheep were driven up to the top of the hills to crop the fresh grass.

Greenland, eagerness for Vinland, good weather, love. At that time, while Leif was so stirring and active, his younger brother, Thorstein, was scarcely to be seen. Nor was Gudrid. Husband and wife were such lovers that, not content with the nights, they went to bed together at midday. Perhaps the good and beautiful Gudrid – and Thorstein too? – had in her heart the words of the Little Knowing One that her first match would not last long.

On one such warming afternoon of spring we heard a great rushing noise followed by what seemed a thunder-clap. 'That means Gudrid has come off. Bravo!' said a man, laughing. Soon afterwards, as often happens at this season when one slide loosens another, there was a second such rushing noise and more mighty thunder. 'This time it's both together!' he said. And we all laughed heartily. Now that Freydis was teaching me things, I think I knew what he meant, but I also was sure that Gudrid was softer and sweeter in her love making than Freydis.

Thorstein and Gudrid would only come out from their room in the late afternoon, and return not so long after sunset.

I do not know what Thjodhild thought of this, but she said nothing against it. She spoke rarely about her dead husband, Eirik the Red, and never in praising words.

Since his younger brother was so entirely wrapped up with his bride, Leif turned more to his elder brother. Thorwald had been left life master of Brattahlid, but in his soul he was still eager to show he was no mere scholar despite his round-shoulderedness and short-sightedness. Leif, caring not only for the future welfare of the family, but for all the people in both the settlements, was keen that his own success should be quickly followed up by another; for otherwise, so he feared, the people would lose interest.

It was agreed between the brothers, Leif and Thorwald, that Bjarni's ship, now unladen but still moored below Brattahlid, should be once and for all wholly bought and taken over by the family as a first step. Bjarni Heriolfsson, though he made a show of reluctance for the sake of striking a better deal, was in fact pleased to have the ship off his hands for a good price. He had no mind to undertake any more sea-faring. All he wished was to thrive quietly at Heriolfsness. He would need to give his full attention to that since his father had become suddenly much frailer during the past winter. Neither was Bjarni shrewd enough to guess that the ship he sold to the men of Brattahlid would be used to lessen his, and his father's, trade with ships from the eastern lands.

8

DEATH OF THORWALD
IN VINLAND

The title to the ship sold to Brattahlid, and Bjarni's interest in it altogether gone, Leif called a meeting of his brothers, and of all the other chief men on Eiriksfjord, who had shown eagerness in the good prospects of Vinland. It was still early in the lovely new year, still spring not yet turned to summer. So now was the time to resolve.

Leif reminded Thorstein that their father had bequeathed Sandness in the West Settlement to him when he had taken a bride.

He said: 'You have a bride now, well and truly, and if a bride be but a newly-married wife, I judge – since we but rarely see you, brother, among company – that she will be a bride always.

'Nevertheless, even newly married grooms have to leave their beds sometimes to take up the work of the world.

'I suggest, Thorstein, that you and the beautiful and lovely Gudrid – for why should I ever wish to marry since Gudrid is another's? – why should I be called "The Lucky", "The Happy", when you are the husband of Gudrid? – take up the gift of our father, and journey up to Sandness.'

'I put into Sandness on my way back from Vinland. For that is the short and right way to – or from – Vinland. All ships, it is my thought, passing between Greenland and Vinland, will call at Sandness; and this will make it an important place – which will be a blow for poor Heriolf and, after his death, Bjarni.

'You and our father, on that hunting trip last summer, found that our caretaker, Thorstein the Black, was too surly a kind to make Sandness as thriving as it should be. He and his wife need a hand over them – yours. It is not so much the farm that matters but how well, or how badly, he works the forge there for the iron ore drawn from the bog in that part of Greenland. Men going to Vinland will need a sharpening of their weapons for killing, if need be, skraelings. They will need axes freshly ground for the felling of timber in Vinland.

'Farming at Sandness must be of second account to this.

'But Thorstein the Black, as I found, like yourself, and our father earlier, is surly, too sad not to be lazy. An able man only when driven. Neither is he helped to be more active by that gaunt bent wife of his.'

Thorstein, speaking for himself and for Gudrid, agreed that fate pointed to this course, and that he and Gudrid should go forthwith.

But then Leif turned to his elder brother, Thorwald. He said:

'I have been thinking, Thorwald Eiriksson, that though you are the eldest son of our father, and that therefore you are bequeathed Brattahlid, and have full right to Brattahlid, yet you are nevertheless still wanting to prove yourself by deeds to be the son of Eirik, and grandson of our father's father, Thorwald, whose name you carry.

'Our father, I know, pretended to look on you as a bookish man, but that was his crafty means of urging you forwards, for he knew you in truth to be a brave man – though more thoughtful than most.

'Now it is right that more than one of our family should know Vinland, and the way to there and from there, for otherwise if there be only one who has that knowledge, and he dies, then hard will be the fate of all in Greenland – judging by what I hear of last winter, and what I know of earlier winters.

'You take the ship, brother, and gather a crew, and I will look after our mother, Thjodhild, and hold Brattahlid in trust till you return.'

Thorwald saw his chance to win a reputation by such a venture and agreed.

So the plan was that the ship should be got ready as soon as possible; that Thorwald should be in charge of a crew of thirty men, of which I should be one; that the ship would first follow the coast up to Sandness in the West Settlement, where Thorstein and Gudrid, carried as passengers, would be left; and that from Sandness, Thorwald, equipped with the fullest sailing directions from Leif, should make his great voyage to Vinland.

For myself, this was an exciting prospect. I had been named by Leif as one of the thirty who should go to Vinland for what had seemed the good reason that I had been in that ship when it had been Bjarni's ship, and we had sighted the new countries when trying to find Greenland from Iceland. That appeared, as I say, a good reason, but yet since I had been so very young at the time – though I but guessed at this, for he said nothing – it was possible that Leif was concerned to put space and time between me and his half-sister, Freydis. If he had that wish, it may have been because he had a kind care for my health of body and of soul, or because he had a care lest Freydis should attain through me, with her boldness and her greed, too great a grasp of affairs as they were going on at Brattahlid.

The time came when we should embark, still early in the season. I had been with Freydis the evening before for two hours, and though she knew – as everyone in the whole fjord knew, for there was much talk – where we were bound, yet in spite of her pleading, wiles and angry passions, she got no more from me as to the expedition than was fit to be generally known.

We made splendid headway along the coast off Greenland, threading the floes in a calm sea and fresh breeze, and without needing the aid of oars, reached Sandness on the third day.

Thorstein Eiriksson and Gudrid went ashore, taking over control of the house which Eirik had left to them. Under the management of Thorstein the Black and Grimhilda the place was no better than when I had seen it last summer, both going to, and coming from, the hunting in the far north, but they had the excuse that the winter had been as hard to them as it had been to the people in the East Settlement.

Thorstein the Black sharpened afresh our weapons and tools, and we re-embarked on the great venture westward. As I took leave of Gudrid and her husband I wondered, by the manner of her gaze, whether she was seeing into the near or the far. It seemed that she was seeing trouble in store, whether for herself or for others no one could say, for she herself would not say. But she took a farewell with Thorwald with an air of sorrow.

All of us were in good spirits – there were thirty of us – and we were ready to give full trust to Thorwald. If he frowned, we thought, it was due to poorish sight, as he strained to see, rather than to worry, still less to fear.

Guiding our path by the sun at its noon height, and steering almost due west, with a little northing, as Leif had counselled, we soon came upon the ugly Helluland, or Slab Land, and turned south and east, following its coast. Next, after a run over open water, we came upon Markland but, not deigning to land there, followed that coast and then, travelling over another stretch of water, and veering course to something of the west, came upon what we took to be Vinland and, from that point, kept close watch all daylight hours – heaving to at nightfall – lest we miss the landmarks and sea-marks Leif had warned us about, – until we sighted the houses he had reared.

Seeing these, with great joy, we made for the shore, and moored our ship by the bank of the stream which flowed into the sea below the headland where Leif's houses stood. We were fortunate that their shelter was awaiting us so we could give the more time to scanning the land. And it had been an easy voyage, helped by a good sea and weather. And I had been of some use, remembering the sea-marks from my first coming to Greenland.

But great ill luck was to follow. After a few days spent settling into Leif's houses, and catching and eating the salmon which abounded in that river, and of foraging the country close to the houses, noticing its riches, Thorwald decided that we should board the ship, and sail along the coast, entering such fjords and creeks as he thought most promising.

As we were running alongside the coast on a south-easterly course, a storm blew up.

With wind and tide behind us, Thorwald, standing look-out, ordered that we run straight and at speed at the clean white sand that lay but a short way off, seeking to drive, with the aid of oars too, the nose of the ship as far up on that soft bed of sand as we could. We were near to the end aimed at, when a great wave lifted up the fore-part of our ship. The wave rolled on before us, but thereupon the stem and bows fell as quickly as they had risen, and the leading part of the keel, in the fall, hit not soft sand but a hard thin reef or ridge of rock. The thudding drop to the fall jerked us forward so that a man broke his teeth on the thwart before him, there was a sound of rending.

The keel had struck the ridge, at a distance from the stem that cleaved the water, equal to the distance of a tall man's long stride.

Thorwald ordered half his men over the side of the gunwale into the water. The rest were to crowd into the stern so that by their weight they might lift the bows higher. Those who were wading leaned and shoved with main strength, and pushed the bows clear of the ridge on which the keel rested, the tide still advancing.

When the ship, mounted on the log rollers which we carried, was on the shore above the tide's reach, it was seen that the keel had been shattered where it had struck, the leading pair of ribs were damaged, and the strakes – from the garboard strake upwards – were wrenched from the stem-post.

Now, if we had not mended the ship, not one man of us would ever have made home to Greenland again. The night was spent in wet and chill garments, foodless, with that thought in mind. And some spread fear amongst us by talking of the likelihood of skraelings. Nor could any mending of the ship have been carried out, but for the forethought of Thorulf who had borne the wright's gear into the ship before leaving Leif's houses. The knowledge that such gear was on board was the one rare thing to comfort us that night, and I silently thanked Thorulf even as I silently blamed Thorwald for not spying the reef as he stood look-out bidding us drive the ship up and onwards to the shore.

It was Thorulf, who had risen early, who grimly told us that there was no hope in unfastening all the timbers, and laying a wholly new keel. The most, which was the bad best, that could be aimed at, was the cutting away of the leading length of the keel, at the place where it had broken, and the splicing of a new length in its stead. But that new length would be of unseasoned timber, the ship thereafter would be weak at the join. We would be lucky if we should regain Greenland and, if we reached home, we could 'thank God or Thorulf, as we pleased', he said.

Five men were told to find food for the whole party each day. The rest, under the charge of Thorulf – for Thorwald had never been a shipwright – worked to make the ship safe enough to carry us back, for after that it would never be trusted.

The ship hoisted on stones below the break, bulwarks supported by poles, the nails pinning the strakes and the stem-post were taken out. A bough of a tree was chosen by Thorulf for grafting with the main keel, and the adze shaped two saplings, bent under fire, and tied with sinews, to serve in the stead of the wrenched ribs. The new stem-post was a mean affair, rising but a width of a man's hand above the top gunwale strake.

By the time the mending was finished, it was judged that it was too late in the year to venture home. And to return to Greenland with an empty, leaking and broken ship would have been a hurt to the pride of us all, not least a hurt to the pride of Thorwald, for he would suffer chief reproach and the shame. Besides which, this worse than failure of the expedition would lower the heart of every man and woman in Greenland who rested the strongest hope that they might continue to live in that country on the goods that might be fetched from Vinland.

Thorwald would be scorned and laughed at; he would be a discredit to his renowned father; and to his illustrious brother, Leif the Lucky.

Better to die than face a welcome of that sort. Moreover, his crew of thirty had to be paid for the hardships they had borne and the separation from their families.

And it was too late in the year, the summer given to the mending, to risk the journey.

It was resolved to refloat the ship and, holding close to the shore, to return to Leif's houses for the winter. In the spring we would gather a freight load of some sort, rich enough to earn a welcome home, despite the stunted stem-post and the weak keel.

This plan we acted upon. The last thing that Thorwald did before we went into the ship, was to take up the length of the keel that had been fractured on the rock and to thrust it into the sand, but above the tide's reach, where the harm had happened.

'I call this place Keelness,' he said, 'and this timber, shaped like a swan's neck, this, hooded and broadening where it joined the stem's post, I plant as a sea-mark, a warning of wreck upon a small spine of rock which a man of poorish sight might not see for all his straining.'

That sad sign, fronting the sea may still stand, may not yet be rotten, and I tell others – through you, my son – that we should not forget Keelness.

There were falls of snow but they were less than in Greenland in that winter. The sun at noon stood higher and the short days were not so short as in Greenland.

The stream, in which our gravely hurt ship lay, curdled over with thin ice but never starkly froze. There were always fish to be caught for our food, birds to be snared, amongst them ptarmigan, and an abundance of wild game to be killed. We peeled the hides from the bodies of the deer to take home as a sign of this abundance. There was fuel for cooking or for warming without limit. We told stories, and we played chess. Thorwald was an excellent player of this game, ever the winner, but he brooded long between his moves, and the brooding was not always on his next move in the game of chess he was playing.

As soon as spring came we were all in favour of gathering all kinds of cargo that we could, and hurrying back to Greenland. But Thorwald overruled us. Whether it was folly or daring, he would have it that we sail once more along the shore, despite the weakened keel. He said it would be a test; for if the ship withstood it, then it would brave the open sea. But his true purpose was to add somewhat to the knowledge of Vinland, beyond what Leif knew, to be able to tell of this or that headland, of this or that fjord, and so to be able to claim before his brother and all men that his party had explored – and mapped – more than brother Leif knew, for the benefit of later comers.

Some of us grumbled that he was further risking lives and limbs, and Thorulf, to whom we owed most, said, 'Thorwald Eiriksson, your bad eyesight led to the breaking of our keel, so take heed lest it lead not to the breaking of your life, if not ours.'

We sailed south from Leif's houses, passing landmarks which we noted, till we came to another headland above a stream. And Thorwald's heart was moved, and he said, 'I love this beautiful headland. If I had my will, I would set up my house there, and there live and die.'

The ship was moored in the stream below the headland, and we climbed up above the grassy slopes. 'This site could be made richer than Brattahlid,' said Thorwald.

Reaching the crown of the headland, one of us spied three low humps by the shore on the seaward side. A man's head and shoulders were poking out from beneath one of the humps according to the one amongst us who saw best and furthest.

Thorwald split our party into two, and we descended the slope so that in matched numbers we would reach the shoreline on each side of the humps. Then with our weapons we rushed on the humps and, finding skraelings asleep underneath, we killed. The skraeling who had been crawling out, fearing us from the weapons we carried, dodged our strokes and fled into the woods landward.

We had killed eight skraelings who had been lazily asleep under three little boats made of the bark of trees wrapped over a light frame and sewn with animal's sinews.

If the boats were not very like the boats of the skraelings in Greenland, neither were the men.

As we judged, their faces were narrower, though they had the same stiff black hair on the head. Their noses too were narrower. Their eyes were black in the main, but the eyes of one were light brown, and another's blue. Three of the dead had a pair of raven or ptarmigan feathers knotted in their hair at the back of the head; another had a longer feather of a different kind bound by a band about his forehead. They were clothed, not in sealskin, but in animal hides that had been treated.

We left the eight bodies lying there and went back to the stream where our ship was moored. Thorwald said we should go upstream on foot, along the bank, which was thick with bushes, some about to leaf. We were to look for the different kinds of berries, fruits and vines.

Though so early in the year the sun was warm and we all felt a great drowsiness. It was about noon, or soon after. We lay down in the thickets near the edge of the stream to rest in the haze of beams of sunshine that reached us through the net of the branches that were still bare. We dozed.

Then: 'Get up, you scoundrels, or you'll be dead men!' banged in our ears.

Who called that out – whether Thor, or Thorwald, or Thorwald's three-in-one new god – none of us afterwards could tell. But we sprang up as one man and saw, coming downstream, a vast number of skraelings in their boats, one skraeling in each boat, paddling rapidly towards the very place where we had lain on the bank. Seeing that we were awake, some of the skraelings put down their paddles, and with their bows shot arrows which came horribly near.

Thorwald sized up the situation at once. At his word we made for the ship as hard as we could, stumbling among the bushes and roots. Jumping into the ship we took up our shields, while our right hands grabbed any weapon that was near.

The skraelings, screaming hatred, came abreast the ship, shooting their arrows, stopping their screaming and shooting only to back-paddle so as not to be swept by the current past us. Luckily, not any of them was intelligent enough to draw alongside the bank to alight and pour down arrows upon us from the land. We ranged ourselves, man beside man, along the entire length of one side of our ship, and let our shields take the stinging strikes of the arrows.

We had done the right thing. By standing on the floor of the ship, the deep bulwark protected each man up to the level of his crotch, while our shields were to ward all above.

Thorwald, quickly realizing that every arrow that sank into our shields was another for us to shoot, gave order that every other man was to stoop below the ship's side, tug out the skraeling arrows from his shield, and was then to shoot two or three at a time.

The evil ones, feeling the smarts we gave them, mixed howls with their screams. And several of their boats, in some of which still sat a dead skraeling bending over an arrow in the middle of his breast, were carried past us in the swift current to the sea. We sorely wounded many more for, in their miserable little boats, they were open to our shots from above, standing high above as we were, the lower parts of our bodies were covered by the ship's side, and we used our shields well.

At length the skraelings, whether still whole or wounded, gave up their attack, and turned their boats around and paddled upstream.

Thorwald asked if any of us were hurt, and then: 'For myself, I have a wound; and it is sore enough to end in my death. You will see where that wound is.'

And he slowly swung his left arm away from his body at the level of his shoulder so that the inward side of the shield, bound with a thong above the wrist, showed.

Between Thorwald's body and his arm was the shaft of an arrow and the head of that arrow rose above his left shoulder close to his neck.

'The skraeling's arrow flew upwards between the gunwale and my shield into the armpit,' he said. 'Had my sight been clearer I would have seen it coming, and the shield would have taken it.

'But I spoke more wisely than I thought when I said I loved that headland and would set up my home there, and there live and die. I shall have my will – by a half.'

And he told us to put his body into a grave on that headland, and to plant a high cross at each end of the grave. He would rise at the last day, looking eastwards to Greenland. And: 'let that cross at the head be yet higher than the one at the foot'.

We did as he wished, and the two great crosses, the one inland the loftier, mark the place: Crossness. So a later seaman will have three marks to lay by: Leif's houses, Keelness and Crossness, and when he lays a sight on the two crosses so that these are in direct line one behind the other, he will have a true east-west bearing.

After this, we called to mind what else Thorwald, dying, had advised: which was to sail back to Greenland with all speed, and to give the charge of the ship to Thorulf.

From Leif's houses we loaded on board in all haste the hides of the animals we had killed, such grapes and vines as we could lay hands on, eggs of different kinds of birds that we had gathered from the nests, and set out for Greenland as soon as there was a likelihood of a settled spell of calm weather in our ship with the weakened keel.

We had named two places on the map of Vinland.

With our scant cargo we fared back to Greenland by the route we had gone out, the one Leif had counselled, passing Markland and Helluland now in that order. The ice, from the spring melting of the glaciers, was thick; the air misty. But Thorulf was a skilled skipper of keen sight and we made Sandness in the West Settlement safely.

Looking on the beautiful but sad eyes of Gudrid, I wondered whether she had foreseen the death of her brother-in-law. I wondered too whether their sadness betokened grief only for Thorwald or whether she had fore-knowledge of far greater grief in store.

When I was with Gudrid, I lost all desire for Freydis; when I was with Freydis, even in her bed, I could not forget Gudrid.

Our ship made a mean showing when we sailed up the fjord to Sandness. The great proud stem-post was now in Vinland, and the mere stump in the front of our ship cheered neither ourselves on board nor those who came to welcome us. Our leader was dead, our cargo paltry, and there had been disappointment in the waste of hope, strength and wealth.

Neither was the husband of Gudrid, Thorstein Eiriksson, so happy with the way things had gone since taking over Sandness. Handsome and virile man as he was, next after Leif, the handsomest in Greenland, and once, after Leif, thought to be the best catch for a girl, he seemed unhappy and slack in Sandness, despite the nearness of his wife – whom, I thought, was scarcely less a bride than before. But she drew me into a room one day, kissed me, and sighed, and then wept, but would not tell me the cause of any of these things.

Thorstein told me that his namesake, Thorstein the Black, was a lout, his wife – Grimhilda – an ugly slattern, and that the bailiff – Gurdar – was the devil, the very one that Christian priests talked of, come back to earth – the one who had brought death and hard work to all men, through getting the first man's wife to eat something in a garden that was forbidden. Gurdar was as wicked as that.

After a day and a night's rest in Sandness, we resumed our journey, and after another five days, sailed up Eiriksfjord in the East Settlement to reach Brattahlid.

A mass was said for the quiet resting of Thorwald's soul whose body lay far off in Vinland among wretched heathens.

Thjodhild took the loss of her eldest son in this way. She said: 'Had it not been for his father he would not have attempted deeds for which he was not fit.' So:

'Eirik will have this sin upon his soul. His eldest was born fit to become a priest, but his mind was turned to other things because of his father's wicked folly. More: Thorwald would have become a bishop, because of the greatness of his family and the piety on his mother's side. For those that make bishops out of priests pay more heed to the piety of their mothers than the wickedness of their fathers.'

A man, to comfort her, pointed out that Thorwald died fighting heathen skraelings.

'That at least will be judged to his credit in heaven,' she replied.

Leif, on the other hand, blamed the ill success of the expedition on the rashness of its leader who had allowed the killing of the eight skraelings sleeping under their boats. No doubt, it was the ninth man who had fled to his fellows and told them of what we had done; and that is why they had attacked.

'Better to have killed all rather than some,' he said, 'but better still to have killed none. For now should any of us sail into Vinland again, the skraelings will remember the harm that was done to them, and will make our dealings with them more difficult.

'I grieve for my brother, but it was ill done. The work of a fool rather than of my brother; and a few weeds and skins of animals in a broken ship are no fair return.

'Yet Greenlanders must go to Vinland again, despite the hatred stirred up against us by Thorwald and all who went with Thorwald, for if we do not go there – either to settle, or at least to fetch goods from there – there our settlements in Greenland will not last beyond the lives of our children's grandchildren.'

Indeed, to give point to what he said, a ship came up the fjord to Brattahlid, a few days after he had spoken, laden with wooden boards. It had sailed from Bergen. The merchants demanded outrageously high prices for these boards, and they were backed up by their skipper who alleged that timber was such a bulky article for its comparatively light weight that a ship carrying it would find hold-room for little of high worth that, compared with timber, took small space, such as wine. Therefore if we Greenlanders wanted timber so much, we must pay for it, he said.

So in exchange for Bergen's timber boards, we parted with Brattahlid's last season's haul in the northern hunting grounds of walrus ivory – eighteen tusks, and a live white bear cub – a huge gift for any Norwegian king or an earl in England. Fair-for-fair it was a bad bargain, but for a crying need of timber for our shipwrights and boatwrights, for the building of our doors, rafters for roofs, staves for whey barrels, wood for coffins. And that does not take account of the shavings of the boards to start the fires for the cooking of our food and the warming of us in winter.

Yet there was timber for the asking in Markland and Vinland, if the heathen skraelings could be made to allow our free taking of it.

Thorwald dead, Leif was now the master of Brattahlid. He confirmed Thorstein in the ownership of Sandness. Nor did he forget what his father owed to Thorbjörn. He settled him on a good piece of land, and he rewarded Thorkel for the house-room he had given the father and Gudrid.

None of us who had sailed with Thorwald earned much credit, not even Thorulf. Yet Thorulf did earn some praise, not from Leif but from Freydis. Humbled by the scolding we received from Leif, I took comfort in believing that Freydis would welcome me back as a travelled man, and would make amends for all the hardships undergone and for doing without, for many months, what all men most delight in, and what young men especially need.

Now it is my belief after my long life that men, who may speak truth in all other matters, are still not to be trusted when they speak to other men of their dealings with women. I have found it thus: that those men who brag and boast of having lain with women up and down the land, and in other lands, have in truth – if one thinks about their boastings with care – known only one or two, or none, to lie with; that those, on the other hand, who say nothing in these boasting gatherings of men, and who seem to the boasters little and contemptible fellows, those – I suspect – are the ones who have been in bed with more naked women than the boaster boasts of, or rather dreams of. The quiet one has, it is not unlikely, lain in bed with the noisy boaster's wife.

And I had made some sad findings of the ways of life in Greenland. Who would have thought, for example, that the round little old Archdeacon from Bremen, who said 'tut . . . tut . . . tut . . .' from the pulpit, and who blushed and crossed himself, and opened his breviary if he so much as heard a man swear, would have shared the bed of Eirik Thorwaldsson's – the Red's – the founder of Greenland's – woman? But so he did and Eirik's former mistress washed his soiled underclothes. And this Archdeacon had done nothing in the way of deeds of real worth to put beside those of Eirik, whom men of all time will talk about.

Well, I shall tell the truth. That woman, Freydis, the daughter of Eirik's mistress, received me coldly. If I had returned from a rich voyage, and with many gifts from that voyage, it might have been otherwise. But in truth, when I went to her dwelling, I found her mother there also, and this, I think, was planned by Freydis, so as to prevent the love-making I had so much looked forward to and had expected. Freydis made nothing of the dangers and hardships of the voyage from wind, wave, ice or even the arrows of the skraelings, but much of the shattered keel and the small mean cargo we brought back. Neither did she show any true grief at all at the death of Thorwald, her half-brother in blood. Nor did I get so much as a kiss.

I took it that Freydis was less eager for love and lust than for wealth and fame and power. She had a great appetite, when it was aroused, as I had known, but this violent lipping and clasping would only be given, I now knew, to those men whom she guessed would aid her to advance herself as a lady of riches, and who would – through those riches – become a great and influential person.

Thorulf was an unmarried man of middle years. He was a quiet sober man, stocky but of average height, and he had saved us all from death in Vinland with his cunning and skill. He was both seaman and shipwright.

You must learn however, my son, that a man hitherto blameless, can be much changed in his nature should he come under the power of a bad and strong-willed woman. This is the more likely in the case of a man who has lived into middle age with but scant knowledge of womenkind.

It was Thorulf who was now often seen going to Freydis's door.

And it used to open to him.

9

THE GREAT THING
AT GARDUR

It was still early in the summer. The sheep had been driven up to the fells; the cattle in the byres, too weak to stand after months of feeding on scant fodder, had been lifted from their stalls to graze on the fresh grass; the glaciers were thawing and with thunderous sound were calving their enormous ice-children into the fjord; women sang at their looms, shifting the frames into the rays which slanted through the stretched bladder skins covering the small windows. Despite the harsh winter in Greenland (or my less harsh winter in Vinland, except a failed voyage and the death of Thorwald Eiriksson to grieve for) all of us felt happier because of the warming sun of this sweet lovesome season.

And talking of love. Even the old felt gamesome enough to laugh about it good-naturedly, while the young felt eager and the middle-aged single ones restless enough. The path to the Little Knowing One's dwelling was trodden by a stream of callers: by young women, asking for the recipe for the making of the cake or Sweet Lovebread – and for a demonstration of its making, and the giggles of the girls, as they watched this operation, could be heard at all hours. Even young men called on the Little Knowing One to ask whether there was not some kind of love food which would act on the girls in the same way as the cake acted on men. Middle-aged men too went – but when it was dusk lest it be thought that they be judged credulous and their behaviour laughable.

So you see that however grim the long-term outlook for Greenland was, as far as the future supply of the bare necessities for the support of life through harsh winters went, yet not one of us could help but be happy and hopeful in the bliss of that short but so lovely month.

Even Thjodhild would smile in her thin and tight-lipped way, while Leif would smile often, and broadly, open-lipped – showing his teeth – while he would plume his gold beard, and pat the heads of little children.

If I was sad for an hour now or then, it was only because Freydis, reckoning perhaps that I was of no further use to her in her determination to search for wealth, would have no more of me. The quiet Thorulf, who had lived to himself so contentedly before, was now surely her man. I wondered what Thorulf and the Archdeacon would say to each other if they met – one going to the daughter, the other coming from the mother, say. And the fun of picturing them in my mind lightened my own gloom. Thorulf, I pictured, might tug at his forelock, or greet 'Sera Peder, your reverence', while the Archdeacon would hastily look down – peering to see if, below his fat belly, his dress was properly fastened up. The Archdeacon would mop his sweating face – or the kerchief was to hide his blushes – and he would mutter something like, 'Just coming from strengthening the faith of the good women within', or 'Avoid the occasion of sin, Master Thorulf', or 'I trust to see you at mass, Thorulf'; and Thorulf would think, 'Better keep to the dam, you two-faced shuffler. You're puffed enough after a bout with the mother. Go to the daughter, if you dare, and you'll come out an all but a dead man.'

Concluding that Thorulf had cut me out with Freydis, I resolved – so enlivening was the sweet warm season – to look out for another girl, or other girls. But this I will say: that some of them were willing enough, but none was anything like an equal to Freydis – with the dark red hair mixed with tresses of black, and of the pale skin, the daughter of Eirik the Red – in the game of the bed. And will add this: that with them, as with Freydis, it was the thought, the picture in the mind, of Gudrid Thorbjörnsdottir, that came when it was over, or which came even before it was all over.

The sixth week of summer. This was the week of the meeting of the Great Thing.

Already the place of the Thing had been moved, following the death of Eirik, and despite the greatness of his widow and of Leif Eiriksson, from Brattahlid in Eiriksfjord to Einar's stead in Einarsfjord. Einar's stead was the most central place for the whole East Settlement with all its farms. Moreover, here by Einar's stead, was a wide plain – the only large stretch of flat land in all Greenland – and it reminded all who had been born in Iceland, but had come to Greenland, of the Thingvale in the land which had been their home.

So it was in the middle; it was flat; it reminded us of Iceland.

We, from Brattahlid, had a simple journey. The journey was but a short crossing of the fjord to below the glacier at a spot where the mountains fell away. There was an easy landing and then a footpath to the plain of Einarsfjord, later to be known as Gardur.

All the chief men set up their booths, the place of each booth marked by the booth-stones of the man to whom it belonged. The booths when set up made up three-fourths of a ring, every one of them facing towards a mighty mound in which steps had been cut. On the flattened top of this mound was a fine stool for the use of the Law Man.

On the death of Eirik Thorwaldsson, 'the Red', Einar Einarsson had been elected Law Man and, on the opening of the Great Thing, he would read out, so that everyone could hear them clearly, the Laws.

After the saying of the Laws, any man who had a case in law against another man, brought it forward so that it could be heard and tried, and then a judgment would be given according to the Laws as they had been read by the Law Man. If I remind you of this, my son, it is because, since you were born, things have changed. Since you were born the Church has claimed the right to set up its own courts. And the Church did set courts up; and they were set up, moreover, hard by where we held our Thing. The Church was saying that cases in law pertaining to adultery, fornication, buggery, devil-worship or the black arts, breaking Lent fast, man-killing and theft were their affair and not the Thing's, not even the Great Thing's.

This trample of the Church upon the rights of our people to hear and decide cases in law at the Thing and Great Thing had started at the time I speak of, and it lessened the might of Thing and Great Thing.

The Church courts heard their cases at Gardur in the house of the Archdeacon, who was the judge. He was the man from Bremen you know about, but the Bishop was now a Swede, Greenland having just been shifted from the see of Bremen into that of Lund.

Many of us could allow the Archdeacon, on behalf of the Swedish Bishop, to poke his nose into adultery affairs, the breaking of Lent fast, sodomy with cows or sows, and so on, but we did gainsay the Church's claim to hear cases of man-killing, theft or trespass – the shifting by a neighbour of a farmer's boundary marks on land burned over by fire by the farmer when settled. We held it was a matter for the Thing or Great Thing if a man had his calves stolen, and he later found those calves on his neighbour's land and branded with the mark of his thieving neighbour.

And as for killing, this should be no Church matter either. If a great man killed the bondsman of another great man, on finding him bestride his favourite horse, the quarrel should be between the great men, and the Thing should settle the rights and the wrongs of the case, and how many cattle – if any – the owner of the horse should pay to the owner of the bondsman he slew.

Now many men could see why Eirik Thorwaldsson had been so bitter against the Christian priests, and how it led to a breach between him and his wife, Thjodhild.

Also, but this is by the way, it was known that the Archdeacon did not try himself before his own court for fornication with the former mistress of Eirik, the mother of Freydis. Rather, it would be likely that he would have summoned anyone who suggested that he should do so on the ground of 'bearing false witness' and he would have deemed the matter so scandalous that it would be heard in secret.

The West Settlement had its own Thing at Sandness, and so the East Settlement had its own Thing; but at the Great Thing, in the sixth week of summer, the chief men of both settlements gathered at what is now known as Gardur, in spite of the Archdeacon's house being nearby.

The gathering was not done by taking horse and riding, from all quarters, as was done in Iceland – to the Thingvale. The older men remembered that, but in Greenland, because of the nature of the land, there was little or no riding beyond any one fjord, and we had to gather from all quarters – from Heriolfsness, from Hrafnsfjord, from Einarsfjord, from Eiriksfjord, from Hvalsey, from Icyfjord, from Broadfjord in the East Settlement, and from Lysafjord, Rangafjord and even Fishfjord in the West – of both settlements by journeying, down fjords or along coasts, by ship or by boat. But still when we had reached Gardur, the loveliness of the plain – the mountains around topped with snow against the bright sky – reminded us of who and what we were, that those of us who were not bound to a master should stay free.

After the reading of the Laws by the Law Man, the first case concerned the rights and wrongs between three men over a white bear. Ulf, nicknamed 'Flatnose', Egilsson, had lured the animal, which was scarcely weaned, into a trap he'd laid in Icyfjord. His fellow, Skuf Skufskaldsson – who like his father in name was like him also in being something of a poet – admitted Flatnose had done the trapping, but it was he who had shackled the animal and had since fed it with fish, and now it was ready to be shipped to the King of Denmark. The bear would fetch a great price and the greater share should go to the one who had borne the cost of feeding it. But the rights of either Flatnose or Skuf to any of the price was contested by Helgi, their neighbour in Icyfjord, who claimed that the bear had broken its chains and so mauled the leg of a bondsman of his, before the animal was shackled again, that his man had since died. The price of the white bear for the King of Denmark should be his compensation for the loss of his man.

Flatnose and Skuf shook hands to end their quarrel in order to jointly resist the suit of Helgi.

Another case was to be against an Icelander, Thorgrim Kolbrun-arskald, who had travelled from his own country to avenge the killing of his foster-brother, Thorgeir, by one of our greatest men in Green-land, Thormod, who dwelt in Einarsfjord. Thormod, a very rich and stern-hearted man, a slow-mover on his feet, had struck Thorgeir dead when that man had been a guest on Thormod's ship when he had taken a great cargo back to Iceland and lay in harbour. Thorgrim, following the killer of his foster-brother back to Greenland, had killed one of Thormod's servants in mistake for his master, and now Thormod meant to render Thorgrim an outlaw at the Great Thing, his own killing of Thorgeir notwithstanding.

As the case was about to come up there was a thunderstorm with heavy rain and all men retired to their booths. It was while Thormod was in his booth, preparing his case, that Thorgrim entered the booth where Thormod was sitting, in a sealskin cape, under which he concealed an axe. Thorgrim cleft open Thormod's skull from above, so that his head was divided to his shoulders.

When the case was called, the body of Thormod was shown in evidence, and for the death of Thormod, if not for that of Thormod's servant, Thorgrim was declared an outlaw. Thormod, for his stern loftiness was not liked, but all houses would be shut to the Icelander, and since there were few caves to hide in that were not well known to us in Greenland, Thormod's son had little doubt that he would avenge his father.

The next case would make me unhappy, unsettled in mind. Among those who had come up from Heriolfsness were Heriolf himself, now frail because of his years, but crafty still, a stickler for his rights, and Bjarni. Despite my old friendship for them, I had hoped they would not attend the Thing, but feared they would.

The truth was that they had come up to forward a case against no less a man than Leif Eiriksson. And the prospect of this was not pleasant

to someone who owed a measure of faith to both families. I had
thought that Bjarni had in truth relinquished the whole of his rights in
his ship, in return for a good sum, to Leif. That was my plain understanding, but I had not been by when the dealing took place, and got
my tale of it from Leif Eiriksson. But the men of Heriolfsness now
claimed: that Bjarni had but leased his ship to Leif and Leif had lent
the ship to his brother, Thorwald, and Thorwald had broken the keel,
and Thorwald was dead; and Leif must answer for it.

The claim of Heriolf and Bjarni was for the return of the ship as
whole as it was before she sailed. But since, 'as they heard', this was
no longer possible, they asked for a ship, if not new, then 'in as good a
trim' as that which they had leased or, failing that, the price of such a
ship.

Further, they claimed a half of the cargo which Thorulf – the
skipper in charge on the death of Thorwald – had brought back, and
which, 'they had heard', was very rich.

Of course the cargo was poor rather than rich, and what there was of
it had been split up among many. And of course the building of a new
ship to replace the one with a broken keel could not be undertaken in
Greenland.

As it happened, after the case was called, there was another down-
pour of rain, so the hearing was delayed by the Law Man until the
following morning.

Bjarni and his father had brought a large number of witnesses from
Heriolfsness, but I doubted whether these would count as anything
when weighed against the word of Leif. Leif had a double advantage.
He was renowned throughout the land for his uprightness and honesty
of dealing. Next, following the death of his father, who had founded
Greenland, and of his brother, Thorwald, he was without doubt the
greatest man in the country.

Thereto, he had a third advantage. He was 'lucky': nothing would
ever go wrong for him.

Near to Leif's booth were the booths and tents of all who backed
him in his suit. They were sure he would win. All the great men of
Eiriksfjord were behind him, and would swear that Leif had bought
the ship outright. Thorkel would support Leif, but so also would
Thorbjörn, the father of Gudrid – and well they both might, for they
could hardly do other. Over against this position were the booths and
tents of Heriolf and his son and their supporters. I was sorely troubled.
Leif would take it for granted that any oath he swore to would be

seconded by me as true, but Heriolf in my early years had been towards me as a father, and would count on my standing by him.

After dark I left my shared booth and under the damp cloudy sky went to Heriolf's booth. He rose and embraced me heartily. His son, Bjarni, however, greeted me with coldness, his face showing that he still carried some ill feeling.

Heriolf bade me sit among the men from his fjord who had crowded into the booth. They sat on benches or lay closely on sheepskins on the floor. These men closely watched this meeting with the caller who was known to depend on Brattahlid. They watched the old man and myself in the light of two lamps burning from seal-oil.

'Odd – that your friend, Leif Eiriksson, should take it on himself to fancy that his brother Thorwald could wreck my son's ship – a hired ship at that – and do nothing about it.'

Then Bjarni:

'And he lies if he swears he owes nothing of the cargo brought back, in the ship his brother wrecked. Now you, my one-time foster-brother, Ingolf, for my father reared you, can tell us about that cargo – for you were with Thorwald on that trip.'

'But in truth, Bjarni Heriolfsson,' I said, 'it was a wretched cargo, hardly worth the sharing out.'

'Odd that! Such a long trip for such a poor cargo, a dead skipper, and a broken ship,' Heriolf replied. 'Odd that! Are you so sure that the cargo was a mean, a worthless one? Come, from what I remember, you always spoke the truth – to me, at any rate.

'Whatever the matter, you must eat with us. It's some years since I saw you – but I can still see in you my foster-son.'

And so I ate and I drank – not that there was much ale at Heriolfsness, but what there was had been saved up and had been brought with them to the Great Thing to give them heart in this test at law, and to feast such friends as they would woo – and Heriolf, the old man, was all kindness, though his son still stood off somewhat.

Heriolf had asked me about my last few years, not dwelling much on the last bad voyage, and though I answered shortly at first, yet – as the feast went on – I told him more and more, and my friendly thankfulness towards them both grew strong again, and I said to Bjarni:

'When I saw you at Eiriksfjord, I was hurt when I saw that you saw me and feigned not to see me – '

And Bjarni: 'Let us be friends; if not as great friends as before, then still friends.'

I asked Heriolf how matters had gone with all those in his fjord the last winter, and the winter before that.

As he replied at length, I began to understand, though not from anything he said plainly, that in truth he was well aware that the last trip to Vinland was a bad one: yet I grasped that he was not displeased at that. On the contrary rather. He said he wished the lucky one of Brattahlid to stay lucky, of course, but 'the more often each attempt –'

Here he broke off to ask whether I had 'yet found a girl to settle down with and marry?' looking at me sharply as I answered, 'Well, not yet.' 'That's odd,' he answered, 'that you've found no woman friend, no girl in Eiriksfjord.

'I think the more often each venture from Brattahlid ends like the last, the better. . . . The better for them at Brattahlid, I mean.'

'Why?'

'So they will stop this loss of lives and the breaking of ships, like my son's. Odd, that breaking.'

It came to me that the crafty old man and his son meant to hold on to their fjord, come what might, and, since their fjord was barren, Heriolf rested his whole hope, and that of his son's, on his outlying home being always the first landfall for ships from Norway bringing the timber and grain which he and all Greenland needed, and for the sale of which he, and after him, his son, would act as middleman, and so survive with wealth. Any wreck or failure of a ship plying straight between the West Settlement and Vinland would make him glad.

Bjarni said: 'And you will back us in this suit against Leif – tomorrow?'

Heriolf: 'What my son has sworn is truth and that's not odd, though Leif will say otherwise. Where do you stand? What will you do tomorrow? It's odd that, if you can't say – or won't say – where you will stand.'

I looked at him and remembered how much I owed him.

'Well, are you going to speak? I'm rather deaf, you know.'

I said I would turn it over in my mind in the night.

'Turn it over! Odd that! Turn what over? We need all the friends we've got, you know. Who brought you to this country? Your father, who then abandoned you. Who looked after you when you were brought? I did. Bjarni is your foster-brother.'

I said that I could attest that I believed that Leif had truly thought he had bought the ship outright, but that he was certainly mistaken.

'That keel now, stuck up in the sands at Keelness, is no good to me, you know,' said Bjarni. 'But that keel was more than good when it was on my ship; but no good to me now is my ship without it.'

Heriolf asked me to drink again; and I drank. I left Heriolf's booth, having given an undertaking to both father and son that I would support them, but without clearly knowing what I would do in the morning, and hoping that somehow I might do nothing.

Skirting the booths set up three-fourths of a ring on my way back to my tent near Leif's booth, I wondered what one of those priests would say to a Christian in this sort of trouble. From what I had learnt from Christians I think the priest would say something like this:

'You've no worry, my man – or my good woman – or my son – if you just do, or say, what the innermost part of you tells you is right to do. I call it, my son, the Back-Biter, because if you don't do it, it will bite back.'

That, or such like, I am told is what a priest would say, and it would be thickheaded nonsense, because the choice before me was not between doing right and wrong at all. The choice was between doing wrong and wrong – wrong to Heriolf and Bjarni or wrong to Leif. And if I did wrong to Leif, by saying he was not so much a man who did not tell the truth – which no one would believe of the upright Leif – as a man who mistook the terms of a deal, I would be made to feel it. And no one would credit that either. It would be saying that Leif was dunderheaded. And for that, Leif would look upon me with scorn and hatred, and would see to it that my life was scarcely worth living. And I knew too that Leif had an understanding of the plight of all the people in Greenland. On wood and corn coming into Greenland in plenty, and without being bought, rested the lives or deaths of all in Greenland. But the bringing in of wood and corn from Vinland would mean the end of Heriolf and of all in Heriolfsness, of the poor and rocky soil, who looked to its only profit in the coming of ships from the east.

On my way back to where I would sleep, I passed the booth of Thorstein Eiriksson and Gudrid Thorbjörnsdottir. They had come from the West Settlement to the Great Thing in a suit that so much concerned the credit of the whole family.

Gudrid was standing at the entrance to their booth, waiting, she said, for the return of Thorstein who had gone to attend Leif's meeting about the morrow's business.

Part of the sky had been cleared of rain-clouds, and the stars in that part shone in Gudrid's eyes.

She took me into the booth, then let go my hand to clasp me about the neck. She said:

'I've wanted to do this. I saw you go to Heriolf's, and sent Thorstein to Leif's, and I waited for this.'

And she kissed me as though all her heart and half her soul were in it, and then she said:

'You will stand by us; and you will swear that what Leif and my father, and Thorstein and Thorkel too, will say is true. And you shall be repaid – by my love. And I tell you this: that Bjarni Heriolfsson weakened the keel of that ship, before he sold it, with the intention that it would break as it did break. How do I know this? I know it because I can see a ship's keel when it is deep down in the water though no one else's eyes can.

'And I tell you this: after you have sworn as you say, you will leave Brattahlid and sail with us back to Sandness when you will be paid like this, and with more – much more.' And she kissed me again, in the way she had done before, and yet again.

And so, you may believe how I attested at the trial, though that morning was not divided from the night before by any sleep.

And you may guess, and rightly, how I tried not to meet any of those from Heriolfsness after the trial.

Leif stayed until the end of the Great Thing, but I, with all haste, accompanied Gudrid and Thorstein to their house at Sandness in the West Settlement.

I hope, dear son, your mind will at all times be happier, and, if not, that at any rate it will not have to look back on what you have done, or not done, and repine.

It was rumoured that soon after the loss of his case, Heriolf, one of the fourteen founding fathers of Greenland, died; and that Thjodhild had a mass said for the quiet resting of his soul. Leif, it was said, had other affairs on his hands, and could not attend any church on that day.

10

ILLNESSES AND GHOSTS
AT THE WEST SETTLEMENT

Men in Greenland, no more than in Iceland, do not readily admit to fear. Such men would be jeered at and told to doff their breeches and put on a woman's skirt. But one of our women overhearing such an insult – 'take off those breeches and put on a skirt' – would hurl the retort like a stone: that 'if any cowards are to be found, they are only found among the husbands, or bondsmen brought from Ireland, or skraelings'. And in truth, as we know, some women can be crueller, and of harder mood, than any of our men.

So it is not easy, my son, to have to own to a time when I knew fear that was so great that it became something beyond what is called fear. What we underwent changed me so much that I remember it in my guts to this day. But there was joy at the end.

But first you will need to see in your mind, as though it were cut with a knife into rock, the layout of Sandness at Lysafjord in the West Settlement. Not as it is now, for the house has since grown, but as it was in the winter of the illnesses and of the ghosts. Not only has the house changed, but there now belongs to it a church, a churchyard and a priest. But at the time I speak of the Christian dead were buried in a patch of ground without rites, but a rod was driven through the earth at burial so that one end rested on the dead person's chest. Whenever chance brought a priest into Lysafjord, he plucked out the rod and poured holy water down the hole, saying a prayer the while, to soothe.

This patch of ground is now within the guard of the church which has since been built, close to the water. So the faithful have an easy walk down to mass, but quite a slope to face coming back.

Between this burial ground and the house of Sandness was the hut of Thor. It had not yet been pulled down, but he received no more offerings, and no one would dare to go inside his enclosure. Not even animals would stray into it, so the grass and weeds grew rank. At night a knocking could be heard inside the hut, and it was put down to the idol of Thor coming down from his stand and thumping the walls of his hut with his hammer.

Sandness was about a hundred and fifty man's strides above the fjord, which was called Lysafjord because of the strange milky sheen, or light, which it showed at some hours. At certain other hours it seemed to shudder with a grey and choppy swell, and then it was that trolls were below it, and heaving – or their bodies, though unseen, were hovering close over it, and they were gasping their troll breath down on the water. Yet it was an excellent fjord for the number and kinds of fish which it could be relied on to yield.

The door of Sandness opened to give a view of the fjord. Sandness is built half-way up the slope, and a man or woman, standing in its passage, with the door open, could have a good view of the fjord, both seawards and landwards, and of anything going on in the fjord – of boats approaching, or departing, or, by the rufflings in the water, of shoals of fish, or, by the plunging of their swarthy heads, of herds of seal.

Entering Sandness – so named after a belt of sand on our side of the fjord – there was a passage-way beyond the door, narrow enough for a man to have to flatten his shoulders against the wall for another to pass him, and from this passage there were entrances to two large rooms, one on each side of the passage.*

You must not think that either of these rooms were of the great size of the much renowned hall of Brattahlid. How could they be? Sandness

---

*In the margin of the manuscript at this point is a small, crude drawing, whether in the hand of this particular scribe, or some other, it is impossible to determine. In reproducing an enlarged tracing of this drawing I have superimposed 'legends' – none exist on the original.

was built seven years later, when it had already been found out that in the West Settlement the winters were yet harsher and longer than in the East Settlement, and that there were fewer trees, and those smaller, to hew down and burn – for cooking or for warming, warming rather than for heating. So the rooms were smaller, and the hearth-pit for the fire – unlike the long trench in the middle of Brattahlid's floor – was in a corner of each of the two rooms that led from the passage at Sandness. True, more driftwood could be gathered at the West Settlement than at the East, but these tree-trunks were often jumbled among the ice, to which they froze, and it was hard work separating trunks from ice; then splitting and hewing them, then lifting them home.

But still the two rooms were of fair size, especially the one to the right as one entered the passage through the door. This was Thorstein Eiriksson's and Gudrid Thorbjörnsdottir's – and was to be mine, and others' too, as it turned out.

It was the very same room that I had been in earlier with Eirik himself, and with Thorstein and Thorkel, on my return home from that trip to the northern hunting grounds two years before.

This room had one window to let in light. It was small, and the break in the stone was covered by the membrane of the stomach of a sheep, fixed taut and nailed to the timber lining of the window. The light through this window was dimmed and yellow. Yet through it one could peer and see a little. If one wished to see more than that little, one went into the passage-way and opened the front door for a clear view of the fjord – when it was free of mist; and in winter it might be too cold.

The other room that led from the passage was smaller, but still of good size. It had no window, but it had a fire-pit, no less than the larger room, and the embers, if not flames, would yield not only heat but a little light. So they ought to have been contented with that – Thorstein the Black and his wife, Grimhilda – since they were but the caretakers; but, as you shall see, they were not.

Their room was of the same breadth, but not so long. Still, it was a very good room and, window or no window, it had a hearth; and that hearth was as much in a corner as ours was. As Thorstein Eiriksson's, and Gudrid Thorbjörnsdottir's – and as mine, at the last, that is.

At the rear of the main room was an opening to the store-room and the larder. Here the salted meat was kept, and the dried fish, the barrels of cheese, wooden trenchers, soapstone dishes, tubs of fresh water, fishing gear and weapons. No brook flowed in a runnel through the house as it did at Brattahlid, but there were two wells fed by springs at the back of the house. In the worst of the weather, snow had to be brought into the house and melted.

At the rear of the passage was another door; and then paths leading up the slope to a byre with stalls for fourteen cattle, and to a barn. Still higher were sheepfolds and huts for the shepherds, but these were distant on the fells.

In front of the house, to its right, fifteen or so paces distant, was the privy. This used to be behind the house, and this was its position when we were on our way to and from the whale-horse hunting grounds, but it had been shifted by the time we called there after Thorwald's voyage to Vinland – where we had left him dead.

I think it had been shifted from behind and above the house to a place in front and below because Eirik, in his boisterous way, had told Thorstein the Black, 'Your sour look, and that haggard stooping look of that wife of yours, come, my good man, because what your two backsides put out leaks into the springs feeding those wells. Shift your privy, my glum one, and you will be less glum and your old woman won't be crouching all the time.'

The contents of the privy, at proper intervals, were to be taken by Thorstein the Black or his wife and carried up to the homefield. This was their duty. But they were an obstinate grumbling couple.

Up fjord, or to the right of the house, was the forge where the iron brought from the smelting furnace, further to the right where it had been made soft over glowing charcoal, was hammered into shape over the anvil.

Those who did not believe that it was Thor's hammer thumping the wooden walls of his temple, said instead that the sound came from Thorstein the Black's hammer at the forge and that the sound was rebounding from Thor's wooden walls.

Now that, thanks to Leif, it was made clear that the best way to Vinland was the short way, it was widely thought that the West Settlement at large, and Sandness in Lysafjord especially, as a home of the great family, with its ownership of an iron-working smithy, would become of utmost importance – and must become so, indeed, if the people of our Greenland were to survive.

Though the West Settlement was only a third of the size of the East, it had – apart from its bog-iron and its nearness to the new lands – its happinesses and its gains. If the farmsteads were smaller, the people in them were friendlier, less keen to outwit or out-do one another. Its dwellers came not so much from one quarter in Iceland or from any one region in Norway but, arriving later, drawn by reports of the 'green' of this Greenland, came as much almost from the Faroes, the Western Islands, from Shetland, even from Orkney, as they did from Iceland or Norway, and so they had to find ties among themselves. There were even some thralls who had been brought from Ireland. Some women had actually been seized and brought from Ireland too. Judging by his low brow, swarthy and broad countenance, and uncouth ways, it might be thought that Thorstein the Black was begotten by just such an Irish slave-woman in Iceland – and so, in fact, he had been. Weddings took place between people whose fathers had come here from different lands; and together the fathers dug deep foundations for smaller houses for their newly-wedded children.

People in the West Settlement too were bound more together in trust, because the West was all the nearer to the detestable skraelings, whose devilish whoopings could be heard, giving a warning, when they were daring to think of making a raid. Of course, they make far more raids now, but they tried it more than once in the time of which I speak. The devils captured two young boys and took them away with them.

Another gain of the West Settlement, though, was its greater closeness to the walrus and seal grounds, and its greater richness for land-hunting: not merely for white bears for shipping to kings and earls, but for the herds of caribou which made excellent meat.

The lack of a church and a priest was felt. A priest from the East Settlement might arrive once or twice a year to baptize or to celebrate at marriages and to lift up the stakes protruding from the ground of the dead for the pouring of holy water from vials, but the people wanted a Sera Tomas or a Sera Jon to live among them.

What names – Tomas, Jon, Pál, Mattias! Names of Hebrews or Jews far away and long ago, every one of them. But it was said that people of our blood and kind had no saints as yet to be named after, though it was also said that King Olav of Norway was likely to be made one through killing all his people who would not turn Christian.

Sandness was looked upon by the rest of the householders with some dread and respect, for the reason that its master was Thorstein Eiriksson who had come up from the East Settlement with some of the strength and – who knows? – some of the wrath of his mighty father.

Servants, and others bound to work at Sandness, lived in a number of little dwellings nearby, mostly beyond its forge and smelting furnace, but the shepherds lived upland, and the dairy workers had lodging near the byre.

In addition a number of otherwise free households were bound to pay rent in kind to Thorstein, the son of Eirik, as they had done to Eirik before him.

Gurdar was the name of the bailiff who collected the dues owing to Sandness. And I must say that if there had been any darkening of the happinesses of the West Settlement as a whole, it must be mainly laid against this Gurdar – against him and against the knocking sound heard from inside Thor's hut. Whereas the bad moodiness of Thorstein the Black, and the glum sorrowing air of his wife, angered the hearts, or irritated the tempers, of those in Sandness alone, for in the forge Thorstein the Black was a good workman.

Gurdar was both hated and feared. He carried a whip, and as bailiff to the owner of Sandness, he would enter the dwellings of its tenants and its bondspeople while they were yet in bed, and drive the latter to work. He had an eager and lustful interest in women – not only young ones, but middle-aged wives too – and, as bailiff, would go from one dwelling to another, usually while husbands were working out at Sandness, under the pretext that this or that needed to be done to the property – which had to be paid for. The payment would be a kiss, otherwise a threat to report to Sandness. A kiss at least, if the husband were there, more should the husband be out.

One cannot fault Gurdar for height. He was a tall person, but ugly and ungainly, since his shoulders were much narrower than his hips. He had a high, slanting forehead, a hooked nose, a huge upper lip, but his chin ran backwards towards his neck so as to be scarcely seen. One of his eyes seemed dead, the other would rove and settle its gaze so as to cause unease in the person so beheld.

Gurdar's usual trick when entering a house, whether or not the husband was present, was to say that this or that wall needed plugging with pegs for the hanging up of a horse's halter, or some such. With encouragement, he would lay his whip down and, from a bag suspended over his shoulder, he would produce one of the bones of the walrus – that which enters the female when it fathers its young – and hammer it into the wall. In the room at Sandness occupied by Thorstein the Black and Grimhilda there were three such pegs. Grimhilda believed that Gurdar loved her.

Strange too about Gurdar were his thighs. His legs from knee to foot were no longer than any ordinary man's, but his ham-bones – his thighs – the length between hip-bones and knees – was very great. And his thighs too were bulky. This was made clearer by Gurdar's way of tying strips of cord just below his knee-caps. He stuffed his trousers above the knee with cloths. This is why his thighs looked as burly as they were long.

I had seen enough of this frightening and wicked and feared man when I had stayed overnight at Sandness after the hunting with Eirik Thorwaldsson, but now I saw this man – and too much of him – when I came with my darling Gudrid, and her husband Thorstein, third and youngest son of Eirik Thorwaldsson and Thjodhild, to Sandness in the West Settlement after the Great Thing where the Lucky Leif had won his case against Bjarni and his father, Heriolf.

And I wondered, as we travelled north in the boat, whether the Little Knowing One's prophecy that Gudrid's first marriage 'would not last long' would be proved right.

Something in Gudrid's eyes, as she looked at me, told me that it was likely that it would turn out that way.

There were still two or three weeks, perhaps a whole month, of summer to hope for, in which time the grass – or green hay – would be reaped for winter fodder for the cattle. The hunters from the northern grounds, after the walrus and the seal, would soon pass us on their way south to the East Settlement, sure sign that winter was near.

And already thin and chill mists hung over Lysafjord in the morning, and were slower to go each morning as the days shortened. And the mists came earlier, too, each evening as the days passed, and some said, 'We can see the forms of the trolls hovering in the mist over the fjord and breathing down upon it.'

The joyful part of the year had indeed passed.

When Thorstein Eiriksson and Gudrid had reached Sandness, they discovered that Thorstein the Black and his wife had dared to occupy their room in their absence at the Great Thing and had even slept in it.

Now *the* Thorstein, our Thorstein, already had the look of a man who foresaw his own doom, perhaps because of the prophecy to Gudrid by the Little Knowing One; or perhaps because he thought he must soon follow his elder brother, Thorwald, into death. Others might think he had become a weaker man since he had married, it for was wrong that he spent afternoons, as well as every night, serving Gudrid in bed. As to that, I would reply that even if he did spend too much of his man's strength doing this, he did it because, believing the prophecy, he pledged himself to have Gudrid and to hold her to himself, and to rejoice in her as long and as much as he could. Whatever the cause, the man who, after Leif, was the tallest and handsomest man in all Greenland, with plenty of fire in his heart and spirit in his mind, and strong force in his thews, had become almost a hangdog, even though he was still so young. He slouched instead of stalking upright; his voice was faint instead of bold. He had looked up at Gudrid beseechingly when he sat on the thwart of the boat. He was still a comely man with hair the hue of tow, or brined rope, so I did not like it.

Nevertheless even Thorstein roused himself to anger when we entered Sandness and found the signs that his ugly namesake and his wife had been occupying the best room. Incited by the look in Gudrid's eyes, he drew himself up and said to them, 'Get out.' They were to keep to their own half of the house.

The blundering wife dragged out the offending, and offensive, bed-clothes. There was the question of where I was to sleep.

I said I would not sleep in the room beyond the passage since it had no window, and I did not relish the company I would have to keep. Moreover, I guessed, though I did not speak my guess, that Gudrid, who promised me such rewards for testifying as I did at the case in law at the Great Thing, would hardly wish to inflict on me such a fate as to lie in that room with those two low-born people.

In the upshot I did sleep just one night in the same room as Thorstein the Black and Grimhilda.

I decided to have no more of it; and so the next night I slept on the earthen floor in the passage between the rooms.

But later I was to sleep in the room with the window – but then all five of us were to sleep there, as you will hear.

The wooden bed of Thorstein Eiriksson and Gudrid Thorbjörnsdottir was, in the hours of daylight, their bench, the curtains concealing it being swept back. This bedframe was in the corner between the hearth-pit and the window. There was another bed in the opposite corner without hangings.

Gurdar came round to Sandness to see the youngest son of Eirik the Red the morning after Thornstein's return. He came to tell what dues he had collected and of how he was enforcing the work on the home-field, the byres, barn, the upland fells. He carried his whip, put it down and started to hammer a penis bone of a walrus into the wall of the passage – 'a peg', he said, 'for a halter'.

It was Gurdar who caught the illness first. Yet he did not stop going his rounds on those huge-thighed legs of his, carrying the disease in him, as he did, from farm to farm, large or small, along the shore of the fjord, and roaming among the upland dwellings too, spreading it – the vile illness – through all Lysafjord. Then the illness spread further and people in the neighbouring fjords, on either side of us, caught it. They started to die.

Days shortened and the milky sheen on Lysafjord curdled and seethed under the moon before it settled into ice.

People of all ages, whether of good birth and householders, or low-born and in thralldom, sickened. Even in the farm furthest from Lysafjord the entire family died. In other houses, though all the members of the household fell sick, a son or a daughter, after a long and terrible fever, might recover, while even those who survived were rendered unsightly with their scars and some were left blind in one eye or both.

It was Gurdar, with his cruel wickedness or grinning spite, who wrought or sowed this curse of illness. Perhaps it was the Great, or Wickedest, Fiend of all, of whom the clergy often talked, who was actually inside Gurdar's vile and ugly body, doing this harm.

The earth was still wet and soft enough for an hour or two after the noon to dig graves, even though the sun was now very low in the sky at noon, sometimes appearing as a mere gash or stab in a rent cloud. Soon a whole thicket of poles of varying heights were seen sticking up from the ground chosen for the dead. Where a stouter pole rose nearly to the height of a man above the ground, this was to be a sign to the priest, whenever he should come round in the next year, that three or four people, whether of one family or more, were in the one grave. When he plucked up the pole he was to pour more than one vial of holy water and to say the prayers for as many people as he thought were in the grave.

Then Gurdar himself died. People gladdened at this; he deserved to die, and since he had opened up himself to the disease from the Great Fiend and then maliciously spread it around, he had earned hell and dire pain for ever.

Gurdar was not put in the Christian burial ground, for he would trouble the bodies and souls of good people and give them unrest.

Rarely had any sensible words, or notion of any kind, come from

Thorstein the Black's wife, but it was in truth Grimhilda who suggested what should be done with Gurdar's body.

And it was a good suggestion and was acted on. The body was lifted up from the place where it was found by means of thongs which were passed under it. It was then carried to Thor's enclosure and, with a great effort, it was then swung and tossed over the stakes guarding that enclosure. Among the rank weeds that grow in such places, Gurdar would lie and rot.

'And if Thor doesn't like it, he can come out of his hut and thump and beat dead Gurdar with his hammer,' they said.

But it is doubtful whether the idol did come off his platform and out of his hut. Instead, Thor remained where he was, but showed his displeasure in having Gurdar within his enclosure by knocking more angrily and shaking the timbers of his hut.

In Sandness itself the first person to catch the illness was Thorstein the Black, which was the less unexpected since he was one of the four who had helped lift the body of Gurdar with thongs into Thor's own place. He lay in the smaller dark room but beyond quietly groaning now and then he did not trouble us much because, for all his swarthy ugliness and uncouth ways, he was brave. Not only had he pluck but he was of sturdy build, thanks to his regular labours in the hot smithy. So he recovered, and with his pockmarked visage, and the lid of one eye disfigured, he was only slightly more uncomely than before. But the knowledge that he had suffered the illness, and so was likely to pass it on to Grimhilda, was reason enough for me to stop wishing to sleep in the passage. I did not want to hasten my own death by lying so near to sick people.

I explained this to Gudrid. She said she understood and would speak to her husband about it. She was as good as her word for, sure enough, I soon was told that I could sleep, not indeed in Gudrid and Thorstein's – her husband's – room but in the store-room that led from their room.

There was no door separating, but I do not think that mattered. There were curtains surrounding their bedframe, but Thorstein Eiriksson, though not stricken with the illness yet, was a changed man, seemingly too languid and sorrowing to go on honeymooning. Yet, from her tender care, it was clear that Gudrid still loved him dearly, but more as a mother loves her child.

Grimhilda next caught the illness, while her husband, though he had endured with hardly a sound, was still bed-fast.

That night the moon was staring through a thin cloud. The fjord was now stark frozen; and the great Troll-Woman was seen. She was sitting cross-legged on the ice in the middle of the fjord, her lower half wrapped in wide-spread skirts that stretched out far on each side of her, of the hue of grey smoke. She waited for us to see her from Sandness. Then, when she knew she was being watched, she swivelled round on her haunches slowly. Her skirts revolved with her like two oars, held idle over water, while the ship turns slowly about in the turn of the tide. She presented her back to us. She revealed herself as the Cleft One. For what the Troll-Woman showed was her back, hollow as a cave, and black as charred wood, from which crystals, unevenly studded in her cave, winked in the moon.

Next day the shape had gone. But we knew we had seen the sad omen.

Unlike her husband, who scorned to cry out, Grimhilda moaned and lamented much, and her fits of sobbing mixed with cries were so loud, that one or another of us was obliged to cross the passage to look in on her. She called on saints. She called on Thor. Besides, she craved water, and it was needful to humour her – her cries were so pitiful, and by giving her what she clamoured for it was hoped she might lessen her noise. And then we would take food in to her on a trencher. If she were too weak, we reckoned that if her husband, who was on the mend, wished to eat the food brought to her, he could.

It was I who first looked in on the distressed creatures, but it was mainly Gudrid who took in the water and food, risking contagion. She said that Grimhilda was raving about the fatal Troll-Woman squatting on the ice; that Grimhilda's face was all blubbered with tears; that she was as fiery red, blotched and swollen as anyone could be and yet live. At other times she had shivering fits as though she were cold.

Thorstein Eiriksson was not overheated at this time yet: rather the reverse. He lay pale and languid and, when he stirred himself from the bed, took slow and mild steps.

Thor's, or his idol's, hammer could be heard knocking by day as well as in the night now. But the thicket of grave-poles had hardly increased, because the soil was now too stiffened with ice for the spade to be shoved down into it without hard work and the use of much strength. Besides, the men left in Lysafjord, strong enough even to walk, let alone split open frozen soil, and lift the heaviness of its frozen clods on spades, were now few.

In Sandness, Grimhilda grew more frantic and distraught. We would have wished her husband had regained enough health to hold her down. One night she left her bed, staggered across the passage, and fumbled at our door, beating upon a panel with her fist. At the gruff command of Thorstein the Black she left off and went back to their own room. But the panel was broken.

The next night was her last.

We knew she was on the prowl. After her wild crying and the sound of her yelling at her husband, who was still too ill to hold her down, she came across the passage. Lifting the latch, she swung into our room on bare feet. The glaring moon was shouting – I know, son, the moon cannot shout, but it was like that – on her long greyish-yellow disordered hair.

She swayed and stumbled towards the bed of Thorstein Eiriksson and Gudrid Thorbjörnsdottir, and fell over their bodies, despite the curtain round the bedframe, rending it from the rod from which it was hung.

Amid sobs and groans, Grimhilda made her need plain. Gudrid, the good and kind, drew herself from her place beside Thorstein. Calling on me to aid her, Gudrid lifted Grimhilda up from where she was lying across the bed. The food and water we had given Grimhilda were raging in her bowels and she was to be helped over to the privy.

Gudrid, standing on Grimhilda's left, put an arm round the woman's bent back, with hand under her right armpit. I took Grimhilda's right hand with my left and lifted the latch of the front door. The moon was four days past the full, and glaring though thin high white cloud. There was a low mist, floating in from the waters of the fjord.

O! how cold the air of Greenland at its West Settlement can be – in spring, in autumn, in winter – and this was winter. Chill to make one gasp on opening the door. And surely it was growing chillier at each step we took.

We had taken but three or four steps on the path to the privy, when Grimhilda stopped and her bent form suddenly straightened, and:

'Look!' she cried, in a strong voice. 'Look at them. All the dead are there!'

'You are right,' said Gudrid, and sharply. 'But of course they are all there – or here. Now you can stand up!' And she withdrew the hand from the armpit and thumped the back. The hump of Grimhilda disappeared, and she stood up straight between us, tallest now of the three.

She shot out her left arm. 'All' she said, 'of them', pointing. And then I, Ingolf, too saw them.

Grimhilda cried:

'There they are – all of them, all these have died from the illness. All are dead people! And that is me! O, I am among all those dead people too!'

And Grimhilda was right. They were running. Or loping. Rather loping than running. Their feet – were they touching the ground? And as they passed the air sighed colder and yet colder. And there was a rustling or whistling but it did not seem to come from them. They passed, or so it seemed, between where we stood and the enclosed place of Thor. Men, women, children. Old men and young men. Children of all sizes. And they all wore grey shifts to their ankles – and yet they could run or lope. Some of the dead went in twos or threes. Some alone. But they all kept step, even the old shrunken bald men. Their loping made no noise, but there was this rustling or faint whistling, and in the chill air there was a smell as of sweetness that was like dank mould. And what was odd was this: when the whole line that had died from the illness, though those were so many, should have passed – when the last had passed – there was a shaking dazzle or glimmer, and the whole long line of dead people was pulled back – their legs and feet, which seemed not to touch the ground, still running or kicking forwards, and they started passing again. Twice that happened, that sort of pull-back, and each time there came a jeering laugh.

When the leaders of the dead people were passing for the third time, their pace quickened – shorter steps, knees not lifted so high – as though they were now running in earnest, and there was a sound of a panting, matching their steps.

'Here is the whole crowd of the dead – and there are more among them now,' cried Grimhilda, 'and, beware Gudrid, here is Thorstein, your Thorstein, among them. Poor lady, there he is, your own dead man.'

'Hold to yourself. I saw him before you did, at the first time,' said Gudrid. 'Stay with your own kind.'

Then Grimhilda screamed:

'Yes, I see myself! I am among them, and near your Thorstein! Look there! That is me with your husband. With your dead Thorstein.' And she swayed, wept and wailed from the deep of her lungs, and then shook, as though her heart would break; and then sobbed and sobbed again.

At the third and last passing of the dead, the rear was brought up by Gurdar. He was urging on all the dead before him, waving his long whip. We saw him coming, but when he reached us, he alone did not pass sideways on to us, but turned. Suddenly the upper part of his body spun round on its waist – but the buttocks and huge thighs, legs and feet were keeping their forward way. Looking at us, he brought down the lid of his whitish eye and sent the light of the other full on Grimhilda. Riding sideways on his hips, as though riding sideways on a horse, mustering, so it seemed, his spittle, he spat at her – a thin, strong, high arch of water. Then, with a bold chortle, his torso clicked around to move as sideways as his legs had run all along. Lifting his head with a hauty jerk and waving his whip, he flogged his dead people forward.

'So! I knew it was always mine he most wanted,' yelled Grimhilda. 'It was my gash he was most after, though he did go among all women here with his pegs. It was mine he was after, Gudrid, and not yours. Mine above all.'

As soon as she said that, Gudrid hit her as hard as she could on the back. And the hump of the old creature rose up again, after the blow. 'Liar,' Gudrid said, and struck her once more, so that Grimhilda fell to her knees.

'I can't go on. And I can't do it here,' she said.

We dragged Grimhilda, with a grasp under each armpit, her heels trailing behind in the snow, back into the house, into Sandness. Inside, she gathered herself into a squat and emptied her bowels in the passage behind the front door. She then crawled on hands and knees away from the mess she had made. Further up the passage, she rolled over onto her back, and died.

The two Thorsteins were in their rooms, each on his bed.

Next day the two men rose slowly from their beds. Thorstein the Black, still swollen but rather pale than heated, knew there was work to do for his wife's body. Thorstein Eiriksson's slowness was the weakness of despair as though he foresaw his sad doom. With the ground so frozen there could be no burying before spring and, come to that, they both lacked the strength to dig deep enough into soft wet ground even. I too felt the illness in the eyes, the forehead, the heat of my skin, but if I didn't become worse it was, I believe, because I had sworn to myself that I would not become worse, and because I had kept away from drinking the milk. I think it was this drinking of milk that made so many of the West Settlement die that winter. If it wasn't the drinking of milk that lead to his death, then it was the drinking of this stuff that had made Thorstein Eiriksson so pale and heartless. It had curdled the life flow in his loins and this resulted in Gudrid's disappointment.

There were some boards in the store-room, where I slept, and some pieces of driftwood.

The two Thorsteins and myself set out to make Grimhilda's coffin. The passage was too narrow a space for men to work in. We needed to stoop with our tools. The corpse blocked an easy movement to and fro. We disliked the stooping to the job. And we needed light too.

So we set about the making of the box in the room of Gudrid and Thorstein. So as not to stoop we wielded adze, nails and hammer, with the boards put up on the bed in the corner opposite to that in which Gudrid and Thorstein slept, using this bed as a joiner's bench. To make our reckoning the straighter – to make sure, that is, that she would fit in her box – we dragged Grimhilda from the passage into the room. She was now stiffening and one arm – it was the one that pointed at Gurdar when he rode past – would obstinately lift itself up.

It was crude labour with one man only skilled to work with his hands, Thorstein the Black. He in truth gave out orders and wielded the tools. We were a sorry team of three: the widower still weak from the sickness was one, the now feeble and weak-willed man, Thorstein Eiriksson – whom I now saw was doomed to take the sickness – another, and myself. I was determined in mood not to die, though I knew I was already assailed by the pest. I fetched and carried timber, but I was a bad and clumsy carpenter.

When we had made the box, it seemed easier to lift Grimhilda from the floor into what we had made for her than to lower the box – thick, unplaned wood – down to the floor to put her in it. The three of us were so tired that we could hardly hear what one said to another. You understand?

Box made, the three of us managed to hoist Grimhilda up from the floor into her box. It was quite a matter of thrusting her into it since she had gone on stiffening and both her arms were now fixing outwards. We shoved her in, but then her arms kept rising upwards, however we kept pushing the hands below the level of the rim of the box.

We had no wood which would fit, for the lid. Daylight was ending and we were sweating and tired. Thorstein Eiriksson indeed was at last red and hot, and he laid himself down on his marriage-bed nearest the wall. Gudrid, sitting on that bed, had been watching us. Thorstein the Black and myself sat down on that bed, one on each side of Gudrid, to rest. Her husband was stretched out behind her. Thus we just stayed for one hour, two hours, more; in truth, though days in winter are short, the nights long, we found we had so sat in this way till it was another fore-noon.

After a long while Thorstein said the two words: 'Eat must.'

He meant that his wife dead or not dead, *he* must go on. He must eat. He even meant more, for he added: 'You must too.'

He was as sound as his word. And if it had not been for him we would all have starved to death, if not died from the disease. For he lifted himself up onto his feet, from where he sat on the edge of the bed, on one side of Gudrid, her marriage-bed. Thorstein Eiriksson, on that bed, prone on the bed, face to the wall, turned onto his right side, his face bowing to where his wife's haunches were resting, and mine. Thorstein the Black moved to the store-room. He left Sandness with a pole-axe and a spear, and went down to the ice on the fjord – to split open and hack a hole in the ice to catch, with luck, some fish. He was right: 'Eat must.'

Gudrid, still sitting on the edge of her marriage-bed, turned to wipe her husband's face of its tears. His eyes were only half-closed and he was crying, though softly.

I looked over at the bed in the opposite corner. What I saw was this: the hands of Grimhilda, which had lifted themselves more and more into the air, came down, and gripped the rim of her box, and she sat up. Next, the dead woman lifted her left leg over the edge of the coffin and the sole of her foot pressed upon the bed on which her box rested. And she sat up and made little short panting noises.

Then the dead woman clambered out of her coffin, and we heard the clamp of both feet on the floor. She reared herself as upright as she used to hold herself in life, and moved towards where Gudrid and I were sitting. Thorstein Eiriksson was still lying and weeping with scarcely a sound.

We, Gudrid and I, felt we couldn't touch her as we rose and stood in the middle of the room. In passing us, Grimhilda made a vain kind of swipe at Gudrid herself, as though she were in her way, or as a repayment for the strokes she had taken from Gudrid when she had boasted of Gurdar's lust for her alone.

The dead Grimhilda knew what she was after. Lifting the covers, she got into the bed with Thorstein Eiriksson and clasped him. Still standing in the middle of the room, Gudrid watched this.

But I ran out of the room and out of the house towards the fjord, shouting and crying all the way, 'Thorstein the Black . . . Black Thorstein . . . your lady is not dead. Not dead.'

From a distance Thorstein looked up. He was crouching on his heels over a hole he had made in the ice. He came running up from the fjord, running with his pole-axe to the house all the way. He overtook me. Following at his heels, I saw him break through the door into the passage-way, burst into the room, and thrust the point of his weapon full in the centre of his wife's breast as far as it would go.

And then she was dead indeed.

Thorstein the Black and Gudrid pulled Grimhilda from out of the bed where she had no right to be, lugged her over into the other corner and, with my help, stuffed her back in her coffin.

If his first strength had been drained out, a kind of second strength now took hold of Thorstein the Black's thick body. He left the room, went across the passage to his own room, and brought in a three-legged joint-stool. This he planted hard by the bed frame which supported the coffin from which his dead wife had lately risen and then been returned.

Then he said:

'Gudrid, come to me over here!'

And the lady Gudrid obeyed.

With her husband's eyes upon her, and as though she had no will of her own, she walked over to Thorstein the Black on his three-legged joint-stool and sat on his lap. The churl's shirt was unfastened to the waist, and the ugly black hair on his chest and belly was matted and tangled with the illness sweat. She placed herself sideways on his lap, the right side of her body against that lover – that Thorstein – her feet not reaching the floor. Gudrid placed one arm around his shoulders. Then I saw the low fellow lift her left arm up by the wrist and kiss it on the inside all the way up. Then he took her right arm, which was embracing him, and started to kiss her deeply in that armpit.

At that moment the dying Thorstein Eiriksson, watching, said: 'Gudrid, don't let him do that.' Then Thorstein the Black said: 'What is that to you? What do you want, Namesake?' But hearing her husband, Gudrid pulled herself from the lap of Thorstein the Black, and said to him angrily:

'Gudrid Thorbjörnsdottir, or Lady, you will call me, or you will call me not at all.' And then she went back and smote Thorstein the Black's face as hard as she could. Then she went over to her husband, who took her into his bed, holding her as closely as a weak man could. Thorstein the Black stayed on his stool, but leaned forward, his hands to his head, his shirt unfastened, but not showing so much of the thick black curly hair on his chest – which was thick and clotted and smelling.

Holding her close to him Thorstein spoke to his wife in a rapid loud whisper. He addressed her as 'Gudrid darling', or 'dearest Gudrid', over and over again. He told her that when he was dead he did not wish to be put in the ground outside Sandness among the thicket of poles – to wait and wait there until a wandering priest should come round to pull up the pole for the pouring of the water and the saying of the short prayer. That would be 'not enough'. Gudrid should remember who he was. He had been the son of Eirik, no less. When the sea was unfrozen, he was to be taken back to Brattahlid. There was to be mass in his mother's church, with 'many singing men', and he was to be put in the consecrated churchyard as became his worth. Besides, Gudrid, who was his dearest, would surely leave this Lysafjord, after these terrible things, for ever, when she could; and his dead body should go south with her. He had loved her body above all things, and though his body would not serve hers again, yet he did not wish them to be parted as widely as the East and the West Settlements were parted.

Then he went on about the illnesses, the ghosts and the hauntings, 'the wicked days and wicked nights'. He said that the bad Gurdar was the root of all the harm; that it was Gurdar who had tried to make the cut between him and 'his dearest'. If it hadn't been for Gurdar she would never have gone 'to that low, dark man Thorstein, when he called, and sat on his lap'. And 'I saw what you did with him. I saw you do it.'

Since Gurdar was the evil root of it all, she was to see to it that he was dug up, wherever he now was. They were to 'burn, burn every bit of that vile lot'.

Thorstein didn't know, or had forgotten, that there was no digging up to be done – that Gurdar was rotting where he had been tumbled – into Thor's place.

Gudrid said she would see all was done as he wished. Then she broke into tears. Then her husband said: 'Wipe your eyes with the back of your hand, and then hold that hand to my mouth so that I may taste and drink that sweet water, those tears.'

And so she did. And so he did.

Then he said: 'Gudrid, dearest, you will marry again as she foretold.' He had in his mind what the Little Knowing One had said about a second match for Gudrid. So he said: 'You will marry again; but do not marry someone like that low-born churl sitting on that stool. Rather than have him, marry an Icelander, though your fate will then part my dead body from yours, which it loved above all, by lands and by seas.'

And then the youngest son of Eirik Thorwaldsson died.

Gudrid stood up, and went over to Thorstein the Black briskly, and as though she were going to strike him again. She told him, as he sat, to remove himself, his wife in her box, and his stool forthwith, and to take all three into his own quarters beyond the passage. Cowed, the man did as he was ordered. He needed help with his baggage – from bed to floor. Then he lugged.

Spring came. The sun, each day, shone, and the more strongly.

Thorstein the Black changed utterly in his demeanour after the death of his master. He was no longer lustful, surly and insolent beyond bounds. By his breeding – his mother an Irish slave-woman – he could not be other than rough in ways and uncouth in looks, but he showed his lady the respect he owed as a servant, never dared to touch her person, and addressed her as 'Gudrid Thorbjörnsdottir', as was her due. Moreover, he vowed to see to it that he would conduct her and the body of her great husband to Brattahlid as soon as ever the fjord became unfrozen and the outer sea free.

Whether Gurdar had indeed been the root and stalk of all the ill-nesses, the ghosts and the strange goings-on in Sandness and the whole of Lysafjord, will never be known for certain, but it was a fact that after the death of Thorstein Eiriksson the illness began to slacken off, and men and women began to behave again as they are expected to behave, when not struck by illness and hunger, by dread and mass deaths, by the fear of evil omens and happenings, the terror of ghosts.

Gudrid and I became friends by strength of all that we had shared. She gave me one night beside her – and a second – and one more. That third was our last night together in Lysafjord. There was no fourth anywhere. And during one daytime, between the first and second nights, we looked into each other's eyes, and each saw in their gaze the other's soul, and knew that, whatever happened, and though parted, there would be a bond of love. When the one died the bond would still hold. When the other died the bond would still hold. We would be near to each other in or out of the body, one or both, for as long as men lived in Greenland. Beyond that, we did not know, and I do not now.

As to the payment or reward hinted at by Gudrid when I gave evidence in that case at law at the Great Thing about the ship: I must say that when she looked at me – the asking look – to join her in her bed at Sandness, the memory of old friends, of Heriolf and his son, Bjarni, caused me trouble. Gudrid saw this trouble in my eyes, and overcame it by saying: 'This is not a reward, this is what I most want.'

Then came the task of fetching out Gurdar from beyond the stock-ade of Thor's enclosure so as to burn him as Thorstein Eiriksson, dying, wished, and so that Lysafjord need never fear that that fiend, living or dead, would rove again. Better the spiteful and dirty skraelings, heathens all, whom one could kill so that they would stay quiet and live the fewer, than this Gurdar of our own race whose shadow walked and ran after spreading the illness, which he begged of the great Evil One, far and wide. The fiends henceforth, all Lysafjord hoped, would be mere skraelings – bad and troublesome enough, but they could be dealt with in a way they and ourselves could understand.

The difficulty was not so much to find enough wood for the making of a pyre, as to recover the corpse beyond the fence without entering the ring of the dread enclosure. With staves, held from outside the stockade, men prodded the earth among the rank grass and poked among the weeds, but they could not smell out Gurdar's meat. At last the points of the staves found the leather thongs which had slung the body and followed it into the ring. But, for all the raking, nothing of Gurdar was found. The points of the staves, middling the thongs, lifted them over. And that was all our poking about could do.

Suddenly a gamesome lad of about fifteen, after walking backwards, took a run at the fence and leapt over. This naughty fellow, rummaging about, came upon, first, the bones of the right hand of Gurdar, then one of his thigh bones, the stock of his whip, his jaw bone with its few teeth, and last, the begetting bone of a male walrus.

As the rascal picked up these nasty things in Thor's enclosure, one by one, he started to pelt us – grown men – outside the fence. We dodged the flying gruesome bits. Then the mischievous lad cried out, 'Thor has eaten up all the rest of him, or the devil has', re-vaulted the fence, and started to pelt us again with bits he'd brought over. But his father put a stop to that. He chased him round and round Thor's ring till at last he caught him by the collar, and beat him over the shoulders and on the backside as hard as he could.

At that sight we turned to look at the beautiful Gudrid who was standing at the open door of Sandness. When we saw that she first smiled, and then laughed at the sight, with a ray of the sun shining on her face, we all laughed as we had never laughed before.

But then I noticed, loving her as I do, that she stopped laughing. Tears welled in her eyes. And she quickly went back indoors.

Still, the things of Gurdar were gathered into a charcoal pit, and the two thongs also, and burnt to ashes. And then the same venturesome lad scooped the ashes, when they were cold, into a bowl, and emptied it into the fjord. One man cried out, 'Look out, Gurdar is going to poison the fishes.' Then we all laughed again, for the man thought he had made a joke. And we clapped the naughty lad who had gathered the bits and been beaten by his father.

Grimhilda's coffin was found a lid, and she was buried in the holy patch of ground when there was a thaw, and a hollow reed went down into the middle of her chest, into the very wound which her husband had made when he thrust her through. The priest, when at last he came round, could pour holy water down this hollow wand.

Yes this winter had passed like all others before it. The days began to lengthen, and those still left in the Lysafjord were drawn the closer together after all they had been through. And because of all the people who had been lost, and the deaths of so many children, the fathers and mothers who were left looked the kindlier upon the signs of love-making among their sons and daughters, and were the readier to breed more children themselves.

The young daredevil who had jumped the fence became a great favourite among the girls of the West Settlement.

He strutted like anything when, say, a group of three girls, out for a walk arm-in-arm, nudged each other, and giggled, when they met – as so they hoped – the blushing young swaggerer. He was a likely lad.

11

GUDRID MARRIES AGAIN

Thorstein the Black was as good as his word. As soon as ever the ice on the Lysafjord had loosened, though but a little, so that paths could be steered between the floes, he took the risk. Reaching the outer sea, we found it was hardly free for sailing, but with cunning and pluck this fellow of the mended manners struck out on a winding course, and brought the ship carrying the corpse of Thorstein Eiriksson, the living Gudrid Thorbjörnsdottir herself, and the one who had loved her for three nights – the same who will love her always – into Eiriksfjord and up alongside the berth of Brattahlid.

Thjodhild, widow of Eirik, mother of three sons, seeing our ship, came from her door to meet those the ship carried. Leaning on her stick, she was yet paler than in her youth but, though stooped in years, she was still stately in bearing.

When she reached us, it was to find that the rough dark box on the deck of the ship held the body of her youngest. Her thoughts were for the widow as well as for herself. She shifted her stick and put her right arm about Gudrid, and said:

'God has taken my eldest, killed by heathen skraelings. And he lies in far Vinland. He, whom you bring back, is my youngest. He at least shall have Christian burial at Brattahlid. God's will be done. I have one son left, Leif, the noblest of all, but he is unwed and I have no grandchildren of any of them. But my two dead sons I trust to see again when I die, if not my man that begat them on me, who died in his sins, and still heathen.'

Then she said to Gudrid:

'Daughter-in-law, I have no kin left now save my second son. As I said, and as you know, he is unwed. Is there a hope that through you,

God may yet bless me? That in you, before he died, my youngest might have sown a child – one whom I might get to continue my line? My husband brought me here. Heathen though he was, he founded this land. I would not wish to die, thinking that Brattahlid would pass from our line – not even to the Church!'

She withdrew her arm from Gudrid, changed her stick back to her right hand, and rapped the deck: 'You must stay with me, my dear Gudrid, for the next few months at least. And then we'll see. I have a right to that.'

Gudrid, knowing that her father, Thorbjörn, was lonely and, though reasonably prosperous, would now begin to ail more often unless he died quickly, would have liked to have gone for a time under Thorbjörn's roof. But she was overruled. Gudrid was to bide at Brattahlid under the protection of Thjodhild and her brother-in-law, Leif.

As you may guess, son, Thorstein Eiriksson had far better rites than Thorwald Eiriksson had.

Thjodhild's new church was not nearly finished then. So the requiem mass was held in the first church of Greenland ever to be built. The dead man's half-sister, Freydis, was allowed into the little church, but not her mother, of course. But Freydis was not allowed at the graveside.

Freydis looked at me, in an asking way, at the mass, but my thoughts, you may be sure, were for Gudrid, not for Freydis. Mainly. For I was still aware that that dreadful woman, Freydis, had most, of all his children, of the blood-strength and liveliness of her once-energetic and ever-resourceful father.

At the requiem mass, Thjodhild of course knelt before the coffin in the front row; Gudrid and Leif knelt on each side of her. Freydis and I were in the third row. Thorstein the Black stood at the back by the west door.

The mass was to have been celebrated by the Archdeacon. But, first Leif, and then Thjodhild, had heard rumours of his visits to the house where Freydis and her mother lived. Thjodhild had held it her duty to send a full report to the Bishop in Sweden, at Lund, of what people had said – and of what she, and her son, Leif, thought to be the case – of the Archdeacon's scandalous behaviour. The Archdeacon had been suspended. He was to take the first ship, by order of the Bishop, for Norway, and thence Sweden, to answer to Thjodhild's complaint. At Lund he was put in irons and then racked. He confessed to have carnally known several other women.

So the requiem mass was said by a lesser priest, but very well, and with some singing, and then just a chosen few went to the burial in the churchyard of Thjodhild's church.

Freydis, not one of those, after the mass came to me to say she was very sad at the death of her half-brother, and would I take her to her house to tell her all about the dreadful winter she had heard we had all suffered.

I said: 'What about Thorulf? Won't he be at your house? And, if you are so sad, will he not strengthen you?'

She had too much spirit not to be angry, and so we parted.

I guessed she had tired of Thorulf, a dull man, once she had drawn from him all he knew about Vinland, and now wished to have me as her lover again. I was not ready for this since I still had a grudge against her for her treatment of me. For not only was Thorulf, for all that he was clever with his hands, thick-witted, but he was also, I believe, a slow heavy lover – not worthy of Freydis. But if she had given up a full-blooded and stirred lover for the sake of information to help along her wealth, she was welcome to the bargain – and could stick to it. And besides, my heart's devotion was for Gudrid Thorbjörnsdottir.

So I left Freydis to wait for a while.

Not long after the burial of Thorstein Eiriksson, and in beautiful weather, a very great ship – and not only huge, but heavily laden – came sailing up the Eiriksfjord to give us all cheer. Leif was delighted and welcomed the master warmly on several grounds. For not only was Thorfinn Karlsefni born of one of the very best and wealthiest families in the north of Iceland, but he had altogether by-passed Heriolfsness in bearing his cargo from Norway, with one call at Iceland, straight to us. Bjarni Heriolfsson would not gain anything as middleman. Moreover, it was a superb cargo that was lifted out of the hull of the ship and stored at Brattahlid.

Almost at once Thorfinn, the master, was attracted to Gudrid. Thjodhild, noticing this, was wary because she still hoped for issue by her son out of Gudrid, and wished for a delay of any betrothal for a few more weeks. But Leif rejoiced to see this attraction. It fitted his plans, and Gudrid was under her brother-in-law's protection.

Thorfinn 'Karlsefni' deserved his nickname 'Manly-Stuff'. He was the son of Thord 'Horsehead', a man of enormous repute in Iceland. Karlsefni had the long narrow head, though not quite so pronounced, of his father. And this told of his lineage. Karlsefni was lean and tall, his eyes were close together, their hue was yellowish brown. He had a high slanting forehead and his tough hair was the colour of burnt honey. He was spry, a quick and good leader, and he had great trust in his own judgment – which he made on any business rapidly.

Thjodhild, the old lady, who kept Gudrid as close to her as she could, did not like the signs, but she was unable to complain that Karlsefni was not a Christian. He went out of his way to conduct her to mass at her church early each morning.

Gudrid in turn had a liking for Karlsefni. His odd appearance attracted her. So also did his abrupt confidence, for this contrasted so markedly with the feebleness of her late husband in his last months. Then too, her brother-in-law, Leif, pressed her to think of Karlsefni as her second mate. In this he overruled his mother, Thjodhild. But Leif had a purpose, good for himself, and for many others besides, it must be admitted, in urging this match between his widowed sister-in-law and Karlsefni.

Leif the Lucky, he who had first set foot in Vinland, and built houses there, had never let go the thought in his mind that Vinland should be settled from people in Greenland. And who else ought to settle Vinland other than the sons of Eirik Thorwaldsson, the founder of Greenland? His kin should stake the claim first. And he, Leif, had already built houses in that land.

But Leif had lost his two brothers, the younger and the elder – the elder had fallen in Vinland. He himself was now the master of Brattahlid in Greenland, the guardian of his old and revered mother, and the master of Sandness in the Lysafjord in the West Settlement following the death of Thorstein. Hungry as he was for fame and wealth for himself, and for his family, he could not venture just now with these cares on his shoulders.

But here comes this most respectable and daring man, Karlsefni, from Reyniness in Iceland, who was keen moreover on Gudrid, his sister-in-law, one to whom he had to afford shelter so long as she remained unmarried.

They must marry. They must found a settlement in Vinland. He had built there for a start; and he must follow when his duties in Greenland allowed. And so he would one day! In default of himself or of blood-kin, the tie with the family would meanwhile be maintained. Besides, Karlsefni, for all his brisk ways, was a Christian, and for this his mother had proof. He was even more of a stickler for observances than Thjodhild herself, and reminded her of some which, in mercy to her own frailty and age, she was inclined to forego.

Karlsefni was rich. I was poor. So I could but envy this Karlsefni, which availed nothing. Neither did I run to Freydis, or even to any of the other girls, though three certainly, and possibly four, would have been pleased if I had, but Gudrid knew the strength of my feelings for her and this was a comfort. If during this time we had scant chance to be alone together and speak our hearts, yet our eyes silently spoke their secrets to each other in the evening in the noise of the hall.

Soon after the betrothal the wedding. I was bidden to the wedding mass, and to the feast after the mass. The mass was celebrated in Thjodhild's church, and the church was crowded. As bride and groom stood before the altar, I wondered what the feelings were in Gudrid's heart, and I guessed she spared some thoughts for the feelings in mine. She would grow fond of the 'Manly-Stuff', son of 'Horsehead', by her side, with his long down-curving nose, yellowish eyes, high slanting forehead, and burnt honey-coloured hair, I believed. But she would also always remember the three nights' sweet 'reward' she gave to someone else. For with the words 'And will you take . . .' put to her by the priest, she did more than turn to look at the man beside her. Gudrid turned her eyes yet further to the right, and though they did not meet mine among those standing or kneeling some three rows behind the groom, this was a sign. And if the sign were put into words, the words would be: 'I must follow my fate.' And then I knew that Gudrid knew that this would not be the end for Gudrid either. She knew that she would outlive her second husband as she had her first. For the Little Knowing One had said: 'Back in Iceland your later lines lie.' Gudrid of the second sight saw that the plan to settle Vinland would fail, that she was likely to outlive the good man by her side, but that it was likely she would not die childless – but whether the father of the child she was carrying in her womb was by her beloved Thorstein Eiriksson, tall and of the tow-coloured hair, or her Ingolf, only she herself might know – or guess. Thorfinn Karlsefni, her new man, who would grow to be well-liked, might think as it pleased him best to think.

Soon after the wedding the plans for the journey to Vinland and its settlement were hastened forward. And while these were being pressed, suddenly there sailed up the fjord a second vessel from Iceland. She looked imposing enough under weigh, but when she tied up at Brattahlid just behind Thorfinn Karlsefni's ship, it was seen she was but about two-thirds of the size of that, but was still handsome enough. She was in the charge of a man named Thorhall Gamlason, whose home was not in the north of Iceland, in Reyniness, as was Thorfinn's, but in the east of Iceland, at Hof in Vapnfjord. So neither Thorfinn nor Thorhall knew the other's designs. Yet, like Thorfinn, Thorhall had rounded the southern cape of Greenland and run up to Eiriksfjord without putting in at Heriolfsness, and likewise had brought in a profitable cargo.

What was in the mind of Karlsefni – and of Leif, and of all of us – could not be kept quiet, so it was put to Thorhall Gamlason straight: Would he in his ship too bear over to Vinland with those intent to settle in that country? Thorhall agreed; and there was much excitement over this. The ships would sail in convoy, Karlsefni's leading. Two ships were safer than one, for if one were lost and the lands peopled by skraelings could not be held, then those daring to venture would not be wretchedly stranded.

So both great ships were prepared.

No less than sixty-one people were to settle, and of these five were women of child-bearing age. Of these women, Gudrid was, of course, chief.

The settlement once founded and thriving, and trade between the two lands established, wives or sweethearts or women seeking husbands would follow. The crews were mainly Icelanders.

Leif, whose hand was everywhere in the arranging, made it plain that I should go on Karlsefni's ship. My experience of Vinland, accompanying Thorwald Eiriksson, would make me useful. But I was not keen to go again for the reason that to hear the words of the growing endearment between Gudrid and her new husband, Karlsefni, would be a sorrow for me – and, still more painful, to witness the acts of endearment between them. Besides, the other four women travelling to settle, though they might be worthy enough to their husbands, did not seem likely, by their appearance, to raise in me any strong interest at all. I thought I might do better remaining in Greenland, whether or not I took up again with the passionate Freydis, wicked woman though she was.

But Leif, by far the greatest man in Greenland now, was not to be crossed. He knew how to get his way. Not only did he point out that as a founder settler in Vinland I would have the pick of the land to make my own – as those who had first accompanied his father out to Greenland had had their pick – and he trusted me to make a better pick in Vinland than 'old' Heriolf had staked in Greenland, but he also warned that I could never hope to have such an opportunity in Greenland, however long I stayed here – no, not as long as I lived.

Moreover, he enjoined his sister-in-law and Thorfinn Karlsefni to add their pleas – which the latter did somewhat unwillingly. Because of Gudrid's plea I consented, but on the understanding that if the attempt at settlement failed, I should not be held to blame; that if the would-be settlers returned home, not able to hold the new country against the vile skraelings, I would receive in Greenland the reward of land I would have earned in Vinland.

Gudrid told Leif that this was fair and just, and a deal was made on those terms.

Karlsefni asked if he could buy the houses Leif had built in Vinland. He offered for them a price as much as a half of the mighty cargo he had brought in the ship and which was now stored in the outhouses of Brattahlid. To this offer, Leif replied:

'I shall lend to you the houses I built in Vinland, but I will not sell them.' This was shrewd, if not foresighted, for it was firm in Leif's mind that he would again, when the time came, stand in Vinland, and own as much there as he owned here. But he also saw that these same houses, if not broken into and despoiled, or burnt down by lawless and heathen skraelings, would form the first base and shelter at hand for all the settlers. They would need to know the sea-way as well as a man could but, while faring on the waters, they could look forward to quarters on landing that were dry, stout and prepared.

All sorts of livestock were to be carried including a bull. A strong and mettlesome beast was selected for the excellence of the future stock. As a further precaution, it was agreed that some of the cows chosen should be in calf.

There was an abundance of farm implements, tools and weapons put on board. Food and water, too, but it was constantly in mind that we should be going to a country rich beyond dreams in timber, wild corn and vines, and that the streams were abundant in fish. When we were established in Vinland the great surplus of these goods was to be shipped, free except for cost of carriage, to Brattahlid, and Greenlanders would no longer have to buy them at the extortionate rates demanded by the Norwegian and German merchants and skippers in exchange for our walrus ivory, falcons and white bears whether or not their ships unloaded at Heriolfsness, Bjarni Heriolfsson taking his cut.

Our design, of course, was to turn north on entering the sea from Eiriksfjord and to make for Sandness on the Lysafjord in the West Settlement. We were to carry as passengers, as far as Sandness, Thorstein the Black, his new wife, and seven other people. These latter were to take over some of the homesteads left empty because of the terrible and sweeping illness of the last winter.

After unloading these nine people, and taking on fresh water and more food, we were to strike due west until we sighted Helluland. Thereafter we would find our bearings from Markland until we came to Vinland. Following that coastline we would look out for three landmarks: the two crosses on Thorwald's grave at Crossness, the one rising directly behind the other on an east-west bearing; next Leif's houses; and then Keelness.

On the eve of sailing, I went to see Freydis. Thorulf, who had been forbidden by Leif to sail with us to Vinland, was not there. Freydis had told him to remove himself when she learned that I was coming.

Why was such a handy man as Thorulf, to whose skill all those who had been to Vinland under Thorwald and had returned to Greenland owed their lives, been banned from our ships? The answer to this was that Thorulf and Freydis had been living together as man and wife. His natural sister's behaviour gave great annoyance to Leif. Not only was she sharing her bed with a man in defiance of Church law, bringing ignominy to the noblest and best-reputed family in Greenland, but that man was a landless one and of such mean account that even had they been joined in wedlock it would have been a disgrace. It could not have been borne by the proud Thjodhild nor by Leif, though Freydis was but his half-sister. No more would she receive support if she married Thorulf. Let her think of someone worthier of her father – and of Leif too.

Thus it might have been thought that Leif would have pressed Thorulf to go on the venture, if only to force a parting, but he did not. Maybe he suspected that Thorulf would make trouble among the five married women. He could of course have given orders to have Thorulf killed in Vinland, and have it sworn that the slaying was done by skraelings, but Leif was altogether too upright for that, though it could have crossed his mind. Before he became a Christian no deed was too hard, too rash, too cunning, or too bloody for Leif.

Not that Freydis lived in awe of the man she lived with. Thorulf would not be back so long as I was there, Freydis declared, and her mother was in bed and had grown deaf.

Freydis was less hungry for love than for news of our plans which would feed her greed for wealth and power. And 'if I came back, she would throw Thorulf over, and we two would go, and, unlike all those other poor-spirited men, *we* would find our wealth'.

I taunted her with her betrayal of me and her love for Thorulf.

'Love for Thorulf!' she said. 'He's a wretch compared with my brother Leif, as a man, or with you as a lover. Don't be fearful; he's out of the house now.'

For all her anger it ended as she meant. In deeds of love Freydis was violent and greedy beyond all other women: but only after she had raised my lust with every possible wile, and I had sworn to be her help if I came back, did she lie on the floor and spread her thighs. She would carve out a settlement in the new rich land as no one else could: for pride in ownership and fame was even stronger in her than the lust for tangling with another body, though that lust was warm and moist enough. The one lust drove the other. In this she was more like her father, Eirik, than any of his three lawful sons. Eirik was ambitious and hot; Thjodhild was ambitious but cold; the mother of Freydis was warm, moist and jolly. Freydis's mother was not very hungry for fame, for after Eirik's death she managed with fat and sweaty archdeacons, and such like.

Those who saw us off in our two ships that bright clear chill morning did so in the belief that if we found luck, they would never see most of us again. Husbands and lovers might return in two, three years' time to fetch wives and sweethearts – if they found luck. The Icelander crews they might hope to see again, and in a ship laden with corn and wine, and some of the girls as brides-to-be might later take passage in that very ship to their men in Vinland – if their men had luck. Only if their men had no luck would they see *them* again in Greenland. Thjodhild said farewell to Gudrid without grief. If a grandchild were born to her of Gudrid, its upbringing would be beyond her care – if the settlers had luck – and her doubt, in that case, as to whether the child's father would be her own Thorstein or this Icelander Thorfinn's would be beyond her ability to conclude though she knew her Thorstein's features were not like 'that Thorfinn's ugly ones' – though Gudrid found them appealing.

Leif saw us off in another mood. The Lucky Leif, with great height, golden beard and hair, with his fame and his Christian greatness, wished us good cheer and the strength of God to assist us all the way. He was sure that he – God – would help the righteous to take land from the heathens to give us Greenlanders new homes; and to bring from the new country to the motherland, and in particular to Brattahlid and himself, new wealth. It was a great deal we were bound for.

Freydis watched us casting off, and spitefully called out, and loudly, an endearment to me which I feigned not to hear. Whereon she made a rude and disgusting sign.

Gudrid's old father, Thorbjörn, watched his daughter, with her second husband beside her on the ship, depart. He looked sad, and was alone.

Thjodhild was not one for watching travellers till they were out of sight. She lifted her stick half-way in farewell and hobbled back up the path to Brattahlid.

Her great son, Leif Eiriksson, the Lucky, with arms folded, watched our two ships till they could no longer be seen.

And some of the old women, simple mothers of churls, held rags to their eyes and wiped away tears. And old men, fathers, who could not see far because of their failing sight, still watched to see beyond the distance they could see – the two ships, the greater leading, in which their sons were sailing.

And then, the bright chill weather of the spring grew still chiller, and it was a time for the watchers of our departure to turn for home – as Thjodhild had done long before.

12

THE VINLAND SKRAELINGS

After three days we sailed up the Lysafjord. There were few enough people there after the last winter's terrible illness. But besides dumping Thorstein and his new woman at Sandness, and six other folk to take over other houses, we had brought – and we were to leave him at the West Settlement – a priest. He was to pull up all the stakes that went deep into the graves and pour holy water down the holes where the stakes had been. Further, when he had done this, Sera Tomas, this priest, was to bide at Lysafjord. For Leif, who was now the godi in place of his brother, had arranged this with the Vicar-General.

Now talk had it that the Vicar-General was being naughty with the mother of Freydis, in the way the Archdeacon had been, and that Thorulf, Freydis's lover, took a bribe from this, the highest of churchmen among us, to keep his mouth shut about it.

Perhaps one should not repeat scandal; or perhaps one should, since it shows what was in the minds of the people, whether true or false. But, speaking for myself, I believe that the Vicar-General, a loftily important man, liked a good fat meal, and a good strong drink rather more than getting between a pair of good fat woman's legs and spilling out his sort of liquor into her cup. But there, good meals and good drink have ever been scarce in Greenland, and he might have gone – to his way of thinking, mark you – to the second-best!

Anyhow, the people of the West Settlement were glad to welcome Sera Tomas, until they learned they would have to pay for his upkeep.

Moreover, they would have to build a house for him.

When there had been but a wandering priest he had been put up for just two or three days and nights at the house where I had spent the last dreadful winter, the house belonging to the great Eirik, and to his sons after him. In those few days, he had pulled up stakes and slopped down holy water, had baptized five or six infants, had read the wedding oaths over their parents, and had said mass.

But now they were to have Sera Tomas for year after year. And a house must be made for him. The men who put it up would have their tithes remitted just for this one year.

The cheek of it! What the men did was to say:

'That bit of land over there is a fine bit of land for your house, Sera. We'll put it there.'

And that bit of land was none other than Thor's enclosure, the grove, with a fence round it, over which the horrid bailiff Gurdar's thing – his body – was thrown, and where it rotted until a sportive youngster took a vault over the fence, and tossed back the fragments of Gurdar.

'That's just the place for your house, Reverend,' the men said.

'But, I hear it was the home of a heathen god, one Thor,' replied Sera Tomas.

'Just so. But a man of the one true god should live and take over from the bad one,' said the men. This shows how we Greenlanders take our revenge on hardships with jokes. So there the presbytery was built.

Also the people of the West Settlement were much heartened by Thorfinn Karlsefni and his lady, Gudrid, whom they wished well on their marriage, when they made it clear that the West Settlement would become a very important place indeed – the first haven of call – when the new lands in the west were settled, and that this great sailing was to do just that.

After taking on food and water, our two ships, leaving behind Thorstein, his new wife, the priest, and six others, set off on the course which we now knew well. The weather for so early in the year was wonderful, and we sighted Helluland, passed it, and then Markland, with no mischief. But I was in the leading ship, with Karlsefni and Gudrid, and first knew that something was odd while scanning for Crossness, the grave of the good, round-shouldered, short-sighted, but clever Thorwald Eiriksson.

When I had last seen them, the cross at his head lifted high above the cross at his feet, and the masts of the two crosses, when sighted in line, gave a true east-west bearing.

Searching at daybreak for this good landmark, I first saw what was Thorwald's head cross leaning afar askew, to the north. It might have been wind and rain that did the slanting except that, hanging from a sinew of about two yards in length, on the down-leaning arm of the cross, hung a round black thing of the shape and size of a man's head. It swung in the mild breeze to and fro, sometimes knocking the upright pole of the cross. Whatever the thing was, it was either the work of what men used to call trolls, or what the Christians now call demons, or it was a warning that the skraelings had been at their nasty games since I had last left Vinland.

But the light was tricky. Driving our ship nearer inshore, Karlsefni waving Thorhall Gamlason's ship to follow, we saw that it was indeed a man's skull hitched to a sinew from the down-leaning arm of the head cross. The lower jaw had fallen away. Thorwald Eiriksson's skull or not, this was but the first omen of the many strokes of ill luck that we were to meet in Vinland.

Yet we still sailed on, until we gained the sight of Leif's houses, whereon Karlsefni gave thanks to the three Christian gods in one, and called on all of us to do the same.

Then at last our two ships were anchored, and later drawn up in the haven beyond the tide's reach. Thanks to the three Christian gods, or thanks to Thor, or thanks to luck, we found the houses of Leif untouched by brooding or squatting troll or thievish skraeling. We unloaded our goods, turned out our livestock onto the grass, and tasted its delicious soft dew. When we had bestowed ourselves and our goods as best we could, Karlsefni, my Gudrid beside him, told us to give thanks to God again. For we had reached Vinland in safety despite the grisly sight of Thorwald's swinging skull on the crossbeam.

When, a week or two later, I was sent to look at the grave, there was no doubt. His head was in a net basket of fibres fixed to the end of plaited sinews. We put Thorwald's head back in the grave and straightened the cross.

My son, our design was to settle in Vinland, and to make of it a rich and healthy land. We had a summer, hot and fiery, and a winter of longer days and of lesser frost than we know of in Greenland, and yet another summer, bountiful as to sun and weather.

At first, Karlsefni had insisted that we deal mildly with the skraelings, even though the unspeakable wretches had uprooted Thorwald's body, that of Gudrid's brother-in-law, from its grave and had harmed the cross with his poll which they had hewn off. These skraelings we found to be even more treacherous, spiteful, dirty and thieving than those in Greenland. Worse: they were far more numerous than those in Greenland.

And because they were so many, as many as flies around a stranded whale, and because they were land skraelings rather than the water skraelings of Greenland, they kept thrusting themselves against us in spiteful war. And they had very good weapons, one of which you'll hear about.

All we wanted was to clear the timber, till the land and graze our cattle like good Christian people.

But these skraelings could not be treated in a Christian manner.

To begin with, they gave their animal skins to us in exchange for the milk from our cattle which they gobbled in greedy manner, never having seen cattle before, nor tasted the like. Not that much milk is good for any man, since it makes him pale of skin, heavy and slow of movement, and sluggish in the action of his bowels. For this reason it is a food and drink better suited to babies, aged folk, weak women, and dolts – and, seemingly, skraelings. Yet, would you believe it, they dropped their bowls and fled when our randy and sharp-horned bull bellowed? That bull gave them a shock. Lowering his head in wrath, and roaring, he chased them. He was a mighty weapon of war to set against the feeble wretches when our need arose.

As they became more pressing, Karlsefni ordered a stockade to be built around the houses for he feared an attack, either against those built by Leif or the new ones nearby since erected by the men in Thorhall Gamlason's ship. So stout and high palings were thrown up around both lots of houses in one ring.

Then one night one of our men had waylaid a wife of the head man of these skraelings and had raped her, and then cut out her tongue. This started a bad quarrel, even though Karlsefni had severely reproved the man for this act which he said endangered us all. But the man was surly and defied Karlsefni: 'What do you expect us to do since there are no women of our own sort here?' Karlsefni was angered by this insolent defiance and, in a rage, ordered the malefactor to be hanged, but few of our men were willing to do this work, even though the man had brought all of us into danger by giving the skraeling chief a reason to be annoyed with us. So fighting broke out amongst ourselves since this man was a member of Thorhall Gamlason's ship. Nevertheless, Karlsefni had his way, even though Gudrid pleaded with her husband for the man's life. For Karlsefni answered: 'This criminal can pay no fine to the husband of the woman as he would be made to do in Greenland, and for him to suffer outlawry, which he would be made to suffer if the husband were a free man, not a bondsman, would be worse for this felon than to be hanged amongst ourselves since the skraelings will practise unnameable cruelties upon him if he falls into their hands, as is certain if he is driven from our compound as an outlaw.'

But we still didn't like it, since a new punishment, one never known in Greenland, or in Iceland, by word of our leader, must now be carried out. It was a strange thing but our women, except for Gudrid, though few in number, were more eager for the exaction of the penalty than our men.

There were many who blamed Karlsefni, but he was undoubtedly in a most awkward situation. Death by hanging, as a punishment, was quite unknown, as we made plain to him, in our Greenland, and in Iceland too, where our great men were all free. And though indeed we had bondpeople, taken from Ireland and so on, yet even those low and simple people had before them the hope that, if not themselves, yet then their children, or their children's children, might one day become, if they were hardworking and faithful, smallholders – churls, free men, if only in a small way. But in other countries such as England, in which lived men of lesser minds and meaner laws, even their greater men were not free, but lived and died subject to the will of a king. In Norway this had happened, and because we would have none of this – we would rather be dead than live under a king – we had sailed for Iceland, and from Iceland Eirik settled in Greenland.

In Iceland, I agree, it is said that a man had once been stoned to death. But this was because he was a wizard who had cast spells on the fields of a farmstead to make them barren of crops, and not because he had killed a man, let alone raped a woman. The crops had withered in the very sight of the farmers and the farmer's wives, and the man, Gunnlaug the Wizard, had actually been spied at night, in the third quarter of the moon, scattering ash made, it was believed, from the burnt claws of deformed cocks and the afterbirths of babes who became idiots. Spied on at his work, he was chased by all the people up into a stony place. They surrounded him and hurled stones at him in the moonlight until he was dead. Then a cairn over his body was made with the stones which had killed him, and you may see the cairn to this day. But this stoning was not after a trial at the Thing, nor after the will of a king or leader, but came from the anger of all the people who knew their crops to be spoiled. It is only in countries like Norway and England or, it is said, even in Denmark now, that a man can suffer such an ugly and disgusting punishment as being hanged at the will of a king. In Greenland and Iceland we had a higher opinion of even the worst men than to carry out such a shameful, as well as cruel, punishment.

But Karlsefni had been in Norway, and in those other lands. If 'Kollsvein Hrolfsson had just raped a woman that would have been no great harm', he said. It was the fact that 'we are in a place where we are so surrounded by wild skraelings, of a more vicious and treacherous kind than ever those at home in Greenland, that is the harm'. Further: 'You, Kollsvein, stupidly chose a woman belonging to their chief man. Why choose that one? Following their chief, the whole crowd of the wretches will be mad for war and burning. That makes the punishment chosen by those English and Norwegian kings the right punishment for you.

'For if the skraelings do not see that we punish what they think was a wrong you have done to them, we can never hope to abide in peace in Vinland, for the heathen devils will become yet more unfriendly, and we will have to go back to Greenland with all our plans thwarted because of your doing. And our Greenland itself may die unless we can settle this Vinland, and send our families and our friends the corn and the timber without which they may not live.'

This Karlsefni said to Kollsvein before us all.

But Kollsvein had sailed in Gamlason's ship. The two skippers disagreed, fighting broke out, and a man was killed in the quarrel. Gudrid sided with Gamlason against her husband, but the other four women, and most of the men, stood up for Karlsefni. They valued their own skins. As they put it: 'We shall stay here or we shall go back home; but, if we stay here, we want to stay here alive.'

So a tall pole was planted inside the compound, rising far above the stockade. By signs Karlsefni tried to explain to the chief skraeling that all his people were to assemble outside the stockade in the morning to see 'very bad man who'd done big wrong to skraeling big man's woman go up the pole'. And he said that each skraeling who watched would afterwards take from him – Karlsefni – a strip of scarlet cloth of a finger's width and the length of a forearm as a token, when it was done. He–Karlsefni–'would do ill to his own man who did to skraeling ill thing'.

All the same I do not think our hanging of Kollsvein was of much use in making the skraelings more friendly. They could not recognize the face in the noose when it rose above the top of the stockade. As we understood later, all of us looked alike to the skraelings. Besides Kollsvein had taken the woman in the dark and even if she had known him from the rest of us, her tongue had been cut out on purpose that she couldn't describe the wrongdoer to her husband. Indeed, when it was over, we concluded the skraelings thought it was our god that we were hanging, for they had a silly and confused notion of what went on in our Christian religion, from a crucifix left behind by one of Thorwald Eiriksson's men. It is even likely that the wretches had dug up Thorwald and slung his head from an arm of the great cross over his grave to make it more resemble the crucifix, thinking it might please us when we came back. So they beat the ground, as though they were in sorrow, and made strange sobbing noises from their throats when they saw Kollsvein being drawn up to the very top of the pole so that he could be seen by all beyond the stockade.

Then came each skraeling to the gate in the stockade to be given by Karlsefni himself his token strip of red cloth of a finger's width and a forearm's length. This was a good notion of Karlsefni's and it worked well. Perhaps the stupid people thought the strips were charms for it gave them a wild delight. Some hung the strips over an ear and grinned; others tried to eat the strips; a few others tied up locks of their filthy black coarse hair with them, clapping their hands and leaping about. They were nearly naked creatures.

Seeing this, we thought they would take more strips of scarlet cloth every day they came to bother us, in exchange for the skins of animals they brought, instead of the milk we had before poured into their bowls. This would have been cheaper for us but, after a while, they wouldn't have it: they threw the strips of cloth to the ground stamping, shaking their heads, growling and frowning, baring their teeth, wanting the milk.

One thing Karlsefni was strict about, and in this he was utterly right. No man of us was ever to trade any of our weapons of war, no matter what or whatever its worth was offered in exchange. Any man who broke this law was to have the harshest punishment, for by his deed he put us all in danger. Far fewer in numbers we were than the skraelings, but at least our weapons were far stronger – except only the skraelings' terrifying war-sling, of which I shall tell.

Then a man broke this rule. He told Karlsefni that he had not traded the axe, but had dropped it after felling a tree. Despite his 'seeking for it', he said, he had 'lost his axe – not meaning to – among the grass and the branches after felling'. But Karlsefni ordered a search into the man's belongings, and there was found in the man's coffer a big collection of the skins of squirrels and of a kind of large grey-striped cat. And a pelt of a brown bear. The man's answer to Karlsefni was this: 'But an axe is not a weapon of war but a tool for a husbandman, Karlsefni.' Scolded for such a lying snake-tongued answer when the skins were shown him, the man next said:

'But since, Karlsefni, we are all bound for home, Greenland, and soon enough, on account of these skraelings, and your ill-managing of them – and of us – I see no harm in taking back a few skins. They will be all I have to show for a voyage under your leading.'

I had never seen Karlsefni so wrathful before. His yellowish face darkened, his eyes became blood-red, and the vein stood out just on one side of the middle of his forehead; and the great vein each side of his neck became swollen. The man was one of those in Karlsefni's ship, not in Gamlason's, and Karlsefni would have his own will without any fighting from Gamlason's lot. Karlsefni, in his rage, shouted for the rude man to be tied up and thrashed until he was so bloodied that if he be given one more stroke he would die. And so it was done.

That, no less than the hanging, had been a punishment not known in Greenland or in Iceland, where all free men had their rights, but flogging was a practice, no less than hanging, in the crueller and slave-like king-ruled lands of Norway and England.

It may be explained in this way. When our forefathers settled in Iceland, there was none to resist them; when they settled in Greenland, there was none to resist them either – for it was only later, in our summer hunts in northern waters, that we first met skraelings. On the other hand, it is said that the English, who are kin to us, though somewhat smaller and weaker, when they first began to settle their land, encountered vast numbers of people who resisted them, and who were not much better, even though many of them were Christian, than the skraelings in Vinland, and whom they had to kill or drive out. They did drive them out – to Wales, to Cornwall, parts of Scotland, to Ireland, where they are now permitted to live. But the English had to impose harsh penalties on them, because of their numbers, until they submitted; which penalties the English still shamefully impose even on their own kind. So we too, far from our own kind, and among a wicked and low people, and beset with perils, had to do outrageous things.

Yet the trading of the axe proved rather laughable than otherwise. Next day, from within the stockade, we saw a skraeling finger our axe and then try it by smiting it with all his strength on the shoulder of a friend. He took his arm off, and the friend fell down and died. The skraeling next tried the axe on a stone, whereon its blade flew into splinters. Then he threw the stock of the axe away.

In a hard time it is good for the mood of the heart to see a sight to make us laugh and be merry.

And after the flogging, Karlsefni addressed the man on whom it had been carried out thus:

'For trading or, as you lied to me, for losing an axe, in Greenland you would have suffered nothing but to have been thought a fool. But if you had killed a man in Greenland, you would, if he were a mean man, have been fined, or, if he were a great man, you would have been outlawed.

'But here, where we are now, in Vinland, you could not be fined. For what', and he scoffed, 'is the forfeiture of a few squirrel skins, if none of us make home? You may have killed no man, but by your deed, you meant, as by a token, to put at risk the life of every man of us here, great or mean.

'If I had put it to the vote, you would have been outlawed. You would have been thrust outside from us to shift for yourself among the skraelings, whom you aided with that axe. But if they had tortured you, or promised you food for a day, or shelter for a night even, you would have betrayed us all to them. Or, if you had been stout-hearted, instead of the base man that you are, and you had not given us away, the rascals would have killed you cruelly.

'I had you flogged out of pity, for my wife, Gudrid Thornbjörnsdottir, begged that you be not outlawed – for then your fate would have been to live or die among wretches, among whom you share neither a faith nor a speech, and you would never see Greenland again. That is what was made known. But since, under a roasting fire, an outlaw would yield up our secrets, despite the difference of tongues, my lady and I agreed rather that you should be flogged so severely as the fellow who had traded his axe, and lied.

'As it happens, the axe you sold was broken by the skraeling: that loss of the axe to us was no gain to them, thanks to luck. And that is the only good of the matter: for what is to the skraeling no gain is still to us a loss.'

And then both Thorfinn Karlsefni and Thorhall Gamlason made it well known that henceforth if any man traded either weapon or tool with the skraeling, or even lost such a weapon or tool blameworthily, he would be tried and, if found guilty, he would be outlawed and that man would never see Greenland again.

Autumn came on. The skraelings had had their fill of strips of scarlet cloth, and of some beads we had brought, and as the yield of our cattle slackened off, which we explained by signs, they no longer came pestering us for milk, a food which strengthens women and babes, but which weakens men. So this was a good time. The weather was still warm and parties of our men would go out felling trees for seasoning, or for fuel, without being disturbed; or they would harvest the wild corn; or they would catch fish, which were abundant; or they would trap game, or they would gather fruits and berries. We all loved this land for its great richness, and only hated it for its skraelings.

And it was about this lovely and fruitful season that the lovely lady, Gudrid Thorbjörnsdottir, now the wife of Thorfinn Karlsefni, gave birth to a son. He was named Snorri after Thorfinn's grandfather, Snorri Thordsson. Gudrid's baby, Snorri Thorfinnsson, as he became known, was the first child – and he was a man-child – of our kind and kin ever to be born in Vinland.

Great was our pride at this truth, and I shall be proud of it to the end of my life. For my belief is, that though we had, after another year, to go back to Greenland, yet in the long run, once the hideous skraelings are subdued by greater strength of weapons, if not of numbers, many, very many, of our men and women will in time settle in Vinland, and there they will breed and rear children without number, making of Vinland a greater and richer country than either Greenland or Iceland, greater and richer even than Norway or Denmark or England.

And still, in my old age, I believe that, my own son. You see what hardship is before us in Greenland now, so that, if we don't look to it, we shall starve. Yet if not you, nor your son, yet your son's son, may yet have the richness of living that Eirik Thorwaldsson wrongly thought that he had found for himself, and for those who came after him, in Vinland.

It was in the warm and calm dawn of a tender autumn day that Snorri was born. There was a mist, sweet with earth-scents, through which the stars shone.

Now we had brought four other women with us, who had come with their husbands, and three of these were good-hearted women, though nothing to look at, and each of them was ready to perform the part of a midwife. So the lady Gudrid was well aided. Only the fourth woman was unwilling to help. But, though more comely than the

153

others in looks, she was the wife of the man who had been flogged for selling his axe, and she gave that as a reason for refusing her aid. She sent an answer by another that 'tending the hurts given to the back of her own man by Karlsefni, the husband of the mother-to-be, she could not be spared'.

That may have been so, but it is more likely she was sullen out of pride. Besides, it may be thought she cared less for her husband than for some others. Because of her better features and figure, she received much attention from many of the single men. Her husband, in fact, may have done the dastardly selling of his axe in order to be able to boast to his wife of 'how much better and more cunning he was than the other men in his dealings with the skraelings. He would be able to dress her more finely with the squirrel skins than the other women's husbands could.'

All the signs and stars, and the moon too, waning and low in the sky, as it was discerned through the dawn mist, but still large and shapely – signifying capacity for learning and wisdom – stood for health and luck at the moment Snorri was born. I prayed he may become a great man.

As I have said, he was named Snorri Thorfinnsson by our leader. Whether the old lady at Brattahlid, Thjodhild, would have been pleased at this, I did not know; but I hardly thought so. The child was born within nine months of Thorstein Eiriksson's death, and the proud widow of Eirik, the founder of Greenland, had sorely longed to see, before her death, a man-child that owed its being to her own blood and bone through one of her three sons.

Thorfinn or Thorstein? Of that no one can be sure. Or was the father some other? However, I rejoiced, like all the good men amongst us, at this birth, and even more so in later years – as it came about – because of the greatness and distinction of this Snorri. He had the best and dearest of women of all those I have known, except one, for his mother.

And not only the best and dearest; but the most gifted, as has been shown, in her second sight or far sight, just as the Little Knowing One perceived soon after the lady, and her father, Thorbjörn, first came into Greenland, during that very hard winter – though there were to be winters that were yet harder. An instance of this weird gift of Gudrid will soon be told.

It came about in the spring, a season when the skraelings, it was feared, would be back again to pester us. So leaving about half our band under the leadership of Thorhall Gamlason at Leif's houses, Karlsefni and the rest took ship with the purpose of seeking a part of this same country that would be as equally fruitful as the part we were now in, but free of or, if not free, then less troubled and marred by these dirty people. For the skraelings were foes, the only bar to our happiness and wealth in this land.

There were many days at sea. We passed the ness on which the stempost of Thorwald's keel had been planted, Keelness, and then held on south. At times we lost sight of land altogether, but our good seaman said he believed we were passing a vast gulf into which a river flowed. He declared this on the strength of the outflow thrusting us from the west and because the water tasted and smelt less salt, because trees and branches were swept past us, and because of the freshwater birds being harried past us to be lost in the main sea.

That it was a gulf was proved when we saw land again, a seemingly endless layer of white sand beach which we called Far and Farther Strands. Still we held on, and at last, rounding a cape, we came on what looked to be an island.

And a most promising one at that. A deep haven ran into the north of this island. Into this haven we brought our ship. There was a very great number of small hills scattered all about in this place, and, what was better, there was a plenitude of freshwater pools, of all sizes, in which throve many kinds of fish, excellent for eating. There was fine grass for our cattle, freshened by sweet dew in the early mornings; and much woodland. Surely this was the best part of all Vinland we had seen. And here was but scant sign of the skraeling. We hewed timber and put up houses. But, since we could not trust in luck too much, we built a stockade about the houses. Yet we were not left untroubled for long.

We had called our island Fast Stream Island. For between us and a tongue of land we could see some four or five miles away, a tidal water streamed so fast and with such strength that we judged we were secure from attack from that tongue of land. 'No paltry craft of bark or hide', we thought, 'pulled by oar or pushed by paddle – or anyhow – could reach us athwart that streaming flood. Rather, it would be swept past, up or down in a vast hurry, depending on which way the tide ran. We were safe on Fast Stream Island.'

We were mistaken.

After a short while, it is true we had met a few skraelings. But these we deemed inhabited our Fast Stream Island and, because they were so few, we would soon master them. Not that they were not annoying since they wanted to finger our beards – their own men were so feeble that they grew none – or gaze and wonder at our weapons. And when they saw our women – we had brought the three who attended Gudrid when she had given birth, beside the lady herself – the wretches made all manner of lewd gestures and silly cries. We had to push them away when, giggling and grimacing, they tried to pick away or peel off their clothes. When they brought their own women these went naked but for a mere piece of bark or cloth the size of a man's hand, over the organ, supported by a string about the waist. These women tittered, clucked and clapped when they saw the little Snorri.

They were meddlesome people, but docile, and few in number, and we believed we were safe on this beautiful and fruitful Fast Stream Island. Richer than the land around Leif's houses, we would bring the rest of the expedition here; and here we would settle.

Then one early morning we looked out over the streaming course of water between us and the tongue of land. It was littered and thick with small boats making towards us from Tongue Land athwart the run of the tide. They were so many and black that the sight resembled a mass or hoard of shattered charcoal faggots scattered after the ending of a smelting fire.

And, as they came nearer, we saw from our houses, built on a low hill above the stream, that in each of these little black boats, beside the man paddling athwart the tide, was another with a long pole which he wagged. As they came still nearer to us, we saw that at the top of these poles was a kind of blue bag of cloth which resembled a ball when it was filled with the breeze. Nearer still, we saw that around the foreheads of the men were tied bands into which, at the backs of their heads, red-streaked feathers were planted. Their faces were painted with reddish paint, but they had whitish-yellow stripes on each cheek.

Certainly the whole crowd of boats were driving towards the beach below us, and the men in them were in no friendly mood when they had disembarked, judging by their pointing to us with both arms at full stretch, screaming and stamping, while those with the long poles swayed and nodded them towards us as we watched from within the stockade on our low hill. And as the blue bags, at the top of the poles, swung to and fro in the breeze, they made the sound of a limp sail suddenly filled to bursting by a sudden great squall.

The skraelings, their boats on the beach, strung themselves out in an immense line along the shore of a long but narrow pond which lay between the foot of our slope and the strand.

After a while, seeing that the wretches did no more than squat, plant their poles in the shingle, babble and make hideous high-pitched howls from their heathen throats, Karlsefni made his plan.

He made sixteen of our men, and I was among them, leave our stockade with our shields, blades and our spears. We were to go slowly but boldly down the slope, and when we reached the flat, we were to line, each man five strides from his neighbour, our side of the long but narrow pond.

'Meanwhile', said Karlsefni, 'I, with our remainder less two, will stand outside the fence of the stockade, showing our weapons too. The gate will be open. If the wretches swarm round the ends of the pond to attack you, then through that gate will storm and trample our great weapon of war. And with all speed we'll follow him.'

So our sixteen left the gate. And I was frightened no more than the others. We reached the flat. We spread out, each man five strides from his neighbour, lining our side of the long and narrow pond, facing the wild and hostile people.

Next we perceived the purpose of those devilish and frightening poles, which were three or four times the height of a man even when their stocks were sunk far into the shingle or sand. Strings were fixed to the heads of these poles, and these strings were pulled with such force that the poles, or saplings, were bent back to make hoops, the blue cloths reaching the ground. Each hoop minded me of some agile clown, eager for praise at some drunken feast, who springs from his bench, to run on his hands and feet, the fellow's back arched over the floor, his pouted belly heaving towards the rafters. Into each blue bag was loaded a stone: the strings were let go; the saplings sprang up straight, and with a terrifying loud huffing sound, like a sudden blow of wind smiting a woman's washing hung out to dry, or the sudden roar up of a fire that has been sleeping, flung balls of stone, or wooden blocks smeared with flaming pitch. Then the poles swayed and wagged, flapping their cloths, until their heads were drawn down to be loaded again.

While these stones were hurled at Karlsefni and our fellows by the stockade, other skraelings in great numbers slunk around each end of the long and narrow pond to fight the sixteen of us at near quarters. When he saw the devils had rounded the ends of the pond and were close on us, Karlsefni brought out his great weapon of war. Two men, trotting, brought out our bull from the gate, one man on each side of a long sinew threaded through its nose. The two men then ran as hard as they could, pulling at the sinew, to give smart to the bull, to madden it with pain and rage.

Half-way down the slope, the two men, at a word, released their strings and, trailing them, the great warrior plunged down the slope, followed with brave shouts by our leader, Karlsefni, and the rest of our men with shield, spear and blade.

That high-mooded charge saved us on that day. Not that our bull knew friend from foe, but he brought stark terror to all the skraelings, who had seen none of his kind. Except for those who lofted their stones with poles planted on the far shore of the pond, the devils were caught between us and the helping raid led down the slope by Karlsefni. And our mad bull did great work for us on that day. We laughed with joy as, towing the long strings from his nose, he thrust a horn into the loins of this or that fleeing skraeling.

Many were killed; and we lost three good men, and one was so hurt by an arrow in the groin that we thought he, too, would die. He did not die, despite the bleeding, but was no longer a man, though we stopped the bleeding, because of that skraeling stone arrow. We tried to cheer him with funny jokes, telling him that he would have no offspring to support in his old age. Yet he was sad.

'A high voice means a low outlay,' one said, 'but if you want them, I'll do the job for you.'

Besides this man, and the three killed, another of us had had an eye knocked out, and another had had a stone arrow-head in his throat. When it was picked out, he could never speak again but in whispers.

It was on the evening of this fight that Gudrid Thorbjörnsdottir, she who is more mine than Thorfinn Karlsefni's, whose wife she was, saw what was given to her alone to see.

The sun had set; our three dead had been brought up the slope before burial on the morrow; the gate had been shut. The men were eating what there was to eat. They were sour in mood. They cursed this Stream Island which had promised so much. They cursed it for being 'so rich, and so full; the land above all that is fair, but turns out a liar'. They compared Stream Island to a woman who gave earnest of being true and kind in marriage but who was false and hard. What they meant was that this island, more than other parts of Vinland they had

seen, and far beyond all that had been hoped of Greenland, had green-
ness in its grass, had food for cattle, timber enough and to spare; it
had wild corn for bread and for ale; it had deer, and fish, and birds,
and the eggs of birds; it had warm summers and mild winters; it had
all that our hearts and our hopes had wanted. As a Christian among us
said, it had seemed a kind of heaven gained as a reward before death –
but now was to be taken from us by reason of the skraelings. Such was
the bitter mood of the men in the calm evening of that day of cruel
fighting.

But Gudrid was alone in her room, before an open door. She was
sitting on a bench with Snorri, her son, beside her in his cradle. As the
dusk deepened, a lady – and she was not one of the other three women
we had brought with us – appeared softly on the threshold of the open
door. She wore a long gown of grey cloth that reached to her ankles.
She had a belt about her waist. She had the largest eyes that ever
Gudrid had seen in her life; and she had a headband to bind her long
hair.

This woman was standing framed by the jambs and the lintel of the
door of the room where Gudrid was sitting on the bench beside her
baby in his cradle.

And this woman said:

'My name is Gudrid. What is your name?'

And Gudrid said:

'My name is Gudrid.' And Gudrid made space for the strange woman
to sit beside her on the bench, inviting her with her hand.

And the strange woman said: 'Rather come and sit beside me here.'
And she moved into the room from the doorway and sat on one of a
pair of stools that were set on the other side of the open doorway.

Gudrid rose from her bench, gathered her son, Snorri, in her arms
from his cradle, and moved before the open door to sit beside the other
Gudrid.

And as soon as she had done this – at the moment she had done this –
there was a loud crash and a ball of flame flew through the open
doorway and struck the bench on which Gudrid had been sitting.

Gudrid looked to the strange woman with the long gown, the large
eyes, and the headband, but that woman had vanished.

Hearing the crash, men, her husband among them, quenched the
flame.

But Gudrid told no one about this, except me alone. And she
interpreted:

'Not now, but some other year, a hundred years hence or more –
or more still – there will be many Gudrids living in peace in this land,
and your Snorri will be the forefather of some of them.'

Then she took me by the hand, and said:

'But now soon we shall return home to the ill-named Greenland, the
unhappy. There you will die, but I shall go further east from Vinland
than you to die.'

13

I SETTLE AT SANDNESS

Bitter to fail. High the hopes of sixty or so men in two ships when we had set forth from Greenland to find new homes for ourselves, with many to follow, in Vinland. And two summers and two winters we had passed; winners against the land, but against the people of that land, losers.

Not that the skraelings were wise. In all things they fell utterly below us, except in number. As for weapons, their arrow-heads of stone were no match for ours made of iron! Not knowing the use of iron, they had neither sword nor spear, but they used hatchets with blades made of the shoulderblades of animals. In one weapon only had they a skill or cleverness worthy of men: I mean the fixing of blue cloth bags to tall sapling poles which flung heavy stones, with a dreadful noise, dead or burning stones, high in the air and for a long way.

For us to settle Vinland from Greenland, and to make homes there, we need only find a weapon of war which flings further, and with a sharper mark, than theirs. That found, even a very few of us will have the means to kill a very vast number of those skraelings, so as to clear the rich land of them for our own use. Beyond doubt, those people are not only heathen, but they are rude, wicked and dirty in every way. Those skraelings do not know the arts of farming, whether of grain or beast, and they can neither read nor write. Though great in their numbers, they should be all killed, or render themselves our slaves, so that we, who understand these arts, whether still followers of Thor or followers of the new three-in-one God, should be able to use their land as it should be used. We could then send back to Greenland those goods of which Greenland has such need and which Vinland has in abundance – timber, corn, skins of animals, and – they say – wine.

When those of us who had spent the winter at Stream Island, and sailed north in the spring, joined Gamlason's men at Leif's houses, our two ships sailed home for Greenland. A fine load of timber, some grain of the wild wheat, two skraeling boys we had taken, and one skraeling female about thirty years of age, and above two hundred skins of animals of different kinds – bears, wolves, hares, squirrels, foxes, deer of all sorts – was all we could show for our losses. And the skraeling woman we took back was swarthy and ill-favoured, and so dirty that she would pluck scabs from her hair, chattering her teeth. She could hardly be taught to speak one word outside her own tongue, though six or eight of us on shipboard would ring her round, and laying fingers on different parts of her body, say its name, starting with her breasts, and saying 'woman'. But the creature was copious in pointings and gestures and chatterings, rolling her eyes, and muttering 'Valdidadida', and that we took to be her name.

Three of the men, it was said, on Gamlason's ship used her, not with great pleasure I should think, but the needs of all the men, save those five who had brought their wives, in that way were strong – the more so since nearly all dangers were over on land or sea, and we were sailing home to shame. Two of these three men had wives in Greenland, so with noisy threats among themselves they said it was the single man's luck to look after the slut Valdidadida when they reached home. Now I know two of those three men's names but think it wrong to tell them. But I will say that the single man swore it was *not* his 'luck', and wanted to draw lots for it. They drew lots but Valdidadida came to him all the same. The two young skraeling boys were also used in a similar, but not just the same way on our ship, not Gamlason's, and Karlsefni knew of it. Karlsefni knew of this indeed, but tried to keep the news hidden from his wife lest she be ashamed that such things could be. The boys were more apt at learning our speech than Valdidadida. They were to be sold as servants to any who would buy them when we reached Greenland.

But our losses. Of sixty-one men who had set forth for Vinland, one had been killed when fighting broke out between Karlsefni's men and Gamlason's men on the issue of whether Kollsvein Hrolfsson should be hanged for waylaying and raping one of the wives of the skraeling headman. And Kollsvein had been hanged, lifted above the stockade for them to see, so as to make the skraelings more friendly. But the skraelings had thought that the hanging of Kollsvein was a holy deed of worship to our three-in-one God, a cruel deed, and were bent on more fighting. So, while we lost three men, when away on Fast Stream Island, Gamlason's men, during the same season at Leif's houses, lost five in fighting with the vile people. From within the stockade of Leif's houses, Gamlason had seen skraelings cut off one of his men's hair, all the skin of that hair on the top of his head, while his man was yet alive, having fallen with a twisted ankle. When Gamlason went out to aid his man, he could see the bone of his skull all bare.

Then there were those who died, not from blows, but from illness. While we were at Stream Island, a dead whale had been washed ashore below Leif's houses. One of Gamlason's crew, an Icelander, thought he knew all about whales and, licking his chops as though he were tasting a fine meal, declared the monster was good to eat. But this fellow, Odd Oddsson, was an inland man – he dwelt at Mosfell – and his greed was bigger than his knowledge. A great weight of strips were cut from this dead whale. They were carried up to Leif's houses and were boiled by Gamlason's cooks. Of the seventeen who ate, all groaned and were ill, vomiting and idle for several days just when the skraelings were at their most vicious. And of the seventeen who ate, as many as eleven died.

This is to speak of those who died. But we also took back one live man who would never be able to perform with a woman because of a skraeling stone arrow-head in his groin, and another man who would never be able to speak since his voice-box had been broken by an arrow-head. Both had wives in Greenland. To cheer them up they were teased. We said the dumb man was the worse off of the two because he would not be able to answer his wife back. And no one would take any gladness in doing it for him; but, in the other case, it was another matter.

Yet we did bring back one young man whom we did not take out as a man since he was then still inside his mother. It is Snorri, I mean: he would grow, since none but Gudrid was his mother, to become a great and worthy man – though in Iceland – and the father, it would be accounted by many, of a man yet greater than Snorri himself – none less than a bishop of Skalholt.

But when we reached home, we found that during our two-and-a-half years abroad there had been births and deaths in Greenland too. More deaths than births, for such is the hard and ungiving nature of our land, and fewer people now from the east – whether from Iceland or Norway, or from Faroe and Shetland, or from the other islands – knowing this, were coming in to settle. Among those who had died, while we were away, was the father of Gudrid, Thorbjörn Vifilsson. Gudrid loved her father dearly and had looked forward, once it was clear that our plan to settle at Vinland had failed, to his welcoming of herself and his grandson. For that Snorri was his grandson there could at least be no doubt. Thorbjörn, when he died, was not much above middle years, and lived alone. He had been rewarded meanly for his early befriending of Eirik. He was a vigorous and well-liked man, and hale. But one day, a man who purported himself to be a bailiff of Leif Eiriksson, had come round to demand certain dues he said were owing to his master.

Thorbjörn, who had struggled hard to make his livelihood, and had succeeded – even though he merited a great deal more from the family of Eirik than he had received – strode in hot haste to Thorkel's. It was under Thorkel's roof that father and daughter had found shelter when they set foot in Greenland and Eirik had turned a cold shoulder. It was at Thorkel's that Gudrid had sung the Spirit-Songs or Ward-Locks which had enabled the Little Knowing One to reveal what was to come.

As Thorbjörn was telling his friend, Thorkel, of the outrageous demand on his scant wealth the same man who made the demand came hurrying up. At the sight of this man, a blood vessel burst in Thorbjörn's head. With this stroke he was rendered speechless. He died at Thorkel's house within three days.

This is the account Thorkel had told to others, but Thorkel too had died before we came back from Vinland. But it is only fair to state that Leif denied that he had sent any man to gather dues from Thorbjörn: 'For the sake of my father, I would have done no such thing. Further, he was the father of the woman who was my brother Thorstein's wife – before she became another's. The man was a friend; and he who asked money of him, in my name, an impostor.'

No wrong-doing could ever be traced to Leif, the Lucky, the Happy. He was renowned for his uprightness.

Thorbjörn's body was taken over the water and buried in the churchyard of Gardur. Gudrid went to see her father's grave and had a stone put over it in which runes were cut. Interpreted, these runes say:

> Thorbjörn Vifilsson, helper of
> Eirik Thorwaldsson. Died with
> some help from Eirik's son.
> Mourned by Gudrid Thorbjörnsdottir.
> God gladden his soul.

The old lady, Thjodhild, was still alive, but had fallen and broken her thighbone and now kept her bed, food being brought to her. But she had herself borne on a litter of wooden boards to her church each Sunday and Holy Day. The frame was put down right before the altar. Leif stood tall beside it. Her knowledge of the Latin mass was better than the priest's. She lay flat on her back, her head on a pillow. But she would lift her head and correct the priest, while he was saying mass, and loudly. He was one of our half-taught Greenlander priests, not a German or Swede. When he said something like 'In nomine patris et filiae et spiritus sanctus', Thjodhild would lift herself on to her elbows and say: 'Not "filiae", wicked man, but "filii". Our lord was not a girl. Learn your grammatical genders, Sera Mattias.'

Some said Thjodhild was a saint. She certainly gave money for the priests and the Church which she had founded in the land, and the Bishop in Rome would praise her for that. But Rome was very far off and the men who made saints there did not know how hard she was on poor people.

Others said her son, Leif Eiriksson, should be the saint. It was he who had brought the faith into Greenland, had stopped killing Christian English and Irish, and had converted his mother, if not his father. Besides it was he – the Lucky, the Happy – who had set foot on Vinland, finding there innumerable heathen souls who might one day both own the faith and confess us to be masters for bringing them that wisdom.

Thjodhild ordered Gudrid to bring Snorri to her as she lay in bed at Brattahlid. Gudrid and Karlsefni, our 'Manly-Stuff', took the babe to be closely looked at. The old lady looked over Snorri from head to foot, seemingly ever more critically. Then she said sharply:

'He's not mine. That's no Thorstein. Still, he'll do. He may become a bishop. But can my own sons do nothing? And is he yours, Thorfinn Manly-Stuff? He doesn't look so much like you either.'

'Be that as it may, I want to die. God has made me ready.'

Leif Eiriksson, the Lucky, took the news of our ill-starred attempt on Vinland with calmness. Nothing was allowed to upset him when he was in the presence of others. I guess that even when he was alone he was full master of his mood. He was still unmarried. He asked about the state, when we left, of his houses which he had built in Vinland. He said:

'Even if we may not settle in the land by reason of the vile skraelings, yet God will allow us to go there each and every summer to cut and bring back timber. And that will not please those who live in Heriolfsness.' And he added:

'I shall still be known as Leif the finder of Vinland – so as to set foot on it, I mean; unlike Bjarni Heriolfsson who did no more than spy from a heaving ship.'

Apart from widows, and the wives of the badly damaged men, the one most moved by our failed venture was – Freydis.

Whereas Leif was calm, lofty and well-tempered, his half-sister, showing much more of the father of both, was distraught with passion.

Her mother had died before our home-coming. Taking over the fees her mother had earned from the Vicar-General and, before him, the Archdeacon, as well as the precious objects given her by Eirik himself, the daughter was well set up. In addition to these goods, Freydis had now her annual money from Leif. Hating harlotry, Leif still honoured what could be considered to be a moral charge laid on him, to help to maintain his father's daughter. Moreover, Freydis had won – and was still winning – sums from this man or that man – and many another too. Her lovers were not only Greenland men. When a ship came in from the east, whether from Iceland or Norway, the Greenlanders suffered a 'No, not today', and a slammed door from Freydis. Such was her reputation that, as soon as the ships that reached us wharfed, the skippers and merchants stepped ashore, randy after a long sea-voyage, and made for her dwelling 'to pay their respects to the daughter of Eirik himself, no less'. These outlanders had to pay a high fee for the privilege, more than Greenlanders could pay, and therefore at these times Greenlanders themselves were not welcome.

With these resources, on her mother's death, Freydis had left her dwelling above Brattahlid, and bought herself a fine farm on the plain of Gardur, between Eiriksfjord and Einarsfjord. Her feeble common-law husband, Thorulf, moved over to Gardur with her.

Hearing that our ships were coming up the fjord, and that they looked less well-manned than they did on setting out, Freydis crossed the water, and was standing on the wharf at Brattahlid before our ships tied up.

Before we had so much as tied up to disembark, she was crying out wildly, so that all could hear, such things as: 'The men are back! Frightened of skraelings? Put them in the garments of women! Their mothers mistook these things. Undress these weaklings and you'll see they haven't got what it takes to be a man. Their mothers mistook!'

We were milksops in her view. When she spied the two skraeling boys as they came down the gang-plank, she seized the wretched youths by the scruffs of their necks, one in each hand, then glaring at those of us still on board, she spat towards us and called, 'Cowards to be afraid of warriors like this pair of weaklings.' Then letting go of the brats, she smote one on the ear, and cried out:

'I am only a woman, and I'm not afraid of you.'

The lads were afraid of her. The one struck, bawled out in terror, and, holding his hand to his ear, he ran back up the gang-plank to the arms of the man who had used him most in bed. But Freydis was mean-hearted and cruel, for she then yelled:

'That's right, champion, running away to protect your wife' – whereas, of course, it was more like the other way round.

For all her wrath and scorn, Freydis was eager to find out all she could about Vinland, for she had a will to go there herself, and to succeed where others had failed. To that end, in the following days, she waylaid as many of us as she could. She had a quick mind, and would take up and compare what one man said and with what another said. Few could withstand her, even those who had just joined again with their wives, either because of the offer of her body for an hour as a reward was such a lure or because of her threats to those who would resist that lure.

She well knew the irresistible appeal of her body, and to feign not to acknowledge those charms or – worse – to laugh at her was highly dangerous. If any man laughed at her she would seek ways to have him wounded by her paid fellows, and wounded in such a way that the wounded man would be shy of laying a charge at the court of the Thing.

I had resolved that, when my turn came, I would have nothing to do with her. She had given me over for Thorulf, and I would say:

'I know of Vinland more than all the others. I saw it even as a child with Bjarni Heriolfsson before your brother did, and I have twice since been there – with Thorwald Eiriksson when he was slain, and now with Thorfinn Karlsefni. You could have asked me before the others who have come back, and you have not. And you live with Thorulf – against the law of the Church. You can do without what I know of Vinland.'

Though that had been my plan, I fear it went otherwise. (Beware of such women, my son.) Through her wiles – she wished to show me her new home in Gardur and to treat, she said, about a business deal – I rowed over the fjord to Gardur to see and praise her new dwelling, which was in truth a handsome property near the Vicar-General's house. I knew her mother, the mistress of the ever-to-be-renowned Eirik, had died, but she said Thorulf would be at home. So indeed he was, but he was no protection, for, when I was brought in, he was ordered outside by his common-law wife, and told 'not to be seen for three good hours' in a manner most galling to the pride of a man. Yet the lily-livered fellow, with a lewd wink, as much as to say 'A better ride than you had in Vinland, mate, from what I hear', did as he was told.

I confess that like many of the others who had travelled to Vinland – for I had no taste for a skraeling woman all the while I was near Gudrid – I had not clasped a woman while in that land. But, unlike others, I had memories of times of Freydis to think of as the woman unequalled in all the acts of love, while in the wildernesses of Vinland. So when the door was shut, with Thorulf the other side of it, and with the nearness of Freydis as she bared her breasts, I lost my resolve. After, I told her all I could tell, she managed to raise my lust again, as her 'thank you', she said. During this second time, the base-hearted Thorulf, deeming 'the three good hours' were up, lifted the latch. With a mock show of manners – that is, with a low bow – he retreated.

I tell you this, my son, though it is to no great credit to myself, only that you – and through you – others may better understand what is much spoken of, the later deeds of Freydis in Vinland. Though these were evil beyond all reckoning, it would be unjust not to grant that she had more of her mighty father in her than any of her lawfully begotten three brothers, and that she was of high temper, fearless and strong in energy of heart – no less so than her father. But some would wish she did not use such reckless oaths and rude words in her speech. Yet, unlike many who swear 'by Thor' or 'by Christ', the one's 'Hammer' or the other's 'Blood', Freydis used oaths which indeed expressed her boldness in love or, if it came to it, in fighting, while others who use the same oaths as Freydis, do so because – unlike Freydis – they scarcely know their meaning, yet the brains are so thick they can utter nothing else.

But though she was to call me a 'breakfaith', I did not accompany Freydis to Vinland, and I am glad I did not. And if she laid it about that I got from her something for nothing, yet I am confident that the 'nothing', which she had from me twice that day in those three hours, beginning that noon, was yet a deal more in good measure, as one measures water or wine, than the nothing that the feeble Thorulf gave.

Yet I must own that Thorulf was a craftsman with his hands – a good wright – and had he not made a new keel for Thorwald's ship, neither he nor I would have made such payments to Freydis.

Yes, she spread it abroad that I was a 'cry-off', but I am glad that I did cry off. For it was then that Gudrid, who must have known my quandary, pleaded with Leif, her brother-in-law by her first husband, on my behalf.

She put it to him that, since the Vinland quest had failed, at least I should be given land in Greenland, as a token for all I had done for his family: 'He was on your side, Leif, in the case at law against Bjarni Heriolfsson and old Heriolf; he served your elder brother, Thorwald, in Vinland, as best he could, and was first to see his head, when it was hanging in a net of hair, and swinging in the wind at the end of a thew from the down-slanted limb of a cross, and buried it afresh. Our Ingolf served your younger brother, Thorstein, again as best he could, when Thorstein starved and died in that terrible winter of illnesses and ghosts at Sandness in the West Settlement.'

And Gudrid also spoke up for herself:

'Your great father, Leif Eiriksson, before his death gave his house, Sandness, in the West Settlement, to Thorstein.

'I am Thorstein's widow still, and though I am now married again, but to your friend, Karlsefni, I ask you to seal that house and land as mine, and my husband's, through my first husband.'

Leif, looked up to by everyone as the most upright and just man in Greenland, could not but agree to Gudrid Thorbjörnsdottir's pleading – and she had reminded him of what her father had done for his father. Further, she won from Leif the gift to me of the house and land next to Sandness in the West Settlement.

In all this, apart from pleading for me in law and justice, Gudrid, I believe, was striving to keep me near her, and away from the reach of Freydis.

So it came about that within seven weeks of our return to Brattahlid, Karlsefni, with Gudrid and Snorri, and myself, set forth from Eiriks-fjord to the West Settlement.

14

FREYDIS IN VINLAND; A PARTING

Since my mother had died at my birth, and my father, after bringing me to Greenland as a young child, had left me and returned to Iceland, never to know me again, and I had therefore been reared in the houses of others, it was a great happiness to be at last rewarded with a home of my own. For, as a child, I had at first been with Heriolf, that good old man, and his son Bjarni at Heriolfsness. Later I had lived at Brattahlid, where I had been so overborne by the wills of the members of the greatest family in the land that my friendship with those at Heriolfsness had been ended – a breach, stemming from the case in law at the Great Thing at Gardur. The ending of that friendship troubles my soul still. I owed loyalty to both sides, and whatever I did would have been a wrong to the one side or the other. But, acting as I did brought me the dearest of rewards in Sandness in due course.

But I had worked well and long for those at Brattahlid, so it was right that I should be given at last this house and land, next to Sandness, in the West Settlement. This was one of the houses whose owner, wife and children had died in that winter of the illnesses and ghosts which I have told you about and which I can never forget.

And I knew I owed this home to my good lady, Gudrid, more than any other, and thank her with all my heart. For she had persuaded Leif, her brother-in-law by her first husband, that this was my right and due. And I think she kept in her soul the memory of three nights.

Karlsefni, I felt, was not so eager to have me as his next neighbour.

But though not the leader, I had done almost as well as he in Vinland. And not only at the Stream Island. Born of this great and wealthy line back in Iceland and with the hair like burnt honey, yellowish eyes like a hawk's, and his slanting forehead, Karlsefni was now inclined to be touchy since his venture to Vinland had failed. His tawny skin became yellower still. He would fall out with Gudrid, and blame her for his feeling ill, for the food she put before him, for making me his neighbour. She was not to blame. The truth was that my body had been better able to drink the bad water in Vinland than his. Besides, I took care not to drink the cow's milk there, whereas he had drained a draught of it every day shortly before noon. This led to the yellowing of his skin, a laziness in his walking, and of his thinking too, a blocking of his bowels, and a surliness of temper.

Besides, I lived a virtuous life alone, even though the bondsmen on my land had wives and daughters. It was a sweet thing to be near Gudrid and watch the growth of Snorri, the child.

My house, like Sandness itself, overlooked Lysafjord. And while Karlsefni busied himself with Sandness, getting men to add two more rooms on the easterly side, the side of the property nearest mine, so that the room in which Thorstein the Black and his wife, Grimhilda, had so groaned and sickened, had now a hole in its wall to lead into more rooms, I meanwhile often thought of the room of the three nights, of which Manly-Stuff knew nothing, in Sandness, and of the illnesses, the fear, the ghosts, and the jokes of that winter and also of the shining hoard of love that lay in the black earth of that winter, and which was shown at last.

And I saw the changes.

A church had now been built by the north side of the burial ground. The dark side of the yard, ever in shade, lay between the church and the fjord. On its sunny side, this churchyard girdled within its wall the hundred or more graves which I had seen as a bristling thicket of poles after the illnesses. The poles had all been pulled up, except for three or four which stood high; but, if you walked in the long grass a month after midsummer, you would find the stumps of other poles which had broken off nearly a knee's height above the ground but which would be overtopped by the highest grass of the year.

There was now a house for the priest of the church on the very ground I remembered as the god Thor's holy enclosure or grove. The hut of the god had been pulled down, his idol burnt on a bonfire, his fence uprooted. The priest's house was a square house on mown land, and it had a flat roof. The people had been made to build the house by Leif himself, though that greatest of men lived six days' rowing distance away.

Our people had also been ordered to find a woman who would keep

the house and cook meals for the priest. They sought out the ugliest
woman they could. She was born a Christian, and had been brought,
against her will, from Ireland. Her name was Bridget, I believe.
Priests were not supposed to marry, but they could take a concubine,
as it was called, if their flesh was so strong they could not do without.
By choosing ugly Bridget – which we changed to Birgit – our people
trusted to keep their priest pure and not too strong. Birgit was squint-
eyed.

The young priest now was a Sera Jon, and he was said to be better
than the Sera Tomas before him. Jon and Tomas are both outlandish
names – Hebrew names like the name Jesus or Hesus, who is the second
god of the three gods of the new faith. But we must get used to
these names since, as Eirik Thorwaldsson would have said we have
broken truth with our own god Thor. For Thor's idol, who had
thudded and rattled on the walls of his hut in that winter, had been
burnt. And the naughty lad who had leapt over the fence to grab and
hurl Gurdar's knuckle-bones and other bits had skipped through the
smoke and flying sparks of the burning idol, hand-in-hand with his
latest lass – or so I was told, for I had been in Vinland at the burning of
Thor.

All three gods of the new faith are from that far-off land in the
south where the weather is always hot and the dark-skinned folk are
not like ours in Greenland. Some of our people say that those folk are
dark as the skraelings in Vinland, but have longer noses and are very
shrewd in the making of money. I know not as to that, but I will say
that our young Sera Jon was a good man, living with the ugly Bridget,
or Birgit, in the house built for him, saying his mass, and trying to learn
his Latin. He was a Greenlander, so he had to unlearn much as well as
learn much. It would not greatly surprise me either if the daring lad,
who leapt through the sparks at the burning of Thor, were called one
day to be a priest too – if he foreswore the girls among whom he was a
great favourite.

Gudrid, the good and dear woman, was now, despite her upbringing,
for her foster-mother in Iceland was heathen and had taught her the
spells of the Spirit-Songs or Ward-Locks – enabling her to see into the
future, because of what the dead people told her – was now indeed a
strong Christian. She believed and understood the new faith in such a
way that others, by watching her, understood better this puzzling
thing of three gods who were not three gods but only one, and yet not
one but three. And all three of them were men gods, no woman among

them as with our Freya. Or, if they did not understand, yet they wanted to understand for the sake of Gudrid. Fair and comely in person, she seemed yet fairer and more beautiful still from all her deeds. Her fair deeds, she said, came from believing as she did. She knew that Sera Jon was not very clever but, when he saw her listening to his Latin mass with such zeal, he wanted to better his Latin. A good young man he was, but dull.

She was faithful to Thorfinn Karlsefni, of the tawny skin, yellowish eyes and slanting forehead, and grew fond of him, though I believe she never had the longing and craving for Karlsefni's body, nor for the shuddering storm of the sweetest wine from his body's root, which she had craved from Thorstein Eiriksson – until he had weakened. Nor for someone else's. Still she bore Karlsefni a son, and a daughter too, before he died and left her a widow for the second time. Those births and the death all happened after she left Greenland for ever, to go back to the land of her own birth, Iceland.

The daring Gudrid, before she left us, put into the mind of Sera Jon, the priest, the thought for a good custom which no other land, outside Greenland, has to this day, I believe.

It came about when Sera Jon left his house at about noon and walked to Sandness. He said to Gudrid: 'Though I am a priest and you but one of the laity and only a woman at that, yet nevertheless you might be able to help.'

It appeared he was troubled in mind, so much that it kept him awake, despite having to say mass early even on the coldest mornings, about the fate of those who had died baptized, and those who had died unbaptized, and who lay mixed, baptized by unbaptized, side by side, in the ground of his church – 'ever since the winter of the great illnesses'. He understood she had been there at that time.

'When the lord comes again,' he said, 'how shall he – this guardian of loaves – tell the man, or the woman, or the child, from the ones who died still believing in Thor? And how shall the dead man tell him, "But I did have the baptism, the water?" For where is his proof? Or hers even? I baptize all of you people now, but in my graveyard there are those who believed in Thor, those who believed in the Lord but were not baptized, for you had no priest living with you then, those who believed in the Lord and had been baptized, those who believed in both, those who believed in neither.

'How shall they, when they rise in their flesh again, be able to say, "Look, I was baptized, but this man next to me, was not? He swore to

Thor even while dying. I am the one to go up to the heaven; he is the one to go down there into hell?"'

Gudrid, in her lovely winning way, smiled at this, and said she thought Sera Jon had 'rather come to her at this hour for some good food and drink'. As I had indeed come too. 'If I can't answer your grave question' – and here she smiled again – 'I can at least do better for the living and hungry body of Sera Jon than he is likely to have set before him by the good Bridget – or Birgit is it? – who keeps house for him.' Would he not put that to the test?

The crafty young priest, without either owning or yielding that a good meal was stronger in his mind than the fate of those in his churchyard, sat down, patted Snorri on the head, and asked me some silly things about Vinland. He did not heed much the answers. His mind was rather on the trencher of food before him than on those in his graveyard, or on Vinland. Sera Jon, alone of the five of us, had not been to Vinland, and it was perhaps more on the wretched meal, cooked by his Irish slut, that he had missed, and the fine one before him, that he thought, rather than what he was told about Thorwald Eiriksson's head in its basket of fibres, twisting in the Vinland breeze. Karlsefni himself, our leader in Vinland, of the tawny eyes and yellowish face, said little. He had on his mind the thought that his father, Thord Horsehead, had, as he had just heard, died in Reyniness in Iceland. Thord was a very rich man, one of the three or four greatest in the north of Iceland.

Then Gudrid said:

'Let each one who dies a Christian here have a stone on his grave. And let his name be cut in the stone, and let a rune be cut in the stone below the name, which will tell that the man or child below was a Christian, such as "Here dwells Vigdis daughter of Magnus. Hesus gladden her soul."'

Sera Jon, who had rightly enjoyed the good cooking of Gudrid, said:

'But will our Lord, an Hebrew man, be able to read our runes? Besides, Gudrid Thorbjörnsdottir, it may be pitch black and there will be such a rumble and jumble of stones, with thunder in the sky, when all the dead in Greenland suddenly heave up all the earth that is massed on top of them, that the lord will surely not be able to tell which stone belonged to which man. So he may take a heathen up to heaven with him, leaving a baptized man to go down into the earth again, but deeper still – into hell. And with this thunder going on, he

174

would not hear when the Christian shouts, "I am the man you ought to take, not him."'

Gudrid laughed, and told Sera Jon he need have no fear, but she offered him a plan which he was free to have if he liked it. The plan was that each baptized person in Sandness should take with him into the grave a little wooden cross. So that when the dreadful time came, and all the earth was heaved off the graves in Sera Jon's churchyard, the man could reach for his little wooden cross with his hand, and spring up, and wave this token, howsoever the headstones were toppled and jumbled.

The good Sera Jon was pleased, and said this was 'a good plan'. So ever since the baptized dead in Sandness have gone into the earth each with his – or her – little wooden cross. And from Sandness the custom has spread into other parts of Greenland, but nowhere outside our country, so far as I know.

This was Gudrid's plan to put at rest Sera Jon's mind after he had eaten well of the fine meal she had prepared.

But, mark you, my son, when a man is caught in a hurry, he may grope around for his breeches before he looks around for a little wand or something to hold up aloft in his hand. He may even want to draw on his skin before he searches for his breeches. Sera Jon did not laugh at my joke when I said a man would need to remember to draw skin and breeches over his bones, and in the right order. But Gudrid looked at me with the light in her eyes. She foresaw that, in or out of the flesh, we would come together that day.

This is a good Greenland custom owing to Gudrid, but in truth she was trying to put at rest the mind of the young man, Jon, who liked being called Sera Jon, because he was a priest. He thought he knew more, or could think better, than all the lay people, but he was wrong.

In later years I played chess with Jon and partook of the boiled fish-meal and milk curds that his ugly woman Birgit made for us when we were settled for a game. I used to beat Sera Jon at chess. After some years the nasty food made him ill-tempered every time he was beaten at a game of chess.

It was not many weeks after this meal that Gudrid Thorbjörnsdottir and her husband, Karlsefni Thordsson, with the child Snorri, made their farewells to Sandness. For, a year after the death of her husband, Thord Horsehead, Karlsefni's mother, Thorunn, at Reyniness in north Iceland, wished her son to return to look after the great estate. The widow would 'welcome her daughter-in-law as though she were her own daughter'. She had heard she 'had a grandson she had not seen'. Thorunn had found all the lands and farms her husband had owned beyond her strength to look after. 'Your wife was born in Iceland, and she should return to her home and help me', were the words brought to Karlsefni. Gudrid was sorrowful, but she had known the Little Knowing One spoke the truth when she said, 'Far back in Iceland your later lines lie.'

Gudrid wished to see me wedded before she left Greenland. My bride had the full blessing of Gudrid. Sandness was then made over to us as a gift. Your mother became the dearest of women. You, my son, were born last. Since your mother's death, I have reared my children as best I could. Before you leave me for ever with your wife, whom you have chosen well, I want to tell you three more matters: what has been said about Freydis; what I have heard has become of Gudrid; and why I believe you are right to leave Greenland for ever.

Freydis, over the years, had found out all she could about Vinland with the design of faring there herself, and bringing back a great cargo of timber to add to her wealth.

She had purchased a ship of her own, and when the brothers, Helgi and Finnbogi, Icelanders, came to Greenland, she bargained with them that their ship and hers, with thirty men in each ship – besides any women they wished to carry – would sail to Vinland to fetch timber to sell. The profits would be shared, half and half, between Freydis and the brothers. They would be fair shares between them. And Freydis on the one hand, and the brothers on the other, swore to be true to the deal; and they shook hands on this.

Then Freydis went to her brother Leif. She said she was resolved to go to Vinland, and would he not sell her his houses?

Leif, who had it ever in mind that the day would come when he himself would return to Vinland, said: 'I will lend you my houses there, but I will neither give them nor sell them.'

Freydis accepted this. But Freydis broke an oath straightway in that she hid in her ship five other men over and above the agreed thirty, dishonouring the deal she had struck with the brothers, even though hers was the smaller of the two ships. These other five were hidden under the starboards, and did not show themselves until they had cleared Lysafjord and were within sight of Helluland.

But I knew of this when the ship which belonged to Freydis, and the ship of Helgi and Finnbogi, put into the Lysafjord in the West Settlement for the taking on of water and stockfish and the sharpening of weapons. Freydis sought me out and urged me to go, saying that the man Thorulf though one of her party meant little to her; moreover she would see to it that, thanks to her cunning, I would come back with far more wealth than I could ever have hoped for. And she confided that she had five men on her ship above what was agreed in her deal with Helgi and Finnbogi; if I would make the sixth I should never regret it – and not only for the wealth I would achieve: I would enjoy her body whenever I wished – and she wished – while we were away from Greenland. But I held firm to my refusal to go, but said I would not betray her ill faith to Helgi and Finnbogi over the five men she had over and beyond her deal with them.

The two ships sailed in convoy, that of Freydis's leading. But because the brothers' ship was the larger, it carried the bigger sail, and it reached Vinland twelve hours the sooner. Helgi and Finnbogi had their men move up all their gear and clothing into Leif's houses as soon as they made landfall.

Then Freydis's ship touches shore. In a furious mood, she says to Helgi and Finnbogi: 'These are my brother Leif's houses. It is to me that he lends them. He said nothing about a Helgi or a Finnbogi or their men having use of them. Helgi and Finnbogi will shift their gear now, so that we can move in.' Then she pointed to the buildings put up by Gamlason: 'Helgi and Finnbogi will shift their gear into there – or elsewhere if it pleases them. Or my men will do the shifting of it for them – or worse.' And the brothers saw that Freydis had five more men backing her than they had, and after some muttering about holding true to a deal, they shifted their gear to the long hut, some way off, reared by Gamlason.

Freydis set her party forthwith to enlarging the clearing. With Karlsefni and Gamlason I had seen many trees felled, and then we had left much brushwood by the lake. It was a warm and lovely autumn, with mist in the mornings. And the brothers, not to be thought either laggards or trespassers, set their men to axe down the trees at another edge of the clearing, three stones' throws away. Feelings were bad between the two parties. The brothers' men were mainly Icelanders.

But Freydis, I own, had a loftiness of mood. When the skraelings attacked – early one morning they came, skulking in the mist from around the lake – her men, with their axes in their hands, fled. But one of her men, hit by a skraeling stone arrow, lay at her feet. Then Freydis drew the blade from the sheath by the dead man's sheath. As the skraelings neared, she pulled open her bodice to show her paps which were now swollen because she was pregnant. Slapping the blade across her paps, with her eyes blazing, and her red hair, with its black locks all disordered, she advanced on the skraelings, calling out to them in her own tongue: 'Dastards! I am a woman, as you see. But if you fight me, it is you who will be the worse off.'

And it is a truth that the skraelings ran away, terrified by the sight. This was not good for Helgi and Finnbogi, though. The skraelings, frightened by Freydis, bent their attack onto the brothers' party at the other edge of the clearing where they killed some.

If that must be set down as a credit to a woman of lofty mood, worthy of her father, her later behaviour was wicked almost beyond belief.

When winter began, the brothers came to Freydis. They said: 'Whether or not you are keeping to your side of the bargain, yet we are all together in this land. It would be better if both sides make the best of our fate.'

Freydis said she fully agreed as to this. And so for the start of that winter the brothers' men came over from their quarters in Gamlason's in the evenings, to play games at Leif's houses. All went well at first. There was chess, there were games bringing laughter, stories were told, and there was no quarrelling about the women in either party. There was shared eating on what the land gave and what was left of the ale that had been brought was fairly rationed.

All went well until Freydis, seeking cause for a quarrel, devised a game which she knew well would lead to anger and bitterness among the men of the two sides who had not brought women into Vinland – and this applied to most of the men by far.

One evening, without asking leave of Thorulf or anyone else, she grabbed a charred stick from the fire, and, with this stick, she drew a picture of a woman all unclothed, on the leaf of the door. To many it resembled herself when naked – with its large breasts and big haunches. When she had drawn this figure on the door, she drove a nail through the charred end of the stick and said that the game was that the men should blindfold their eyes in turn and try to pin the stick where it was most proper it should go.

There was laughter at first when one man pinned the stick into the ear of the picture, and another onto its shoulder, but the game soon led afresh into the bitterness and change of blows Freydis had meant that it should. After that the two parties kept apart in the evenings of that winter.

Having succeeded in this, on a night late in that winter, Freydis rose from her bed, which she shared with Thorulf, and where he stayed sleeping, and went barefoot towards the quarters of Helgi and Finnbogi. On the way, and nearly there, she met Helgi who had left his quarters to go outside to make water, leaving the door of the building unlatched.

Helgi said: 'It is a pity, Freydis, that our two selves and our parties likewise should be at loggerheads. It would please me if this were to end, and we should work together in friendly manner, at least until we reach Greenland and the end of our voyage.'

Freydis said she would agree to this, but only if he and Finnbogi would be content to change their ship for hers: 'For yours is the bigger ship, and mine the smaller, and yet, as you see, my men have struck down the larger number of trees to load and carry back to Greenland.'

Helgi replied that this was no wonder since, though it was against their deal, she had the more men with her for striking down trees.

'Be that as it may,' said Freydis, 'but only agree as to this exchange of ships and there need be no more disputes between us while we are here.'

Helgi said that for his part he would be willing to do this, if it would bring peace, but he would first have to gain the agreement of his brother, Finnbogi. He said he would broach the matter with Finnbogi in the morning.

Freydis said the matter so rankled with her that it could not wait till then. Nevertheless, Helgi refused to wake Finnbogi there and then, but he would leave their door unlatched and, if she cared to call tomorrow evening, she would have the reply of Finnbogi as well as of himself as to the matter of the exchange.

Freydis returned to her own bed, and woke up Thorulf with the coldness of her feet, and the dampness of the dew on her dress. Thorulf asked the reason for the coldness and damp. Freydis replied:

'If I had a man who was known to have enough pluck to have a care for his wife, Helgi would not have dared to have treated me as he has done. But he knows Thorulf to be faint-hearted enough not to avenge insults.'

And she told Thorulf that she had risen from her bed to rouse Helgi. She had called him to follow her without doors, and had sought with even and friendly words to arrange a deal – the brothers' ship for hers: 'We have the smaller ship but the bigger lading. But Helgi became angry and, not content with vile insults, he called his brother and they handled me roughly. If I woke you because I am wet with dew it is because Helgi and Finnbogi flung me to the ground while you lay sleeping. And that is why my dress is damp.

'I must suffer this treatment, I suppose, because Thorulf is a weak coward, but if he were a man, he would kill both Helgi and Finnbogi.' And she gave Thorulf no peace from her taunts until at last he yielded in agreeing to do the worst deed ever done at the urging of a woman.

In the morning, swearing them all to secrecy, Freydis told her party that she had overheard that Helgi and Finnbogi were plotting the deaths of them all. But if they gave her the handling of the matter, 'we will get in first'. None would blame them for forestalling murderers; for she'd see to that: 'Even my brother, Leif, would say we were in the right.'

At two hours and a half after the middle of the night, on the following night, when grown men are at their weakest, and give themselves over to sleep and their trust to the watch of angels to guard them, Freydis and all the men of her party – these under fear of being murdered themselves – broke into the quarters of their enemies, and – for they were more in number – either killed or bound all who lay on their beds. Then those who were bound, one after the other, were led out of the door, and struck down with an axe. Only the women were left alive; for Freydis's men would not touch them.

But Freydis called out, 'Fools! What will these six women do without men? It was they who put up their men to murder you. If you weaken, they will use their wiles to share your beds, and from thence go back with you in our ships to Greenland. And there they will betray what you have done.'

And she seized an axe from a man by the door. The six women were not bound, but they were forced out by men who, holding their wrists behind their backs, thrust them forward with their knees. As they were forced through the door one after the other of the six women were struck on the neck by Freydis, with all her might, with the borrowed axe.

And as soon as the season was fit for sailing, Freydis took the bigger ship, and some of her companions the lesser. They loaded both ships with the timber felled by her own men and by the brothers' and, reaching Greenland, sold the timber for a huge price. And the story she had put about in Greenland was this: that Helgi and Finnbogi and their followers, men and women, were so pleased with all that they saw in Vinland, that they had decided to settle there.

Though that was the story to be told in Greenland, under threats from the good lady Freydis of harm befalling anyone who breathed a word otherwise, nevertheless other rumours spread. Words went about of happenings in Vinland other than those reported. These words and whispers came at last to Leif's ear.

He was a good and upright man who had brought the new religion to our land, and he and his mother between them might still be said to be the most devout in that religion. But because he knew, as much or more than any, about the black-heartedness of his sister, he was determined to get at the truth.

He had three of the men who had been to Vinland with Freydis, and one of those was Thorulf himself, seized. And suddenly. And on the same day. Each of the three was kept from speaking to the others; each was far enough apart from the others in the outhouses of Brattahlid. If one, or the other, or a third cried out he could not be heard by the other two.

Leif had taught his men some devices for plucking out the truth – devices which, as Leif knew, were practised in England and Denmark by wicked men – devices called torture. Torture is the putting on a villain of pains which are at first mild but which become worse and worse, with the threat of still worse to come – far worse – and still worse – if he still holds back the whole truth; or the villain may learn that the pains may ease, or even stop, and he may have some water, if he tells. So little by little Thorulf and the two others told the just Leif the truth of what had become of Helgi and Finnbogi, and their men and six women, in Vinland. And the stories of the three men tallied in the main, though Thorulf had more to tell than the others, though he was not by nature a talkative man. And the stories agreed with what had been whispered about earlier.

And it was revealed that of the brothers' party, three had escaped being struck down. An oldish man, Eyvind – though whose son he was I shall not say so as not to bring shame to his kin – and a young and very handsome youth, Gils Ketilsson, had been in the habit of meeting together in the thicket above Gamlason's where Eyvind made some kind of love to the other for a reward promised to Gils. From this thicket they beheld what happened to their fellows and stayed hidden.

When all their companions were led out to be axed one by one, Gunnlaug the Fleet, a great runner, though with his wrists still bound behind him, and naked, had broken free. He had fled – running as he had never run before – into the wilderness.

How long these three lived, and how they died in the land of the skraelings, no one may know.

Thjodhild was now so old and frail that she had herself carried to her church for mass only on Sundays and Holy Days. A serving-woman, sitting by the old lady's bed in Brattahlid, had heard sharp and terrible screams from the outhouses, where the three were being put to the pain, and had herself cried out, 'O, what is that?' Thjodhild, in the more than half-doze of her old age, had replied: 'I hear the blissful singing of the angels. Soon, I hope to see them with my own eyes before the stool of God.'

Leif, having found out the truth, was annoyed beyond all measure. Not without reason: Helgi and Finnbogi were Icelanders, highly respected in that land. Most of their thirty men, and four of their women, were Icelanders too. If the true story of what happened in Vinland got back to Iceland, it would bring great blame upon all in Greenland, and most to Leif himself, since his father was also the father of Freydis. Friends or foster-brothers of the dead might well come over to Greenland to avenge them. And so they did, and there was much bloodshed for many years in Greenland because of the deed of Freydis. It acted to the great disadvantage of Greenland's trade with Iceland and, beyond Iceland, with Norway.

Nevertheless, Leif did nothing to harm Freydis, except to refuse any further annual allowance of money. But of her brother's money, Freydis now had no great need. Such a rich journey to Vinland she had had with her fine haul of timber in two ships which she had sold with abundant profit. But no one had anything good to say about her again.

Thorulf had parted from her and lived in a mean dwelling on his own, as he had done before Freydis had taken him up. He was no longer a wright working with others; for he now had a limp and two fingers were missing on the left hand. This had come about in the outhouse at Brattahlid when he had been put to the pains. Yet he still had some skill and, seated, he would shape bowls out of soft stone for a living, or he would carve little boats out of wood which men would give to their children when Yuletide came round.

I wonder how it came about that of Eirik Thorwaldsson's children – three sons by one mother, a daughter by another – it was the daughter, who had most of the father in her, who brought upon the memory of the founder of Greenland an ill-repute.

If Freydis was of the worst of women, then Gudrid was of the best. As women's bodies may differ, so may their souls. Gudrid was fair in body and soul. From the age of fifteen or sixteen, when, as a girl, she came into Greenland, all men wondered at her, yet they did not lust to have her merely for the short time it takes to beget a child. But the long upslanting grey eyes of Gudrid checked the desire of men even as it was roused by the shape of her body, so that they raised their own eyes to hers. She drew all men's eyes. They gazed at her with wonder. Yet there was that in her soul which spoke through her eyes into the souls of men through their eyes, and her soul said: 'I must want more than your body, though I want that, or I want none of you.'

And when men raised their eyes to meet hers, they knew that Gudrid had the gift of the hind sight and of the far sight. She was kindly and winning to those who were with her but she also saw, even as she looked at you, those who were far away – those long dead or those not yet born. Thus she alone could sing those Spirit-Songs or Ward-Locks at Thorkel's which freed the Little Knowing One to foretell the fate of that winter and of the next year; and freed her to foretell what would be the fate of Gudrid herself. It was through this gift of Gudrid that I and the wife of Thorstein the Black, Grimhilda, saw what she herself was seeing: the ghosts of all the dead people, in the winter of that illness, in the Lysafjord. It was by means of this gift that she saw the woman in Vinland, with the long hair bound in a headband – the woman who said her name was 'Gudrid' and heard her saying, 'Come and sit beside me here', thus saving the life of Gudrid and her son, Snorri, and all who will come after them.

And if men were not held by the soundless speech of Gudrid's eyes, there was no withstanding her voice which was low and sweeter than any other woman's, save when a dead person was speaking through her, so that all who heard her were spellbound.

Gudrid's body and soul became so matched, and each was so much a friend of the other, that they were one. It was this that warded her, keeping her whole through all the threats of harm to life and limb in Vinland.

To have had three nights with Gudrid after the death of Thorstein Eiriksson and the foiling of Thorstein the Black is reward enough for a man's journey on this earth.

Not that Freydis, for all her wicked acts, should be thought of other than as a woman worthy of some respect. There was little enough of sweetness in this daughter of the founder of your land, but she had a stouter heart, and was more fearless in mood, than many a man.

She was a little above the usual height of women, somewhat broad of face, and broad of shoulder. She had scant kindness in her heart. Except when it suited her to deceive with smooth speech, she said what was in her mind. She would shout out foul words and swear unseemly oaths with a freedom few men could equal. Many men were afraid of affronting her, for she would lay traps to have them wounded in their privy parts to avenge herself of an insult.

Yet, when it was to her purpose, she could draw men to her embraces as no other woman could. When she was in the mind for that, men looked at her body rather than her face, and of this she was aware, for this was intended on her part, and the nearer a man came the more helpless he was to govern his lust. It was as though her power to rouse lust in men – whether to satisfy her own hunger, which at times was greedy beyond measure, or to have men under her hold so as to get her own will through them – raised in Freydis a kind of sweet-smelling sweat which drew to her any man she chose to serve her, whether young or old, good or bad, Christian or heathen, Greenlander or outlander. Self-seeking and cruel as she was, and atrocious her deeds, yet there was a kind of handsomeness in Freydis, which she shared with her father. Odd it is, but it may be said that this handsomeness in Eirik Thorwaldsson and Freydis Eiriksdottir was less clearly there for men to see in her three lawfully-begotten brothers.

The good Thorwald, the eldest, was better fitted, with his short sight, his stooped shoulders and the scant hair on his head to have become a priest or a scholar than to succeed in Vinland. Thorstein, the youngest, a tall and most promising man, lost all his strength and manliness in his marriage-bed with Gudrid. Leif, the middle brother, for all his luck, his tallness and fairness of body, his yellow hair and beard, and his uprightness and Christian firmness of rule, was more than somewhat tightfisted and cold. It may be thought that he had too much of his mother in him.

Of that mother, I say it was wrong of her to refuse to share her bed with her husband at the bidding of priests because he stayed heathen. It was on this account, it could be said, that he sought out the woman who gave him happiness and by whom he had a daughter. Indeed, some might thereby hold Thjodhild to blame for the wicked deeds of that daughter.

I have told how Thjodhild from her bed thought that the cries of men being put to the pains in the outhouses were the songs of angels. It was, in this belief the old lady died. But she built the first Christian church in all Greenland.

When the darling Gudrid left Greenland for ever, with her husband Thorfinn Karlsefni, and her child, Snorri, they settled in Reyniness, in the north of Iceland, where Karlsefni's father, Thord, nicknamed 'Horsehead', had been a very great and rich man, owning much land in his own name, while many other farmers held their land from him.

But as it turned out, the good widow, Karlsefni's mother, Thorunn, didn't take to her daughter-in-law at first. The foolish woman called to mind Gudrid's father, Thorbjörn Vifilsson, who had been forced to sell up his land when he fell on unlucky days, and fared to Greenland. She told her son, soon after Karlsefni and Gudrid had reached Reyniness, that his wife was no fair match for him, in family or wealth. Many mothers no doubt say this of their sons' wives with or without justice. In this case, without justice. Gudrid was not only the fairest of women, she excelled in all the arts of the housewife. She had a sweet temper, and a beautiful voice. Thorunn indeed refused to share house with them soon, and moved out to another, one of the many other properties that had belonged to her husband. But so glowing were all the accounts from all her new neighbours of Gudrid's goodness, that after that one winter apart from her son, Thorunn returned to Reyniness and lived very happily there until she died. Karlsefni had brought with him a piece of a kind of timber which only grows in Vinland. Thorunn used to show this piece of wood to all the old women who called in to see her, to boast of her son having been into far lands. After her death, for so I have heard, her son bought more lands, neighbouring on Reyniness, including the property at Glaumby which he then made his own home. He was much looked up to in Iceland as a man who had been in Vinland.

Karlsefni and Gudrid had a son, Thorbjörn, named after Gudrid's father, beside a daughter, Hallfrid. Snorri, I hear, born in Vinland, grew up a good and wise man. He is married, and has a son. This son, we hear, is so learned and wise that he was chosen to be a priest and, though so young, has been made a bishop in Iceland, no less. Whether of Skalholt or Holar I have forgotten, but more likely Skalholt than Holar for that is nearer to their part of Iceland.

And I have heard, and I do believe, that after Karlsefni's death, the glorious and good lady, Gudrid, set out for a journey to Rome where the most important of all the bishops lives. There are bishops in Bremen, and in Lund in Sweden, and in Nidaros in Norway – and the one in Nidaros now looks after all of us here in Greenland, for we are in his archsee, as they say – and there are two bishops in Iceland, of course, and eleven, I am told, in England, but the one in Rome is the biggest bishop of all. So all the most pious and holy people want to go to Rome, if they can, to look at this special bishop. It is a long way from Iceland to Rome. I hear too that when she returned from Rome to Iceland, she used much of the wealth left to her by her husband to found a convent of very good and worthy nuns. Then she left Glaumby, a fine and comfortable house in a large estate, to bide in a bare cell hard by the nunnery she had founded. There she lives, keeps strict fasts, hears mass daily, confesses often, and devotes the rest of her waking hours to holy reading, to heavenly contemplation and prayer. In Gudrid's prayers I trust that Ingolf has a place, for in that place in her prayers lies his greatest help and hope.

Since Gudrid's going from Greenland, I have lived in the West Settlement in this house on the Lysafjord. My house is next to that in which I passed that winter of illnesses and ghosts. After the sailing out of the Lysafjord of Gudrid and Snorri, with Karlsefni, on their way to the East Settlement, from whence they were to fare to Iceland, never to return to Greenland, and I had said my last farewell to Gudrid in the flesh, I went into that house of that winter, and into the room of that house where there was the bed of the three nights. I found in that room three black and gleaming stones which Karlsefni had dug from the ground in Stream Island in Vinland. I took two of these to my own hearth, and put them on the fire. With little or no smoke, they burned hotly, longer and more brightly than any charcoal. Far better than the logs from Vinland, or the driftwood from our fjords, or the dung from our cattle, would be these black gleaming stones from Stream Island for the warming of our bodies in the winters of Greenland, or the cooking of our food.

Since that day, my son, you have been born, and reared and grown tall. And are now married. Seven years ago your mother died. I am now failing in strength. You are right to take yourself and your wife from Greenland and to settle elsewhere for the good of yourselves and the luck of your children, and the well-being of your children's children. But there is no hope of settlement yet in Vinland for all its wealth, on account of the swarming numbers of the skraelings there and their unspeakable wickedness. Acknowledging neither Thor, who would refuse such swarthy and ugly worshippers, nor yet the second of the three-in-one gods of our new faith – in whom Gudrid has helped

me to believe because of her goodness– those miserable folk surely go
into that hell that the new faith tells of. For they surpass in the skill of
weapons, and craft of malice, the skraelings in our own Greenland,
who year by year make our life harder here.

If you should go to Iceland and see Gudrid, and her son Snorri, tell
them they are in my thoughts. . . .

AFTERWORD

FROM THE MEMORIALS
OF INGOLF MORDSSON,
DESCENDANT

Anno Christi 1410

I am that Ingolf son of Mord son of Ingolf the Learned of Sauð arkrokur in the northern deal of Iceland. Ingolf the Learned was the son of Brand the Unjust who was the son of Pál Andreisson. Andrei had flitted to Sauð arkrokur after trouble with Snorri over the farm further north in Siglufjord. Andrei was the son of Tomas who was the son of Olav the Lawman who while alive had withstood Snorri in Siglufjord. Olav was the son of Ingolf Clubfoot who was the son of Harald who was the son of Ingolf the Good. Ingolf the Good was the son of Thorwald the Wise. But when this Thorwald slew Thorgeir from the West Firths, and suffered therefore the forfeiture of the best third of his land, he was afterwards known as Thorwald Unwise.

Thorwald, who lost much land at the suit in law of the kin of Thorgeir, was the son of that Magnus Ingolfsson who wedded Hallfrith. Now Hallfrith claimed descent from Gudrid Thorbjörnsdottir, wife of that Thorfinn surnamed Karlsefni when he came to settle at Glaumby. This Gudrid Thorbjörnsdottir being the same Gudrid Thorbjörnsdottir who had fared far into the lands of Greenland and Vinland in her youth. She had been wife to Thorstein son of Eirik the Red before her match with Karlsefni. Widowed for the second time, she made a pilgrimage to Rome and returning to Iceland built the nunnery for eleven nuns which nunnery still stands at Stad in Reyniness.

In Vinland Gudrid had given birth to Snorri who was the father of Brand who became, while yet a young man, bishop not as some

---

*What follows is a near literal translation of MS. S Ing M1. See Preface.

191

wrongly say of Holar, but of Skalholt. But Snorri had another son, by name Ingolf. Of him was descended this Hallfrith who was wedded to Magnus.

Magnus, who wedded Hallfrith, was the son of Ingolf the Lawman. Now Ingolf the Lawman was the son of Heriolf son of Ingolf Brandsson. Brand the Stern had taken his son, then a child, into Greenland and had there left him, himself returning to Iceland after but one winter.

This Heriolf Ingolfsson came into Iceland soon after his father's dying, and then wrote down all that his father had told him of Greenland and also of Vinland. This book, I, Ingolf Mordsson of Sauð arkrokur, have.

And thereto I now add this, for the better understanding by my son's son, and those who come after him.

It is said that Heriolf Ingolfsson was a tall man and a good; and a learned one; of a ready and sharp wit; but for that he was somewhat slothful in his walk, he was sometimes called Heriolf Slow-of-Foot.

Anno Christi 1412

Last month, after the harvest, came a holy day, and thereto the plighting of the troth between my son Olav and Gudrid Gunnarsdottir, reputed to be descended in the line from that Thorfinn son of Thord surnamed Karlsefni, of Reyniness and Glaumby, a family once of great wealth. However that may be, Gunnar is but of moderate wealth and standing himself, but his daughter is a well-built and comely girl, and shall make for my son, Olav, if God wills, a good wife, the more so for she hath a sweet voice and patient temper.

To celebrate this plighting of their troth, I had all my neighbours, and all the near of kin of Gudrid Gunnarsdottir, and all my friends, and thereto all that were passing and who claimed friendship with any of these, into my house to feast after the noon of this same holy day. And it was at this feast that I learned more in the particulars of what has been rumoured about in this part of the country in these last two years.

Among those at my feast there came unbidden, but forsooth they had as their plea that they were house-guests, between their sailings, of my neighbour, Vigfus Jonsson, two Icelander seafarers and a Norwegian skipper, one Arni.

These three had sailed on that ship from Bergen in Norway which in *anno Christi* 1406 had been bound hither, but driven by the mightily

great wind of that year, had passed Iceland and been carried far west-
wards into Greenland, whereto no ship had been for many years
before – that land, it was thought, now almost wholly given over to
the heathen skraeling. So it hath been said. But this was not so, and the
said ship was stayed in a haven of the East Settlement, that haven which
is called Hvalsey, and among Christian people, though but few now,
for nigh unto four years. For these poor people, to have a ship among
them, with many of us Icelanders aboard, and some from Norway too,
was a great happiness. For they had seen few in truth, themselves
excepting, for a great many years. These few and poor felt themselves
quite cast off by both the King of Norway and by the Pope, and they
scarcely knew which was the worse – to be bereft of the food of the
body or the food of the soul. And in that ship from Bergen there was
much that eased their bodies, though in truth the lading of that ship
was designed for us in Iceland and would have come to us, but for that
great wind and heavy sea taking the said ship far astray into Greenland.

Since these three farers by sea had greatly rejoiced themselves with
my ale and the cates at the feast which I had given for my son Olav
and Gudrid Gunnarsdottir, I thought it not wrong to have of them in
exchange for their welcome what they had seen and heard of in
Greenland in those four years: *anno Christi* 1406 to *anno Christi* 1410.
And I did this, minding my own forebears Ingolf and his son, Heriolf,
without whom I would not have been here nor my son Olav either.
Memo. Neither would Gudrid Gunnarsdottir have been here under my
roof for the plighting of her troth to my son Olav if Olav hadn't been.
And neither – yet neither – would these three seafarers – swaggerers
like all their kind, I fear me – have had all this free ale of me if there
had no been plighting.

They said – though I could follow Arni but hardly, whose speech,
though he is the most gifted with reason of the three men, has moved
far from that we speak in Iceland now – that their ship was long
a-mending in Hvalsey in Greenland, for that a side of the ship had been
stove in by a great heavy sea, etc., but that the few men yet living in
Hvalsey gave them good cheer for the ale they had brought, and the
malt, and this paid for their welcome. 'Yet for all that,' they said, 'we
brought back whale bone and walrus bone of Greenland for carrying
and then carving when we left after the four years.'

Memo. They said the West Settlement had quite gone these eighty
years. To my asking where had the people of that settlement gone,
they said that one of Hvalsey said they 'were all overborne by the

skraelings and taken away by the name skraelings to be slaves'; that another said: 'They were overborne, but yet not taken away, for as to that I say: to what use could our brothers be put by the heathens who flit from one place to another, never abiding in the one place. I say our brothers were all slain – and long ago, these eighty years or more.' Another said: 'Neither overborne nor slain even were our brothers. I say to you rather: hearing of the good lands that were there to be found, they took ship one and all, and went into Vinland, though no one hath heard of them since.' And still another: 'Not so, as to the one and the all. You see me before you. I tell you my father's father's father – and that one was Eyvind Ingolfsson, whom Ingolf begot in old age – came down here to the East Settlement when there were yet people in the West Settlement, though few enough as God knows by reason of the skraelings.'

Memo. Have I one of kin to me, and yet living, in Hvalsey in Greenland?

I gave them more ale, and then asked of them whether they had been to the wedding between Thorstein Olavsson and Sigrid Björnsdottir which was celebrated on the First Sunday after the Finding of the True Cross in 1408. In faith, they had, and Arni, who had spoken less than the two Icelander seafarers, then put in, and he says: 'Of that wedding I was a witness. By Christ's blood it will be in your bishop's book, if it be true.'

I told him not to dismay himself, for that I knew it to be in our Bishop's Register at Skalholt, and that he – Arni, of Bergen – was written in there as one of the two witnesses enjoined by Holy Church in the nuptial ceremonies.

Moreover, I know the very man, the bridegroom at that wedding in Hvalsey. He is the very same as the Thorstein Olavsson, my neighbour at Miklibaer. I like him well, and had bidden him to the feast of the plighting of troth between my son Olav and Gudrid Gunnarsdottir, but he was unable to do so for his wife being in childbed. I told Arni and his two friends of this, but deemed it the wiser not to tell them of where my neighbour lived lest, being exalted by the bounty of my entertainment, and holding much ale in their bellies, they go on to rouse him with noisy mirth unsuiting to a house in which either one is dying or one is being born.

Further, to assure Arni that I knew he was speaking true, I gave from my memory the name of the second witness, and the name of the priest in Hvalsey who celebrated the nuptial mass, namely Sera Pál

Halvardsson. Moreover, since no bishop of Greenland now goes to Greenland – shame to him for that, for that he rather dwelleth in the realm of Norway in comfort instead – I gave the name of the Bishop of Greenland's deputy – his Vicar-General in Greenland, namely Sera Einride Andresson.

As I moved away from these three unbidden guests to converse with other friends, for so it is seemly at these gatherings when one is host to all, my thoughts moved towards Thorstein and his Greenland wife soon to give birth.

Sigrid Björnsdottir, whether or not happy to have been wooed by an Icelander, Thorstein Olavsson, a seafarer but now settled as a landsman, she is nevertheless happy to be now settled as a wife in nearby Miklibaer. The Greenland bride Thorstein brought back, to say sooth, was sweet and comely enough of feature, but she would shy like a she-colt not yet weaned from its mare, and was more timid and frightened lest she should not please than a young woman should be. But what I chiefly noted, when I called on them, when they kindly refreshed me, was how small and thin she looked. And pale thereto from having too much milk to drink of, wherefore my strong ale would have done her much better good but for her being in childbed and unable to walk. This I put down to the poor and scant food of our kinsfolk in Greenland, from which they have sorely suffered many, many years and more so since the Germans in Bergen stop the King of Norway's ship sailing to them with viands for their stomachs and other needful things, yea, even wine for the sacrament. I call to mind Sigrid Björnsdottir's clapping of hands and jumpings and merry smiles when she first saw the fine dresses and apparels and headgear and bodices prettily embroidered and gay kirtles that our women wear as of custom in Iceland, besides another dainty garment underneath which for modesty's sake I forbear to mention. In spite of her poor and weak frame, it is my hope, if God wills, that she, Sigrid Björnsdottir, will give birth in full safety, and that all her children thereafter grow strong and tall in our land, where there is no such shortage.

Leaving my two Icelander friends and Arni, and trusting that Arni would see to it that the two seafarers would not befuddle their senses with unbridled drinking, and at my cost, I went to speak to Snorri Thorfasson and his wife Gudrun Magnusdottir. They were of middle years and stout but were ruddy-faced and of good cheer, linking arms with each other. They wished me happiness of the match between my son Olav and Gudrid Gunnarsdottir.

Theirs is a strange story.

Snorri Thorfasson, no less than my two Icelander friends – for so, I suppose, I must consider them, for they are drinking my ale – and the Norwegian Arni, had been on that ship bound for Iceland from Bergen which had been driven by wind and wave to Hvalsey in Greenland.

Now his wife Gudrun, after three years, supposing her husband, Snorri, and all with him, drowned, sadly goes to her priest, Sera Peder, and she says to him:

'Sera Peder, three years have passed, and my husband comes not back from the sea. I have grieved for my Snorri so much that my soul has sorrowed, but I now look not to see him again, for I know him to be drowned.'

Sera Peder says, 'I grieve for you, my daughter, but it is as God wills, and may God rest his soul. But what then?'

'What then!' our Gudrun cries. 'Well, this is what then!'

She then goes on to say that she lives alone, and that her neighbour is one Thord, and he no less alone. 'And that Thord comes to me and saith, "Your husband must surely be dead. You are alone, and I am alone, so surely we should wed. And I make this verse for you, for "dead" and "wed" chime. So Sera Peder, what may I say to him when he next comes to me? He is a good man, and lonely.'

Sera Peder saith, 'Well, my daughter, you must avoid the occasions of sin, but I will ask our good bishop what is to be done, but I will say – subject to what his lordship says – that you have a case, inasmuch as we presume indeed your husband to be sadly drowned, and that you may perchance marry again. But till I hear from the Bishop himself, pray and watch and avoid all the occasions of all sin, permitting not the good Thord – may he remain good! – to touch you in those places which, as a widow, you know about. Now go in peace, my daughter.'

And it happens that his lordship in Latin writes to his son in the bowels of Christ, Sera Peder, which Latin conveyed into our own tongue saith:

'The *quondam* male spouse, the aforesaid Snorri Thorfasson, the house-bond, must in all reason now, after this lapse of years, be thought to have died in the sea, *ergo* drowned.

'Therefore I instruct you, my good Sera Peder, to inform the poor widow woman so; and to deliver my ruling as to the matter which is thus: she may contract, since she is surely but a widow, a bond of marriage with the same Thord – whose father's name you mention not – and I must in holy duty as your Bishop reprimand you for omitting that fact – and the sooner the better, I say, for the better forestalling of sin.'

Widow Gudrun and Thord, following the Bishop's letter, are wedded by Sera Peder; and Thord carries off Gudrun to his house, neighbouring hers, and so they both live in merry and true fellowship for a year, or nearly, or the more or the less.

And then cometh the news of that ship, which all had supposed lost these four years. It cometh, heaving with pride and joy forsooth on the sea, and making for safe haven in our Iceland haven wherein it drops anchor, and with a rich lading from Greenland.

And I recall, talking as I do now to Gudrun Magnusdottir and Snorri Thorfasson, of what she had said to me almost these two years gone, *anno Christi* 1410.

'Why,' she said then, 'as soon as I hear the news, I fly out of the house, leaving the side of Thord in his bed but in my shift, and get bareback onto my horse, and ride him at all speed to the haven. And there, true enough, is my Snorri, all well and whole of his body, and I trust too of his soul, thanks be to God. I fling my arms about him. And what do I then? Why, I feel whether he is all whole of his body. And then, both riding the one horse, one behind the other, I take him to his own house, my home before I wedded Thord. Poor soul – and poor body too – they needed some comfort from me after four years in that Greenland.

'But I do say to Thord, "I cannot do else; and dear good man you may be, and thank you, but this is my true husband who's come back from the drowned and who was dead. I can no other but leave you and go back to him: So blame not me", I says, "but blame our Sera Peder, aye, and the Bishop too. But God and Snorri be above both bishop and priest."'

And thereto she was right, for both Priest and Bishop declare that the wedding between Gudrun Magnusdottir and Thord, father unknown, be both utterly null and void.

And here they are, the husband and the wife, at the betrothing of son Olav and Gudrid Gunnarsdottir, and they are as merry as two of our eider ducks in the time of nesting, and with linked arms they drink to my good health and luck with my own ale, and then again to those of my son and his troth-plight. They are fat of face and they laugh right loudly.

I thank them heartily and, thinking it seemly, pass on to have the good word with the mother of her who is to be my daughter-in-law.

Memo. I may hope for my dear son Olav's sake that the daughter grow not to be like the mother. The mother is a short woman, and a stout, she may be likened unto two tubs the one stood up on the other. She hath little wit and – which is the worse – is plain of face. I pity her husband Gunnar, and trust my son tameth his wife so that she be sweet and lovely to have with him in bed. Yea, even when she reacheth the age of her mother, I pray she may rather resemble a bos-bum loaf★ than one tub stood up on the other. And whichever my son Olav prefereth the one rounded part of the loaf – the top or the bottom – to be the bigger, then I pray that it may be the bigger.

Such gamesome thoughts a man must needs have when he giveth feasts, for which he has not much liking so that he may appear merry of countenance.

Anno Christi 1416. Second Sunday in season of Advent.† Sad it is to say that the merry Snorri Thorfasson, for so merry he was at my feast, is now dead. He was yet a strong man, and maybe thought to have lived long after coming back from a supposed drowning.

It came about thus. But shortly after my feasting of them, his wife Gudrun says to him: 'It is already cold. Go, dear husband, and fetch some of the turves stacked without, so that we be happy and warm together this cold evening, and meanwhile I shall prepare something hot and nourishing for my love.'

Thorfasson goes outside to gather turves from the wall of turves he had built up for the winter season. But the rain had fallen, and the foot of the wall is rotten, and the wall leaneth. Instead of gathering turf from the top of the wall, which is indeed above his reach, he digs below. The wall of turves bends down on Thorfasson with a big thump and compresseth both sides of the poor man's ribs together. I attended the good man's requiem mass. Well said and sung it was by Sera Peder.

After his burial I approach Gudrun to say such soothing sayings as our feeble tongues can utter on such occasions, and a happy thought comes into my mind, and I add:

★I retain the Icelandic word since 'cottage loaf' would give a misleading impression. A *bos-bum* loaf rather resembles, with its graceful waist, an hour-glass (save that the *bos* and the *bum* parts can be of unequal size) than the loaf that issues from the English bakery.

†This folio has clearly been inserted by Mordsson at a later date.

'But Gudrun Magnusdottir, comfort yourself a little with the knowledge that you enjoyed Snorri Thorfasson as husband twice. For he was drowned but, by the mercy of God, came to be your husband again.'

'That is sooth, Ingolf Mordsson,' she answers, 'and it is likely that I shall enjoy my second husband twice likewise turnabout: first one, then t'other; back to one, back to t'other.'

Though she loved Snorri as I have no doubt, for so merry they were at my feast, Gudrun goeth straightway in her distress to neighbour Thord. He comforts her, and the short and the long is this: she has now gone back to Thord and there she dwells with him. When Sera Peder reproached her, she saith to him boldly: 'Why, you wedded me once to Thord, and now you would have me wedded again to Thord. What did for you once will do for me now. I have done with such things as weddings and bishops and witnesses and Sera Peders and there's an end.'

And that was the sorrowful case. But back I go now to the feast which I gave for the plighting on the Holy Day.

After talking, as was meet, with many of my guests, the two Icelander seafarers and Arni sought me out again, to my great annoyance. For now I wanted to speak with my daughter-in-law-to-be and give her a pretty kiss.

They were now wild, and spoke of the burning at Hvalsey, which burning I had heard of. But thinking they had something moreover to say, I heard them out. Thus the two Icelanders and Arni of Norway:

'At Hvalsey in Greenland there was Thorgrim Sölvesson, and right good was his understanding of ships, and for that reason we had him aboard for our faring thither and made him shipmaster. His wife came with him. Now the forward part of one side of our ship had been all stove in by the weight of the waters on our faring to Greenland. So Thorgrim Sölvesson day after day tends to the mending of the ship; and, having others under him, has all the damaged timbers plucked out so that sound ones may be put in their place. And while he does all this busily his wife, Steinunn, daughter of Rafn – '

'Isn't that Rafn of Langelid, he who was overwhelmed and crushed by a landslide, when snows melted in the spring of last year?' I ask.

'Whether that Rafn's daughter, or another Rafn's daughter, but still a Rafn's daughter,' Arni said, and rudely. 'I say this Steinunn

Rafnsdottir was shipmaster Thorgrim's wife. And so it came about that Thorgrim was so busy about the mending of our ship that he had no eye for wife Steinunn – '

'And wife Steinunn, having no husband's eye on her, walks down the boarding plank, and off she goes to ramble on the Greenland shores, day after day,' said one of the Icelanders.

'And that goes on day after day till that Greenlander Kolgrim puts his eye on her, and – not so long after – puts something else in her,' said the other.

'And not once, and not twice only, Ingolf Mordsson. And may I say this: your ale is good ale, and for it I give you thanks.'

And they told me how Thorgrim Sölvesson, on finding this out, took leave from the mending of the ship to complain unto the Lawman of Greenland's deputy, at Hvalsey; of how this Kolgrim, Greenlander, had lain with his wife. And how, if this were told in Iceland, when they reached Iceland, their homeland – and pray God, may that be soon – few indeed would be the ships and far apart, if any and ever, seen sailing into Greenland again. However great the Greenlanders' need, they could look for such another ship, such as they had brought here, in vain.'

The Lawman in Greenland's deputy took the hint, and Kolgrim was seized, and *in flagrante delicto* as the Latin hath it.

This Kolgrim was a man two ells high, so that if he stood upright in any house his head smote the beams. But he was loose and slack in the knees, and he did not so much as walk as shamble with arched neck. Thereto he was of hideous aspect, of low and villainous brow, of black hair, grim visage, and black brows. And so his name was Kolgrim, for he was swarthy and ugly as charcoal. Further, he would have fits, roll his eyes, and gush out foam from his mouth. It was said that he had suddenly come upon three of the women of Greenland in the past and laid them by force. That was before he was seized by several *in flagrante delicto* with Steinunn Rafnsdottir. This Kolgrim was rumoured to be the monster birth of an Irish bondswoman who had been turned out by her master.

The question was put to the Lawman's deputy: 'How could such a pretty lady as Steinunn Rafnsdottir, wife to the excellent Thorgrim Sölvesson, lie with such a monster as Kolgrim, however overmuch her husband gave his thoughts to the mending of the ship?' The Lawman's deputy could only swear he believed that this terrible Kolgrim was possessed of the control of the Black Arts. From Hvalsey therefore was

Kolgrim taken hence, bound by many and strong ropes, to Gardur. Here he was brought before the Church Court of Sera Einride Andresson, the Bishop's deputy, the same who signed to the wedding between Thorstein Olavsson and Sigrid Björnsdottir, and put to the pains. The judgment of Einride Andresson was that Kolgrim be taken back to Hvalsey, where he should be tied to a stake and burned 'for that he indeed possesseth, and hath practised, the Black Arts'. The good Sera Einride permitted the Lawman of Greenland to hear all that went on in this Church Court, and the Lawman said the Church ruling was true and right law.

Kolgrim was tied to a stout pole set in the earth, and put in a blaze three days after the wedding between Thorstein Olavsson and Sigrid Björnsdottir. The shavings from the new timbers for the ship started the fire, though the old beams, cut out from the ship because it had been stoved in there on the wild journey from Iceland, were slow to burn. But yet they did. And then the blaze.

And this is strange. For while the whole company of the ship, and not only the three guests at my feast, and nearly all the people of Greenland still remaining, watched the burning of Kolgrim, and heard his dreadful screamings to the Evil One to save him, the lady Steinum Rafnsdottir herself, she who had had the spells cast on her, danced around the pole when Kolgrim was being burned. And she sang while dancing. Her husband, Thorgrim, tried to pluck her back among the watchers. But she smote him, and would have her way.

Memo. She came not back to Iceland, but it is said that on the ship she lost her reason and died.

Memo. We should grieve for the fate of our starving kinsfolk in Greenland. Nevertheless we should give thanks to God and rejoice for all good and merry things here in Iceland and in all other lands.

Resolving thus, I then go among my other guests, catch hold of my daughter-in-law-to-be, Gudrid Gunnarsdottir, and give her a hearty buss. I look around then for another lady, better a widow, striving to miss the sight of Gudrid's mother who looketh not unlike the figure of two low tubs one on t'other with two little legs thereunder, and a sour onion placed on the upper tub. So I make for a lady, below my years but not much, whose shape and visage delighteth my gaze. Praise be to God.

Anno Christi 1413. Mikel's Messe. My son's wife, Gudrid Gunnarsdottir, gave birth to a son this day. He will be baptized in the name of Ingolf for me or of Mord following my father, on the morrow.

It was Ingolf. May Ingolf Olavsson, minding that he is of the line of both Ingolf of Greenland and the dead Gudrid, when he is come of good years, cherish these memorials and cherish that other book I have which Heriolf Ingolfsson wrote down. Amen.

APPENDIX

APPENDIX

This translator and editor of the Sauð arkrokur manuscripts received an astonishing communication, seemingly through the post, on 1 February 1973. The envelope was post-marked 'New York City' and the date-stamping was '2 Feb 73'. The letter it contained was unsigned and bore no address for a reply. It was hand-written, oddly punctuated and used upper – and lower – case letters, as shown below (for I reproduce it verbatim):

> DEAR SIR, OR ARE YOU FRANCIS, OR WHATEVER YOU ARE NOW:
> BUT WHERE YOU ARE, AH THAT WE KNOW: SILLY PEOPLE YOU.
> SILLY-WILLY PEOPLE YOU DARLINGS. Keep on. GO AHEAD.
> TRUSTING YOU ARE QUITE WELL ENOUGH. ON GO. WE ARE
> OUTSIDE FRIENDS. REPEAT OUTSIDE. ITS[*sic*] NOT AS WE
> THOUGHT. LOOK OVER. TELL ABOUT US. WE AFTER YOUR
> LANGUAGE YOU, LOOK. We speak Mordson [*sic* for 'Mordsson'].
> All together. Big America. Not bad. YOU ARE, AS THEY SAY,
> CORRECT. OK. G and I HERE KNOW, ETC. ETC. Tell. G G G
> GUD: I Ing. G and ING. LIKE HA AH! GOT WARM NOW.

I make no comment on this communication, for I cannot.